MARK OF THE FALLEN

Book 1 of the Foxglove Chronicles

Jessi Chaulk

To my husband - the love of my life, my partner in crime,

my best friend.

TABLE OF CONTENTS

Chapter 1 – The Before……...5

Chapter 2– The Before...…17

Chapter 3– The Before…...26

Chapter 4…………...……37

Chapter 5…..………...….49

Chapter 6…………...……64

Chapter 7…………...……77

Chapter 8…..………...….85

Chapter 9…..……....…....94

Chapter 10…………...…..112

Chapter 11…...………....123

Chapter 12…………...…..133

Chapter 13…………...….149

Chapter 14……………….164

Chapter 15………....…....181

Chapter 16…………..........192

Chapter 17……………...202

Chapter 18…………..........212

Chapter 19…………....….218

Chapter 20…………....….231

Chapter 21…………...….241

Chapter 22……………....252

Chapter 23……………....265

Chapter 24…………......273

Chapter 25…….....………286

Chapter 26…………....….297

Chapter 27……………....308

Chapter 28…………......320

PRONUNCIATION GUIDE

PEOPLE/THINGS

ADARRA NASSAR: Uh-darr-uh Nass-arr

AERON: Ay-run

AYLA: Eye-luh

AMULET OF VILIN: Amulet of Vill-een

BLADE OF STRATTERA: Blade of Strah-tair-uh

CALLUM ABERNATHY: Cay-lum Ab-er-nah-thee

CASS BRIGHTWOOD: Cass Brite-wood

FALCON FELDSTROM: Fal-con Feld-strohm

LIAM HOLLOWAY: Lee-um Hall-oh-way

REMUS: Ree-muss

PLACES

DRAGORAH: Drah-gor-ah

ELDORIA: El-dor-ee-uh

HILLSBOROUGH: Hills-bor-oh

KLEIDIS: Klee-diss

SILVERGLADE: Sil-ver Glay-d

STALTON: Stall-tun

TRILITHIA: Trih-lith-ee-uh

Chapter 1

THE BEFORE

This was it - the bottom line. My next move would determine victory. The ragged breath in my chest reminded me just how desperate I was. Staring down my opponent, the unforgiving heat of the sun seared my skin. I felt a bead of sweat drip down my forehead as my eyes met theirs. There was a familiar mischievous gleam to them that almost made me feel sorry for what I was about to do.

A flash of the signal from my ally indicated it was time. I nodded, steadying my fingers on the rounded object in my hand. In one swift movement, I pulled back my arm to its full extent, then lunged forward, releasing it. As it left my fingers, it seemed to fly in slow motion. My arm, suspended in front of me as if stuck in time, held steady as I waited to see if the blow would land.

My opponent swung his bat but missed the ball. There was a satisfying thud as my teammate closed his mitt around it. A swatch of old fabric flashed in front of the batter as Elder Maurice called, "Strike three! You're out, Liam! The Diamond goes to the Red Team!" throwing his hands up with a smile. King's Diamond was a popular game in our village, and Elder Maurice organized these competitions for the youth.

I grinned from ear to ear as I imagined how Bram would react to my win. He would be beside himself with excitement. Everyone watching and playing the game started to disperse, milling around, and talking. I felt a clap on my shoulder and turned to see the batter from the game. "Good game, *Cassandra*." Liam snickered in greeting.

My elbow met his ribs in response, "Keep that up and next time I'll aim the ball for your head." Best friend or not, the only ones allowed to call me anything but 'Cass' were my Ma and General Ren.

Liam laughed and ruffled my hair- a dangerous move. Cocking an eyebrow, he said "And ruin this beautiful face you love to look at? I don't think so."

"Just stick with Cass and you won't have to find out." I stuck my tongue out at him. He returned the gesture. "I'm surprised you made the game today. I thought for sure you'd be too tired from traveling." I let my eyes convey the silent question- *Any news?* He shook his head at me and pulled me to his side in a one-armed hug "Later." he said quietly into my hair by my ear so that any passerby may just think he was greeting me after his week away from home.

Liam turned 17 a couple of months ago. He stood nearly a head taller than me, though that had been true since the spring he turned 13. Since then, though, he had filled out considerably, due to his training with General Ren.

I let Liam hold me close for a moment, his citrusy, cedarwood scent flooding my senses, his presence slowly filling the gap he had left in my heart the day he left for Stalton 6 days ago - the longest we had ever been apart.

People often assumed that we were a couple. I would never admit to him that I had come to loathe the look of relief in their eyes when they realized he was single. Like they thought all the cookies had been eaten but then they found some in the back corner of the pantry.

Though it wasn't particularly ridiculous for people to think we were together. We held hands often and spent nearly every second of our free time together. Thick as thieves, we'd say. But there was often that toed line between brotherly affection and romance that neither of us dared to address. Probably the only thing we *didn't* talk about with each other.

His wavy black hair flopped onto his forehead - he pushed it back, revealing those piercing blue eyes. They squinted mischievously when he said, "You know, I think you cheated on that last pitch."

I rolled my eyes and scoffed. "How would it even be possible for me to have cheated?" Before he could answer, I felt a tiny tug on my hand.

"Cass, that was awesome!" Bram had found me and was wrapping his arms around my legs in his tiny version of a bear hug. "You threw that ball, and he didn't even stand a chance!" Bram - my biggest fan.

Liam dramatically placed out a hand of feigned offense, "Excuse me, sir! But I most certainly did have a chance!"

"Nuh-uh! Cass is way better than you at King's Diamond." Bram crossed his arms and stared Liam down like a pup trying to stare down the alpha wolf. This time we both laughed, and I ruffled the mop of curly golden hair on Bram's head - even though he said he hated it when I did that. "Hey!" He cried, pulling his hands over his head. He didn't know that his smile and the shine in his big brown eyes gave him away. I knew that he loved any attention I gave him.

Bram was 4, making him the younger of my two little brothers. He wasn't old enough to play King's Diamond with everyone yet - but that didn't stop him from watching every game and cheering his siblings on. Kolby joined us, elbowing Liam, "I can't believe you lost to my sister."

I used to get sad when I looked at Kolby after Pa died. Now that he is 13, Kolby's resemblance to our Pa was striking. Now though, I smile when I remember Pa's creases next to his eyes when he smiled - or his belly laugh when you told him a joke that wasn't really even that funny. I sigh internally - Pa. The year Bram was born, Pa left town to negotiate a trade agreement with a town a few days away. We never heard from him again. Liam's dad had traveled to the village to see if they could find him, but they said that he never showed up. They found his injured horse limping along a road right outside Stalton. There was a search party for months, but nobody ever found him. I try not to think too hard about what could have happened to him - I just hope it was painless.

Kolby had our father's wavy black hair, same round eyes - although his were hazel instead of our Pa's vibrant green. On the other side of the coin, Bram was a miniature version of our mother with his golden curly locks and chocolate brown eyes.

I self-consciously tucked a strand of hair behind my ear and noted for the thousandth time the color of it. Red. Hair as red as my cheeks would get when embarrassed, as Liam used to tease me. I was the only redhead in the entire village. Not even a shade of red in either of my parent's hair. Any time we had any visitors in the village they would always give me strange looks, though, that was probably due to the section of gold-so-pale-it's-almost-white hair that grew on the very front of my hairline. Ma says I was born with it. "Just ignore them, Cass. People are so rude. Staring at a *child*. Red hair might be rare, but it's not unheard of." She said to ignore them, but they made me feel so…out of place. Like some kind of *thing* on display.

I threw an arm over Kolby's shoulder, "So little brother - did you study the way in which Liam utterly failed in the Kings Diamond field so you can avoid the same mistakes in the future?"

Kolby grinned at me, "I was planning on writing a detailed report," He stepped away from me, holding imaginary papers in his hands, "How To Not Play Kings Diamond: The Rise and Fall of Liam Holloway."

Liam scoffed - "Well maybe if Cassandra here hadn't cheated-" I punched him in the arm.

Liam rubbed his arm and scowled at me as we all walked towards my house. Bram was riding on my back, Kolby walking on one side of me, Liam on the other. "I told you not to call me Cassandra" I smirked as I hiked Bram up further on my back.

"It wouldn't hurt so bad if you didn't train with General Ren twice as often as the rest of us." Liam said, a smile tugging at his lips. He was trying so hard to play the wounded victim. I rolled my eyes at him. General Ren did train me more, yes. But to be fair, I was the most talented.

I slowed to a stop, turning my attention to Bram, "Hop off Bram, my back is tired." I said, gently easing him down.

"Ah come on Cass, can't I please ride on your back?" His sweet little cherub face turned to pout.

But I just shrugged and said, "Maybe if *you* carried *me* around a little more…"

He crossed his arms, "That's not fair! I can't carry you - you're too big!"

Kolby busted out laughing, "Don't you know it's rude to comment on a lady's weight?" I had to laugh at that as well.

"Go on the rest of the way home," I said to Kolby and Bram when I spotted my mother's gentle face peering through the kitchen window, waiting for them. "I have to get to my training with General Ren." I watched Bram and Kolby run off the rest of the way to our house and smiled as my mother opened the door for them.

Liam and I walked in silence towards the back of the village. I had to wait until we were alone before Liam would tell me anything about his trip. We lived in the Kingdom of Trilithia, in the village of Everloom. Everloom has been my home my whole life. As we walked, I basked in the comfort of the familiarity of my surroundings.

One side of the village was the field we had played King's Diamond on, then in the middle was the town square. The town square had shops and homes surrounding it. Behind the square, where we were going, were the training grounds. The village square was bustling with people, some coming home after the game, some just milling about, talking to their neighbors. The village was surrounded by forest, our own little safe haven in the middle of the chaos that was Trilithia.

We finally passed the last of the houses before reaching the path that led over the hill to the training grounds. I couldn't hold it in any longer, "So? What did they say?" I pressed, turning to him and grabbing his arm, continuing our walk.

He grinned widely as he turned to me, "They'll take us." I kept myself from squealing but jumped and hugged him "They'll take us!?" I asked, just to confirm I hadn't heard incorrectly.

It was by chance that we even knew of the small but growing rebellion, Luminous Storm, and their leader, Falcon Feldstrom. A codename, no doubt. We had overheard a traveling merchant speaking to General Ren about it in hushed tones 6 months ago. Over the years, Liam and I had seen first-hand the brutalization the people of Trilithia had endured at the hands of the Shadow Guard.

Two years ago, it had been Liam's parents who had paid the price. Simply because they didn't have enough gold to pay an unofficial "toll" on a road while traveling. After gutting his parents, they beat and knocked Liam out leaving him lying on the road for days before someone found him. A jagged, shining scar still twisted around his arm in a cruel reminder of the injustice of Aeron's rule. After being brought here by a traveling merchant who found him on the road, Grand Elder Ira tried to heal him, but his wound had sat untreated for too long.

If Grand Elder Ira couldn't heal it, there was little hope for it to go away ever completely. Not only was he our oldest and wisest Elder, but he was also a mage who spent his whole life using magic to treat illnesses, and cure any curses or jinxes put on residents by Shadow Guard Mages.

After the attack, Liam had always talked about *doing* something. Getting out of Everloom – a great escape, as he would call it. Then we heard about Luminous Storm. Hearing about Luminous Storm 6 months ago lit a fire in Liam that I had not expected. But seeing him be so passionate about something - something that gave him purpose - I suppose it lit a fire in me too. Knowing that someone was out there fighting to right so many wrongs that had been committed since Aeron took power gave us both hope that we may live in a world where people were not beaten by guards for no reason. A world where parents were not senselessly taken from their children. Other villages were not as fortunate as we were - the Shadow Guard had enough sense to at least stay out of General Ren's way. Needing to make a difference ourselves, we had agreed to find a way to join Luminous Storm together when we both turned 18.

He held my arms and pulled back to look at me, "I told them that we've both trained under General Ren, I sparred with a couple of their men. Then told them you're even better than I am." A beautiful smile graced his face. The smile of someone who got their lifelong wish granted.

"So next year they'll be ready for us?" I grinned back.

His smile faltered as realization and guilt flashed in his eyes, "I…" he paused, "I didn't-"

"Liam?" I shook my head, stepping back from his arms, "We said when we turn 18. You told them next year, right?" I searched his eyes, and only found guilt glaring at me. "Tell me you're waiting to leave." He looked down, and I didn't need to hear an answer from him to know what he said to them. "You know I can't leave my brothers yet." I said slowly, trying to keep my voice from wavering.

MARK OF THE FALLEN

I would turn 17 tomorrow, so even if we left the day I turn 18, it would still be a year from now. "I need to make sure Ma is set up to survive before we leave. I'm the one who sells the bear and wolf traps. I need time - time to teach Kolby or Ma how to make them." The traps were a design that Pa and I had started before he died. Since Pa is gone, I make the money we need by selling them. "Do you expect me to just leave them behind?" My voice dropped low, "Or were you just going to leave me behind?"

He kept his gaze down and his silence was all I needed. I took a few more steps back, raising my arms in defeat. "Got it. You go, Liam. I get it. Our pact means nothing when it comes down to it."

I turned back towards the training grounds, "Cass-" Liam called out. I ignored him and continued walking. I heard him curse under his breath. Suddenly, he grabbed my hand and pulled me back toward him.

Nearly slamming into his chest, I looked up at him "What are you-"

"I'm sorry." He said, taking hold of my other hand, and holding both to his chest in a plea of forgiveness. "I got so caught up in avenging my parents that I didn't think of how it would affect you. I'll write them right now to let them know we need to wait until you can come. Even if it takes longer than a year."

Oh. Of course, this was about his parents. I couldn't believe I made this about me. I shook my head, "No, Liam, I overreacted. I know what losing your parents did to you. I shouldn't have made this about me."

Liam grimaced, releasing one of my hands to tuck the loose gold strand of hair behind my ear, "No, Cass. *I* made it about you when I asked you to join with me. The rebellion will still be there in a year, and Aeron will still need his ass handed to him."

I sighed, "I don't want to keep you from -"

"Hey." He cut me off, and I was surprised to feel a hand under my chin, lifting it to look at him. His gaze was so intense it felt like just looking straight at him would reveal every one of my innermost thoughts. "You don't keep me from anything - and the Shadow Guard themselves couldn't keep me from you."

His tone was serious, but there was something else in there too - like he was trying to keep himself from saying too much. I was suddenly very aware of how close our faces were. His brow furrowed -and with the way he looked at me, his eyes glancing downward for just a second, I almost thought…No, I couldn't let myself think- "Cass-" He started but was interrupted by a shout down the hill.

"Hey, you two!" We jumped apart, my cheeks burning. General Ren was waving from the center of the training grounds. I glanced back at Liam, "Talk later?" I asked. He nodded, and I jogged over to the weapons stand where General Ren was waiting for me.

"See you…" I heard Liam sigh as he walked away. What just happened? Or *almost* happened, I should say. I tried to push the memory from my mind as I approached General Ren. It was time to train.

Chapter 2

THE BEFORE

I approached the weapon rack and General Ren joined me. He looked younger than his 50 years. His hair was silver, but he had a full head of it. While the stubble on his face made him look laidback, the scar that ran across his left eye showed his war-torn history. He *had* been a general, after all. A general in the King's army before the royal family was wiped out by a plague and the cruel Aeron took over. Everyone still called him General though, as a sign of respect.

I'm probably one of the only people who could get away with not calling him General *all* the time. After Pa, General Ren really stepped in for my family and helped my Ma get back on her feet. He helped me finish my bear trap design - and refused to take any of the money from the sales. We'd grown pretty close over the last 4 years.

"Cassie." General Ren said by way of greeting, ruffling my hair. He was the only one who was allowed to call me that. Liam tried once when we were 13 and it took him a week to get the mud out of his ears after I tackled him in the sparring ring. "When are you going to cut that hair?" He nagged, "All you're doing is giving the enemy something to hold onto in a fight."

"How was your trip?" I asked, fully ignoring the comment, stretching my arms out in front of me. I wanted to lose any tension from my conversation with Liam.

"Highly informative." General Ren said, raising an eyebrow at me. *At me*?

Searching the back of my brain for anything I've done recently that I shouldn't have and coming up blank, I asked "Informative about what?"

"Oh, just that some members of our very own village are planning on participating in a particularly bright rain coming our way." he said nonchalantly, picking up a sword. Bright rain…crap. Luminous Storm.

I let out an exasperated sigh, "How did you find out?"

"Well let's just say that if a certain black haired young man name dropped a very well-known war general in an attempt to make him and his friend more appealing to this…bright rain - the bright rain would want to personally confirm the validity of that claim." He raised an eyebrow at me yet again, "You might want to tell Liam to be more careful next time if I'm not supposed to know."

I stared daggers at the spot over the hill where Liam was standing 5 minutes ago. "I'll be sure to let him know."

I grabbed my two favorite short swords, one in each hand. I weighed each one carefully, getting used to holding them again. With General Ren being out of town for a month, I allowed myself to get rusty. I didn't practice nearly as much as I should have. "I have some business to attend to in Stalton, so I'll be leaving tomorrow morning. You should train with Liam until I get back."

"Again?" I asked, more than a little disappointed.

"Cass…" He warned.

"I know, I know." Shaking my head. I was not to ask about his business outside the village. I thought for a moment, "Are you going to tell Ma?" I treaded carefully – I wasn't planning on telling her I was leaving just yet.

"I'm not sure yet," He said offhandedly, studying the sword in his hands, "How about I make you a deal?" He said with a grin. Uh oh.

"What kind of deal?" I asked, not sure I want to know the answer.

MARK OF THE FALLEN

He motions to the training grounds with his sword, "Spar with me. You win, I keep my mouth shut. I win, I tell your Ma. Because if you can't beat me then you will not survive being in Luminous Storm."

I gulped. I had beaten him a handful of times, but not when anything was actually at stake. I turned my attention to the man in front of me, sizing him up, as well as the broadsword he chose to wield. Despite General Ren's age, he was still one of the most capable and respected warriors throughout the surrounding villages.

"Ready to have your butt handed to you, old man?" I teased, spinning each sword in my hands, loosening my shoulders.

Ren huffed a laugh, "Okay kid, let's see what you got."

We sparred. Every strike he threw at me, I countered. Every lunge, I dodged. My lungs were burning as I switched from defensive to offensive. I started striking first. At first, General Ren dodged and parried my blows, but I managed to get through one defense –

His sword started coming straight down on me. I dropped to one knee, crossing one sword across the other, and caught his sword as it came down. I pushed it back up by sweeping my swords upward. He was caught off balance, and I gave him a kick to the chest for good measure. He gave a grunt in response - the kick hardly did anything. But it did give me the split second I needed to prepare for his counterattack.

His sword came at me from the side; I quickly parried, spinning my sword around his and forced it out of his hand. He lunged for his sword, but before he reached it, my sword was at his neck, "check mate" I gasped.

"You got me," he smiled, straightening to stand, "Your secret's safe." He nodded solemnly.

I sighed and plopped on the ground, out of breath. "Thank you. I don't think we're even leaving until next year, though."

"Good." He nodded, joining me on the floor. "One more year of training and you'll be the best weapon they have."

"And then, the knight rescued the princess, and his reward was...he got to eat sweets all day!" Bram finished proudly. Kolby and I laughed.

It was after dinner, Bram, Kolby, and I should have all been asleep in our room. I didn't mind sharing a room, although as I got older it occurred to me that the only way out of this room was to move out. For the time being though, it was warm and comforting to have them in the room with me. Mama had come in, given us each a kiss on the head, and bid us all goodnight. However, as usual, we were each in our own beds, taking turns telling stories.

Kolby sat up excitedly, "Oh! Oh! I heard one today that Bailor next door told me."

I rolled my eyes, "That kid is trouble. He's always lying about something."

"But this one is good! It's scary, and Bailor said that it's true. He said he heard it from his brother, who heard it from-."

"I don't like scary stories." Bram said in a small voice, pulling his blanket up to his chin.

Kolby crossed his arms indignantly and stuck his chin out, "Don't be such a baby. You want to hang out with me and my friends? You have to be able to hear this stuff."

I am NOT a baby." Bram said, sitting up. "Fine, tell it."

"Okay, so here it goes," Kolby started, "A long time ago, there was a wizard who was obsessed with living forever. So, he would have a fortune teller tell his future like every day. So, one day, the fortune teller told the wizard that someone in a powerful family would be the one to kill him. So, the evil wizard raised up a bunch of dead people to go attack that family."

I heard a little squeak come from Bram, "Kolby…" I warned.

Kolby ignored me, to my dismay, "They had holes in their faces and worms coming out of their eyes. They don't talk or anything, all they do is groan like this," he contorted his face and let out a guttural "aaaaauuuughhh". Bram pulled the covers to his chin.

Kolby reverted back to his "scary story" face and continued, "And when he went to go attack them, the undead attacked everyone! The women, the kids-"

Bram dropped the covers and covered his ears, "Nooo!"

This had gone on long enough. I didn't need Bram waking up from nightmares in the middle of the night. "Kolby, that's enough!" I said sternly, getting up and going to Bram's bed. I sat on the edge, and he climbed into my lap. I stared daggers at Kolby, "You knew that story was too scary for him."

Kolby sullenly rolled over in bed to face away from us. "It's not my fault he's such a baby". I wanted to tell him otherwise but knew better than to argue at this point.

I heard the bedroom door creak open, "What on earth is going on in here?" Ma asked, clearly exasperated, "You three are going to wake up all of Everloom!"

I shook my head, "It's nothing Ma. Bram just had a bad dream."

Ma shook her head as she always did when she found us awake when we weren't supposed to be, "It's all those stories that Bailor has been telling. That boy…never mind. I love you three. Goodnight my babies."

MARK OF THE FALLEN

"Love you mama" we all said in unison. She shut the door, and I threw a pillow at Kolby. I could hear a muffled laugh from behind the pillow. I shook my head and gave a small laugh.

I looked down at Bram, "Are you still scared?" He shook his head no, but I could tell from his eyes that he was. "Well, maybe I'll just sing a little something, because I think I got a little scared."

Bram nodded solemnly, "Okay, I don't want you to be scared, Cass."

I smiled, and rocked Bram back and forth. I sang a common lullaby from my village,

> *There once were three that became one,*
> *Their power was compared to none,*
> *A token so fine it turned to fame,*
> *But no one yet recalls its name.*
> *What is the name of the lost treasure?*
> *Its name will soon be gone forever.*
> *But we remain these kingdoms three,*
> *For one day soon we will be free.*

I looked down and saw that Bram was asleep. After gently tucking him under the covers, I got into my bed and closed my eyes, finding myself pondering on the lullaby I had just sung to

Bram. I had always been fascinated with this particular lullaby, envisioning what the lost treasure could be.

I knew it had something to do with the history of Trilithia, but could never figure out exactly what it meant since according to Grand Elder Ira, history books have been scarce since Aeron took power.

I slowly drifted off to sleep, visions of treasure, books, and kingdoms swirling in my head.

Chapter 3

THE BEFORE

Darkness. Utter and complete darkness...but a light? A light that was blurry but was getting larger and coming into focus. I was in a room...no, a dungeon. That's what it had to be, the walls were made of stone, and the light was emanating from a single lantern on the wall. Suddenly, a voice sounded behind me. A furious, booming voice that sent a chill down my bones, "What do you mean a child lives?"

My focus found its way to a man. A broad, strong, man robed in crimson with a solid gold crown atop his head. There was a heavy gold chain around his neck, the bottom of it tucked into his robes. This man, sitting on a throne made of bones and metal. His body seemed strong, but his face was gaunt. His gray eyes were sunken and lifeless, while still encapsulating the very essence of rage.

"A child...lives." another voice rasped. another figure came into focus. Swaddled in a black robe with a hood drawn over their head, the only uncovered part of this figure was their gray, withered hands clasped in front of them. "My visions are unclear. There is a child, but that is all that I know. They do not yet bear the mark - but given the right circumstances, it will appear..."
The man yelled in rage, "Find them! Find the child and bring them to me!" Everything swept away as I was thrown backwards, the room shrinking into nothingness - I was encapsulated in darkness.

I awoke with a start. My heart was pounding so fast I could hear it in my ears. A nightmare. No doubt fueled by Kolby's ridiculous story last night. I was just about to sit up when Bram launched himself on my bed, singing "Happy Birthday Cass! Happy birthday Cass! Happy birthday, birthday, Cass Cass Cass!"

All memory of my nightmare fled my mind as I tackled Bram into a bear hug, "Thank you Bram-Bam." I said into his golden curls, then started tickling him.

"Let go!" He laughed, and I did. He ran to his bed and pulled something out from underneath it. He hid it behind his back and said, "This is for your birthday. Mama helped me make it yesterday." He pulled out from behind his back a crown made of wildflowers. It was mostly falling apart but I smiled and let Bram put it on my head, "It's perfect because princesses wear crowns, and you're nice and pretty just like a princess!" He smiled proudly.

I went and changed in Ma's room, pulling out soft green shirt and brown trousers, perfect for moving around in.

I wore my flower crown all through breakfast and ignored every time a petal fell onto the table. Bram beamed. "Cass, you look just like a princess." he said – repeatedly, staring at me with those big doe eyes.

After breakfast I wove the broken bits of flower into a braid in my hair. My white-gold strands fell out the front, so I had to keep tucking them behind my ears. My morning was spent playing card games with Bram and showing Kolby the basics on how to make my traps. I checked the clock on the wall - 3pm.

"Ma, I'm supposed to meet Liam!" I called to her in the other room and rushed to put on my training gear. I pulled on my brown leather boots and matching arm bracers and laced up my armored corset. I checked myself in the long mirror on the wall. My lips were too thin and my eyes too big, but at least I looked like I could kick someone's butt in a fight. I never cared much about my looks, but every once in a while I would find myself thinking about how I wished I looked more like my Ma, and less like…me.

I went back into the living room, my ma now leaning against the doorframe leading to the kitchen, drying off a plate with a cloth "Be back before dinner, I have something special for your birthday." She smiled. My mama's smile was beautiful – all of her was. Her blonde curls were piled on top of her head, and her soft brown eyes were crinkling in spots that showed how much she loved to laugh.

I gave her a peck on the cheek as I passed by, "I will. Love you." She caught my hand – I paused. I closed my eyes as she pulled me into a tight embrace, my chin resting on her shoulder.

I was slightly taller than her, but still felt like a small child in my mother's embrace. "I love you too, my Cass. Your Pa would be so proud of you- his 'little fox'" I smiled to myself. I liked to think Pa was watching over us from somewhere. I vaguely remembered him calling me his little fox – red and white hair with a mischievous and feisty personality, I pulled away, and she placed a hand on either side of my cheeks, pressing a kiss to my forehead, "Go teach that Liam a lesson." she said, a mischievous glint in her eye. I grinned and headed out.

Since General Ren had business out of town, Liam and I were supposed to meet up. I knew I had some time to spare though, as Liam was always late.

I got to the training grounds first, Liam wasn't there yet. I dropped my bag down by the weapons rack and wandered farther down the dirt road, surveying the woods that backed the village.

MARK OF THE FALLEN

With a sigh, I laid in the grass field adjacent to the training grounds. Closing my eyes and feeling the heat of the sun on my eyelids, I remembered my dream from the night before. The man had looked so…evil, and cold. I willed myself to remember what he had said. Something about a child? And a mark appearing?

I sighed. I hated when I couldn't remember dreams. I opened my eyes and stared at the sky. At the vast, never-ending expanse of blue. What I would do to just live in the nothingness of the sky forever. No rebellions to join, no families to take care of. Just me, floating - content.

I was shaken from my daydream by a two-toned whistle. A whistle I immediately recognized. I answered the whistle - my own unique version, and closed my eyes again, letting the warmth of the sun envelop me. A moment later I heard the crunch of footsteps approaching.

"Why am I not surprised?" Liam said with a smile in his voice. He plopped down next to me, laying in the grass close enough that our hands were almost touching. He jokingly tsked, "Always slacking off, Cass. Even if it is your birthday."

I huffed a laugh and turned my head to face him. The first thing I noticed - "You cut your hair." I said, surprised. I reached out to touch the no longer existent strands of his hair.

His cheeks reddened, "Is it too short? I asked General Ren not to cut it too short-"

"No, it suits you." I smiled, and because I didn't know what else to do, I turned back to face the sky. "You look older."

I saw him touch his hair out of the corner of my eye. So self-conscious.

Shaking off the tingle in my chest, I sat up and rested my elbows on my knees, "You ready to go?"

We were both sweaty and sore - but it was a good workout. Liam was sat on the floor, he stretched and winced as he touched his shoulder, "I thought you might have gone easy on me on that last one." He reached his hand up to me.

Grabbing it and helping him to his feet, I teased, "And I thought you knew me better than that by now." After all these years, Liam still couldn't figure out that all I did was use his own strength against him.

He laughed, but suddenly something in the air was…off. It felt like the air around us was too tight – like walls were closing in. The sounds of screaming and crying reached my ears right as I noticed a wall of purple light pouring down behind us, enveloping the training grounds, extending past the hill toward the rest of the village. Where the screams were coming from.

"Magic" I breathed, meeting Liam's wide eyes. We broke into a run.

We came over the hill that separated the training grounds from the rest of the village and found the source of the screams. Terror - absolute terror. We ran toward the far end of the village - the other side of the hemisphere that enveloped us was surrounded by people on the ground crying out, others crying into the arms of their loved ones. "What happened?" I whispered, more to myself than to Liam. I looked at Liam's face and followed his gaze - past the wall of light. The Shadow Guard.

Clad in all black metal armor, a red stone imbedded in the chest plate, they stood gathered – guarding something. Their black helmets almost seemed like they absorbed any light that touched them.

I tried to quickly strategize an attack plan like General Ren had taught me. First, get a headcount - 10 - no 13. Between me, Liam, General Ren - No. General Ren left that morning. Was this planned? Did they somehow know he would be leaving? It didn't matter. Okay. Between me, Liam, and the 7 or so able-bodied men that were not left in a heaping emotional mess for some reason, we should be able to handle them, right? But that wall - I don't even know if it's permeable…

But then my eyes were drawn behind the Shadow Guard - my heart caught in my throat. The reason why everyone was losing it. There were 5 barred caravans all filled with…children. Our children. Our screaming, crying children. "Quit your yappin." I heard a guard snap and kick on the caravan wheels.

Without thinking, my heartbeat pounding in my ears, I took off for the wall and heard Liam's footsteps behind me. I didn't see Ma anywhere - where was she? I reached the wall and searched the wagons for Bram and Kolby. Fourth one to the left, I saw his sweet cherub face pressed against the bars, tears running down his face.

"CASS!" He spotted me, reaching his arms out through the bars, as if he could grab me using sheer will.

I found myself pounding on the wall. It shuddered at my touch - something that hadn't been happening before…perhaps if we all hit the wall at once, it would shatter -

"Everyone hit the wall!" I screamed desperately. Nobody moved. Why would nobody help me? I continued to slam into the wall with all my might - something had to break through. They can't leave. They can't go with those…with those monsters. "BRAM! KOLBY! HOLD ON!" I screamed, my hands growing numb.

"CASS! CASS, HELP US!" Bram cried from the other side. I saw Kolby's tear-stained face next to him.

"Cass." I felt Liam's hand on my shoulder, "It's not going to do anything. It's magic…there's nothing anyone can do." I hardly heard his words. I continued to pound on the wall. As long as I could see Bram I would do my best to knock down this cursed wall.

My attack was interrupted by a force that blasted me back from the wall, I could feel a shrieking scream escape my throat as I flew from the wall and landed with a thud on my back, the wind knocked out of me.

"Cass!" Liam cried and hurried to my side.

A Shadow Guard soldier stepped up to the wall, but this one was…different from the rest. His uniform was slightly more polished looking, and he lacked the red stone in the middle of the chest plate. Instead, there was Aeron's emblem, a crown rising above whirls of smoke and shadow.

"Now, now." He said with a wave of his hand, dismissing the mage next to him who was no doubt the cause of the blast that put me on my back. "We can't have you…upsetting the children." His eyes were so dark they're almost black, and his slicked back brown hair reflects the light of the purple wall. His cleanly manicured beard made me want to punch him. I was sure he'd never even been in a real fight, and here he was kidnapping children. Coward.

"What do you want with them?" I asked angrily, standing up and shaking off Liam.

"Normally I would have you whipped for this type of insolence…" He trailed off, his eyes glancing over me a little too long, "But since you amuse me, I'll indulge you. *I* don't want anything with them." He said, wiping a bit of imaginary dirt from his blade with his sleeve, "I find children to be unsanitary and troublesome. The orders come from above. *Far* above." Aeron ordered this? What kind of scheme was Aeron plotting? If only General Ren were here-

The Shadow Guard dropped his voice and took a step closer, his gaze predatory, "If you come with me and be a good girl, maybe I'll let you save *one* of your brothers." He said, and an uneasy shiver went down my spine. I felt Liam take a protective step closer to me. But he wouldn't butt in - no, he knew I could fight my own battles.

"Go to hell." I spat.

"I'm afraid I'll have to meet you there." The Shadow Guard smiled wickedly, "Oh, you really are amusing… Cassandra, was it? In the meantime, this wall will keep you all…contained for the time being. Don't worry," He said with a raise of his brow, "It'll wear off in 1 to 2 hours…or was it 22 hours? I never can remember with these things." He chuckled maliciously. Like this was all some kind of game to him. Something snapped in me.

"I'll kill you." I whispered, murder in my voice.

"Look for Captain Remus." He winked, and then walked away, taking all the caravans with him.

Chapter 4

FALCON

It had been a week since the Shadow Guard started sweeping villages, stealing the children as if they were no more than livestock. All my contacts in each city were writing to me, demanding action, asking what we were going to *do* – why had he even taken the children?

"Sir?" Randor asked expectantly, breaking my concentration, his eyes darting between the paper in my hand and the fingers massaging my temple as I read the missive over and over again. 500 children. So far, 500 children had been kidnapped by Aeron...and that wasn't even half the kingdom.

"What is it, Randor?" I sighed. Randor was one of my most trusted men. He joined up 3 years ago, after his parents had been wrongly branded as traitors by Aeron, executed in the town square.

He and his sister happened upon us in the town. She was only 8 years old at the time, but now she was 12, and helped in the kitchen mostly.

Randor shifted nervously from foot to foot. No matter how long he'd been around me, he always flinched away like everyone in the vicinity was a threat to him. "The new recruits are here."

I nodded, tossing my paper on the desk in front of me, "Be prepared to receive an influx of recruits." Aeron had made a grave mistake this time, underestimating the lengths parents would go to for their children.

Randor nodded and quickly dismissed himself. I made my way to the training room, ready to assess these new recruits. Liam and…. what was the other name? I shook my head dismissively. I remembered what the note had said during his interview, that his companion was an even better fighter than he was. I grinned at the thought of putting another overconfident young buck flat on his rear on the sparring mat.

I opened the door to the training room, immediately assessing. First in line, almost to my height, was Liam. I remembered briefly seeing his face when he was here about a week and a half ago. He was broad - he would hold up well in a fight. He nodded as he saw me, "Sir." He said in greeting. I tilted my head in acknowledgement, moving onto the next recruit. Next to him was a much smaller…girl?

I almost scoffed. We had women in our ranks, but this one…she couldn't have been older than 18. And she was tiny. At least, compared to her companion. She would die the second someone laid hands on her. Her red hair was bound up on her head and what in the…. she had somehow lightened the hair growing closest around her face it was almost white.

"They brought a third." Randor whispered in my ear, "She is in the second training room with Bianca to be assessed." I nodded, my eyes scanning the second recruit. Her eyes, the most curious green that bordered on gold, looked at me, evaluating. Calculating. Her eyebrows knit together as she looked me up and down.

"Name." I said, trying to sound as bored as possible.

"Cass Brightwood." She said, her voice serious. *That* was the other name. Cass. Why did it sound familiar though?

"Cass." I said, "You know, your companion spoke very highly of you when describing your fighting skill. I actually thought you would be a man."

One of her eyebrows shot up, "I don't have to be a man to beat one." Liam sighed next to her.

I found myself chuckling, "To the mat, recruit." I waited for protest. For her to request a female sparring partner. But, she simply walked to the mat, and turned to me, "Do you have…uh…wooden weapons?"

I nodded, "Yes, we use wooden weapons for sparring and training." I motioned to the rack behind her. If she was already worried about facing me with a true blade, there was no way that she would last.

I grabbed a wooden sword from the rack and eyed her choice of two wooden daggers, "That's going to be hard to defend against." I said, warning in my voice.

She shrugged, "I guess we'll find out." Too cocky.

I readied myself, raising my weapon in front of me. "Are you ready?" I asked, as she simply stood in front of me with a dagger in each hand, arms limp on her side. Liam was behind her, hand to head as if he was trying to smother a headache.

She just smiled, "Yes, *sir*." I felt a frown tug at my mouth but didn't let it show. I would make this quick. I lunged, sword swinging. In a flash, she sidestepped out of the way, causing me to trip on my missed swing. My gut sunk. *How* did she dodge me? I took a step back, observing her carefully as she sidestepped, slowly moving around me, anticipating my next attack.

"Nice dodge." I said, more nonchalantly than I felt.

"My mentor taught me well." She shrugged, continuing to scan me…no, it wasn't me she was scanning. It was my movements. Then it hit me.

"You're the one who General Ren trained." I stated. I had reached out to General Ren to verify Liam's claims of being trained by the famous general. General Ren did confirm training Liam and added that he had trained Cass almost every day for the last 5 years- twice as often as any of his other students.

She only smirked, and I struck again, this time, I was more intentional. More focused. She parried my stick with one of her wooden daggers, and spun, striking at the opening under my arm.

"Not fatal." I grimaced. The wood didn't break skin, but that didn't mean it didn't hurt. We danced with our wooden blades for a bit, her striking, me deflecting, holding her off. She struck out again this time aiming for my neck, but I was ready for her.

I grabbed the hand with the wooden blade before it reached my throat and bent it, turning her around so her back was to me, my arm across her throat and my blade at her side, "Checkmate-" I started, but she grunted, and before I knew what was happening, she had somehow snaked her arm up around mine, bent forward with all her might, and pulled me flat on my back. I blinked up at her face which was upside down as she held her wooden dagger to my throat.

"I believe the words you were looking for were, 'checkmate.'" She said, walking around and holding out a hand to me. I heard Liam whisper, "Cass…" In a warning voice. Shame in my gut, I ignored it, brushing myself off. Randor looked like he just might burst out laughing.

"That was lucky." I raised an eyebrow, "And it won't happen twice."

Her brow furrowed again, "I thought-"

"Again." I said, pointing to the mat. And we sparred, again, and again, until my arms were sore, and my body ached. I was beating her about one every five times. I knew she was using my size against me but couldn't figure out how to effectively fight in a way that would eliminate that advantage for her. But I would. I would figure it out if we had to spar every day for the next month.

CASS

1 Year Later

"Chancellor, if you want to keep the use of your thumb, I suggest you search your memory." My voice was cold, calculating, "For the last time, what do you know about where the kids are being held? Why did Aeron take them?"

I studied the man in front of me, waiting for an answer. My hood was covering my hair, and I had a mask drawn up over my mouth and nose, so all he could see was my eyes. The Chancellor of Laires, the wealthiest city in the kingdom – or it was before he started leaching taxes from everyone - was sweating in the seat I had him strapped to. "You can't do this to me." He sputtered, "My guards-"

"Your guards," I interrupted him, running the tip of my dagger across the back of his hand, which was also strapped down, "Are otherwise occupied at the moment."

Confusion flashed across his face as I continued, "Maybe they should be careful who they steal their 'tolls' from. Money is always so…dirty. You don't know what kinds of things they've come into contact with." I grinned as I patted the pouch on my side, now empty of everything but the remnants of the poison I had used to coat the coins, "Don't worry. They'll wake up by the morning. But I'll be long gone, and it's up to you whether or not you'll still have 10 useful fingers."

"My servants-"

"Go on. Scream for help. Nobody can hear you. All of your servants received word earlier in the day that they were being given the evening off to spend time with their families." I paused, "Well, their families minus their children of course."

His face went white, "Now." I continued, leaning over the chair menacingly, "What do you know about Aeron?"

"I don't know why you think I would know anything-" He started, but I didn't have time for games.

"You think the whole city doesn't know that the only reason you were gifted this home from Aeron is because of your compliance in his schemes? Your ordering of the Shadow Guard to squash down anyone who raises a word about the children being taken? The fact that you draw out more taxes in this one city than all the other small villages combined?" I raised an eyebrow, "I asked around, and you have made no friends here, Chancellor. Your city folk were more than happy to point me in your direction, and I didn't even have to bribe them."

The Chancellor was starting to turn green. "I've never been praised for my patience, Chancellor." I raised an eyebrow, "Start talking." I slightly dug the tip of my dagger into the back of his hand.

"I don't know where he's keeping them." He started, "He keeps it from everyone except the Shadow Guard who are assigned to it." I raised my brow as he kept talking. All I had to do was threaten his thumb and he was squealing like a pig, "Them and Captain Remus." I cursed. Of course, Captain Remus knew where they were. I hadn't been able to track him down outside of the Shadow Guard barracks though. The Chancellor kept talking, "He thinks one of them has something he's looking for, but he won't say what. That's all I know, I swear it."

I was silent a moment, observing the man. I wished I could tell for certain if he was telling the truth. I kept from speaking a moment longer, long enough to keep the man on edge.

"…Alright." I said finally, twirling my dagger and placing it back in its sheathe. I wouldn't have actually taken his thumb, but he didn't need to know that. All he needed to know was that I was to be feared. I turned to leave out the window I crawled through, but turned back, "What do you know of the mage who accompanied Remus on the day of the Taking?" The Taking - what everyone called the day the children were stolen away.

He shook his head fervently, "He took a different mage to each village. It's impossible to know." I sighed, and turned to leave again.

"Are- are you going to untie me?" He croaked out, his voice wavering.

"Your guards will untie you when they wake. Which should be in a couple of hours." I pushed away from the window and unsheathed my dagger one last time, "And if Aeron finds out I was poking around, or you tell anyone about this, I know where you live." I threatened.

"I- then what will I tell them when they find me tied up?" He choked out.

I grinned wickedly, using my dagger to lift the gaudy gold chain off his neck, "You can tell them you were robbed. That the great Chancellor of Laires was the victim of a home invasion where they stole the most prized item you own. Tell them, the Red Fox paid you a visit." I snatched the chain from my dagger and stuffed it my pocket.

Just then, the door burst open. One of the Chancellors guards stood in the doorway, looking disoriented, "Sir, are you-?" He stopped when he saw me. I silently cursed Adarra, who had apparently given me the wrong dosage for the poison I used. They weren't supposed to wake for hours, and I had no idea how long I had until the others woke up.

"Help me! Help me! I'm being robbed!" The Chancellor screeched, and I begrudgingly thanked the gods that he was keeping his end of the bargain.

The guard immediately rushed me, and I used his recently drugged state against him, barreling into him, causing him to knock off balance and fall to the ground. I winked at the Chancellor, and quickly swung my legs out the window. I quickly climbed down the way I had gotten in, down the trellis, and landed with a thud on the ground. I could hear the guards starting to come to. Shouts sounded from inside the manor – I didn't have much time. I sprinted for the stable, which I knew had at least one horse.

There was a woman tending to the horses. I recognized her. Blonde curls just like my ma – Stella, I believed her name was - the one who gave me the information I needed on the Chancellor. She froze when she saw me. "You're supposed to be with your family." I whispered.

Stella shook her head, "I have none. My husband died at the hands of the Shadow Guard years ago, and my sons were taken."

I looked back towards the stable door, "You need to get out of here, if you get caught letting me go, he'll kill you."

"I'm not going to let you go." She whispered hoarsely.

My heart pounded. "What do you-"

"I'm coming with you." She said with much more confidence. I went to argue with her, but the voices outside were growing louder.

"Are there two horses? Can you ride?" I asked urgently. Stella nodded. We wasted no time, mounting the horses and bursting through the stable doors, earning shouts from surprised guards as we galloped past. Arrows flew haphazardly in our direction, but the full effects of the poison hadn't quite worn off, making their aim atrocious. "Follow me!" I shouted behind me, and Stella nodded to me. Soon the voices of the disoriented guards faded into the night as we sped through the woods. We went full speed for a while, and only slowed when the horses needed water. We would be back at the Luminous Storm base by the next day.

Chapter 5

I startled awake, cold sweat dripping down my face. I had that dream again. What was that noise? Someone was banging on my door - loudly. "Someone better be dying!" I yelled while stuffing my head under my pillow. The knocking continued, "UGH," I moaned, dragging myself from the bed and checking my pocket watch - 5:45. I cracked my door open with a scowl on my face, fixing my death stare on whoever decided to wake me at this ungodly hour. It was two days since I returned from Laires with Stella, but I was still exhausted.

Liam grinned at me through the crack, "Good morning sleepy head." He pushed the door open and went past me, plopping himself down on the chair next to my bed. I yawned, shutting the door behind him, "It's too early for your happy face." I complained, falling back into bed, pulling my covers around me.

"According to your Ma, this is the exact time you were born." He said proudly, pulling a pastry out of his pocket and unwrapping it carefully. He plucked a candle from his other pocket, lit one of the matches from the pack I have to light my candles, and presented to me a makeshift birthday cake. "Happy birthday Cass." Liam said with a sad smile.

It's the one-year anniversary of me pounding on Liam's door in the middle of the night, bags packed, ready to leave for Luminous Storm. He resisted at first, for my sake. But once I told him I was leaving with or without him - he grabbed his own bag, and we left that night.

"I can't believe it's been a year" I said, sitting up and half-heartedly blowing out my sad little birthday pastry. "Is this from La'Bell's?" I asked him, tearing the pastry in two, and handing him the other half.

He took a bite and nodded, "Only the best for you, Cass" and winked.

I scoffed, motioning to my shabby bed, falling-apart nightstand, and cracked mirror on the wall, "Clearly."

He chuckled, and I found my eyes roaming the walls, the dark, cold stone a sharp contrast to the warm, wooden walls back in Everloom. I shook my head and decided to study Liam's face instead. He'd taken to leaving a bit of stubble on his face, and the rugged look suited him. Back in Everloom, he used to keep his hair pretty unkempt, but since joining the rebellion he's kept it close cropped. He'd also filled out considerably in the last year. He wasn't scrawny by any means before, but now he actually looked like a grown man - which I supposed he was.

"I heard you recruited someone on your recon mission?" Liam said knowingly. Recon. The rule was – do not draw attention to yourself and do not reveal that you work for the rebellion- unless absolutely necessary. Considering my actions against the Chancellor weren't exactly sanctioned, if anyone asked Stella how she was recruited, she'd say she saw me poking around and asked me too many questions.

I shrugged, "She doesn't have any family. Her kids were taken. She's in orientation now. Should be ready for assignments in two weeks." I wouldn't see her for a while.

My eyes darted to the cracked mirror behind him - there are more angles to my face than I remember there being - my baby face is gone. Even the gold strands on my hairline have gone paler and my eyes have turned more gold than green. My hair curls slightly when it's this short, cropped to my chin.

I can't say I'm too happy about the way my body has seemingly redistributed my body fat to give me curves where there weren't any before, but at least I'm still fit. My eyes look back to Liam, who caught me staring at myself in the mirror.

MARK OF THE FALLEN

"You don't look that different." He said softly. He knew how hard this day was for me.

I shook my head, "I do. Because I am. I'm a completely different person now."

My eyes were closed - the sun warming my face as I basked in the mid-morning glow. The sound of rushing water drowned any thoughts I had racing in my head. This was *my* spot. Liam and I discovered it our first month in Luminous Storm – a small clearing hidden behind a wall of vines – through a tunnel of rock and you come out to a small waterfall that pours into a small lake. It's surrounded by grass and trees, almost as if someone long ago had designed this place for this exact purpose. To get away. I kicked my feet, the water swishing around them as I dangled my legs into the pond. My pants were rolled up to my knees. I opted for loose linen ones today since I'm off duty.

I had spent the last year researching, travelling, trying to gather information. Making little…visits to close allies of Aeron, like the one I made to the Chancellor and leaving it under the guise of a robbery – "The Red Fox". Nobody could tell me anything. They all say the same thing. Aeron doesn't share that information with anyone, and nobody knows where they are. I just couldn't stomach it. Where could they have taken my brothers – all the children? Every lead I found legitimately I would bring to Commander Feldstrom, but was almost always brushed aside or dismissed. I wasn't sure what I did in the beginning, but he hadn't liked me from the first moment he met me. Since that first meeting, any snark or attitude he throws my way, I give right back to him. If that's how he wants to play it, then so be it – and hey, I was good at it.

Liam had changed since coming here. While I pushed boundaries and questioned decisions, Liam followed every single order without question. Things had changed between us too. We still had each other's back, but that line that we had sometimes toed between friendship and something more…we didn't go near that line anymore. Not since the night we came here.

On days like this, with the sun shining and the slight breeze, it was easy to imagine I was back in Everloom. Pretend that if I opened my eyes, I would see Bram playing in the grass, or Kolby doing cannonballs into the lake. To imagine that my Ma was sunning herself next to me, elbows back in the grass.

So, I kept my eyes closed. I would let myself be content in my imaginary world for just a moment. Let myself be suspended in my little dreamworld just outside reality.

MARK OF THE FALLEN

I heard a crack behind me – a footstep. Without opening my eyes, I called out, "You know, you would think after a year of stealth training you would be able to sneak up on me better."

A small chuckle, and the shifting of grass next me, "Nobody can sneak up on you." Liam's voice said, the small splash of water indicating that he too had opted to dip his feet in the water.

"I'm sure some could – but definitely not you." I replied, a small smile playing on my lips as I leaned over to rest my head on his shoulder, my eyes still closed.

"You wound me." he said, amusement in his voice. I could just imagine the look on his face. On days like this, when we were both off duty, it was easy to pretend that things were the way they were back in Everloom. To pretend that we hadn't crossed that line, and that we could show affection to each other without having to wonder what it meant – because it was just us. Liam and Cass.

His arm came up around my shoulder, and I opened my eyes. He had his pant legs rolled up as well, his legs kicking lazily in the water. I looked at him, his icy blue eyes were on the lake.

"I can't believe it's been a year." I said quietly, staring at the rippling of the water. We both knew I wasn't talking about leaving Everloom.

"It won't be for nothing." Liam said confidently, "They're alive, I know it."

My lips set in a tight line. It wasn't them being alive I was worried about. If they had all been executed, there would have been some sort of news – some statement. Someone would have seen something. No, what I was worried about was why was he keeping them alive? What was he doing to them? What was his purpose in taking them to begin with? "That's not what I'm worried about." I said tightly, lifting my head off his shoulder. I drew my knees out of the water up to my chest, wrapping my arms around them.

His brows knit together, "What are you worried about then?"

"They're alive, sure. But *why*? What is he *doing* to them? What are my poor baby brothers suffering while I'm – while I'm-" I choked on my words. Liam is silent as let out a slow breath. He doesn't get it. He would never get it. Why waste my time with useless words? "It's nothing." I said, "Never mind."

Liam sighed, turning to me, "No, come on Cass. Don't do that."

"Don't do what?" I ask him in a clipped voice, despite knowing exactly what he meant. I was already getting to my feet and brushing the grass off my clothes.

"Don't...don't shut me out. Please." I looked at him, his eyes pleading with me.

"I don't know what you're talking about." I said curtly, "Don't follow me." I added, walking out of the clearing.

I was on my way back into town when I heard my name called, "Hey Cass!" I turned my head, Adarra was running up to me. Adarra was an exotic beauty. Her gorgeously tan skin complemented her midnight black hair, all which made her light green eyes pop - you almost didn't notice her two small gold hoops piercing her left eyebrow. Not to mention the swirls of black ink that run up both arms – she was easy to pick out of a crowd. "Hey! I was looking for you all morning!" She exclaimed, pulling me into a hug. "Happy birthday!" She smiled.

"Thanks." I smiled tightly. I had made a point to not remind anyone that it was my birthday. I suppose I had Liam to thank for that. I hadn't seen her since I gave her a hard time about giving me the wrong dosage for the poison I used on the guards the day before. She and Liam were the only two who knew about my extra "trips" when I would go on recon missions.

"Let's go." She said, looping her arm through mine and leading me back into the forest.

"But I-" I started.

"No buts. You need to hit something." She said sternly. I could only sigh in resignation. Liam and I first met Adarra on our journey to the Luminous Storm base. She had been a part of Cairo's Traveling Circus - a semi-famous circus that would make its way around the kingdom during the summer. One look at her knife-throwing skill and I convinced her to join us.

She led me deeper into the forest until we came to a nondescript cabin. She pressed a hand to the center of the door, and it swung open. This was one of the various safe houses throughout the surrounding area – everyone had to be authorized by magic in order to enter.

Upon entering, the cabin looked like any other- there was a cozy set of furniture in the corner that included a couch and a rocking chair, a fireplace, various pictures, and paintings hanging off the wall. You would never know that there was a secret weapon's stash behind the fireplace. Unless you knew where to look.

Adarra counted from the hearth, 10 bricks up, 2 bricks over, up one, over one, and pressed. The fireplace retreated, revealing behind it a mass storage of weapons. Swords, broadswords, short swords, daggers, throwing knives, axes, maces – any weapon you could think of. I opted for two daggers. Since coming to Luminous Storm, I found that I liked to get in closer to my target than my short swords would allow.

Adarra grabbed a couple of throwing daggers, sheathed them at her side, and attempted to grab a life-sized training dummy from the room, motioning to me to grab the other end. We dragged it out of the room and out of the cabin, "I can't help but think I could use a big strong man right about now." Adarra grunted. I laughed, almost dropping my end.

We got it set up and stepped back to a reasonable distance. "You go first." I said, tilting my head toward the dummy. Adarra grinned, and brandished 3 knives between her fingers, her knuckles clenched to make a fist. In a single arc of her arm, she releases the knives, the first one embedding itself in its head, the second one in its neck, and the third one in its groin. I winced, "Ouch."

Adarra turned, pointing to the daggers at my side, "Your turn. You need to blow off some steam."

"No, I don't." I sighed, "I'm not mad, I just-"

"Well then *get mad.*" She interrupted me, "Yell, scream, hit something. *Stab something* for crying out loud. But don't shut down on me - on us."

"How on earth could you have talked to Liam so quickly?" I sighed, pushing my hair behind my ear.

"Who do you think kept him from coming after you? I told him you needed girl time." She grinned wickedly. "He was following after you like a lost puppy, and I didn't need you withdrawing further into your shell."

"He was following me?" I asked incredulously, fury burning in my chest, "After I made it clear I wanted to be alone?"

"That's it. Get mad." She said, "And aim for its head." I readied myself to launch at the dummy but then –

"Are you girls okay out here on your own?" A male voice called out. I faltered – glancing around. A group of three men, er, boys came out of the woods peering at us. They couldn't have been older than sixteen. They were dressed in the kind of armor that Liam and I would wear before joining the rebellion – mismatched materials haphazardly thrown together.

I raised an eyebrow at Adarra. We weren't in our armor or leathers, so I could see why they would be mistaken, "We're fine, thanks." I plastered a fake smile on my face, just hoping they'd go away. But instead, they came closer.

One of them, a mousy looking one, "Well, Miss, we in the Light Guard dedicate our lives to protecting those who cannot protect themselves. Can we please escort you to a safe place?"

I smirked. The Light Guard? A little on the nose. "Anywhere I go is a safe place." I remarked, "For me, anyway." I move to turn back towards Adarra, who was looking on, amused.

The mousy one grabbed my arm, my amusement going up in smoke and being replaced by that rage in my chest again, "We've spotted ruffians in the area. I'm afraid I must insist-"

"You have 2 seconds to let go of my arm before I break it." I snarled, and the boy's eyes widened in surprise. But still, he didn't let go.

"Woah, woah, woah" Adarra came forward, arms out in a peace-making gesture, "My friend here has not had a good day. For your own safety, you should let go. I assure you, we are perfectly capable-"

I mentally finished counting in my head and grabbed the boy's fingers, twisting and prying them from my arm. He screamed out in surprise as I twisted his arm behind his back, holding my dagger to his side. "Don't. Touch. Me." I snarled in his ear before pushing him forward into his friends. He landed face first on the floor in front of his friends, who were gaping at us.

One of the other ones started helping him up, "You didn't have to be so rude about it. We just wanted to protect you."

I raised an eyebrow, my rage momentarily satisfied by the sight of the boy on the floor in front of me, "You should really work on being able to protect yourself first." They glared at me and retreated back into the forest, no doubt in search of other poor helpless women who needed their help.

Adarra shook her head at me as we watched them walk off, "You didn't have to be so hard on them, they meant well."

"I'd say I went easy on them," I grinned, "I didn't actually use my dagger, and I gave him five seconds to get his hands off me instead of two."

We practiced on the dummy for about an hour after the "Light Guard" ran off, then put everything back the way we found it, locking the cabin behind us. I had to admit, I did feel much better after we strolled into town, passing by various carts selling flowers, farmers from nearby selling their vegetables, and little knick-knacks. We passed by a cart selling a collection of jewelry – which normally I wouldn't pay any attention to. But it was a hair pin that had what looked like rays of the sun that I was drawn to. It was painted gold in color, and for some reason I found myself picking it up and looking at it.

"Do you like that?" Adarra asked, peering over my shoulder, "I didn't think that you liked things like this."

"I don't…normally." I said quietly, turning over the hair pin and looking at it in the light.

"I'll be right back." She said, disappearing around the cart. I was transfixed by the pin. It was beautiful. If I turned it in the light just right-

"Alright! Hair pin is yours. Happy Birthday." Adarra said, coming back around the corner, a big smile on her face.

My head snapped to her, "You didn't have to-"

"I know." She grinned, looping her arm through mine again, "But that's just the kind of selfless, loving, humble friend I am." I rolled my eyes at her.

We traipsed into La'Bells, a favorite bakery in town. While they weren't official members of Luminous Storm, the couple who owned La'Bells provided us with a safe haven and a non-descript passage in and out of the base. We casually walked to the back of the bakery and towards the back door.

Belle, the woman who made all of the pastries, was working hard in the back, rolling some dough, while her husband, Landry, was checking out customers in the front. Belle's chestnut brown hair was piled high on top of her head, her pregnant belly protruding in wild disproportion to her small frame. Belle wiped a stripe of flour across her head, "Happy Birthday, Cass." she said pleasantly.

"Did Liam tell everyone he could find?" I muttered to Adarra before turning to Belle, "Thanks so much!" I tried to say sincerely.

"Don't be too hard on him, Cass, he means well." Belle said, as if she knew exactly how fake my smile was. Which she probably did.

"What's that old saying?" I asked, placing a faux-thinking finger on my chin, "The road to hell is paved with good intentions?"

She just chuckled and wiped her hands on her apron, "I always forget that you're not nearly as sweet as you look."

I shot her a wink as we passed by, "You know you love me, prickly or not."

Shaking her head, Belle just said, "You know I enjoy a good thorny rose but not everyone wants to be pricked each time they get too close." She looked at me pointedly.

Just then, Landry came in from the front of the store, his white-blonde hair curling around his ears, "My love, we need more chocolate puff pastries."

"There's a batch in the oven right now." She said, removing her apron and planting a kiss on his cheek.

Chapter 6

The next day, 7 am hits, and Liam and I were in the briefing room. Well, we called it a briefing room. Luminous Storm headquarters was in an underground base that was built hundreds of years ago. Nobody really knew where this place came from - but our only way in and out was through the sewers. As a result, the surroundings were always a little…dank. Some sets of rooms were actually just one room with a curtain down the middle - some walls crumbled here and there - Everything always felt a little bit…wet. The only upside was the mages managed to somehow keep most of the smell from the sewers out.

We sat among other warriors, all clad in our uniform black cloaks over our armor. In the corner was a small group of green robes - mages. Since Aeron was a mage, you would think that Luminous Storm would be wary of them - but just the opposite. Whenever there is a whiff of a mage that might be a sympathizer, Commander Feldstrom would send his best recruiters. Fight fire with fire, he would say. There wasn't any sort of rule that prevented us all from grouping together, but I could see why the mages would want to stick together. It didn't help that since shortly after The Taking there was a massive influx of people joining our cause – most needing housing within the base.

Adarra sidled into the empty spot next to me. "Have I missed anything?" She whispered, pulling her robe sleeves down and covering her sleeve of tattoos.

I shook my head, "No, the hens are still clucking as always." Every day for the last year, they turned in useless leads and tips that lead to missions that lead to nothing.

Adarra sighed, pulling her sleek braid over her shoulder, and pulling at the strands at the end "I don't know how many more days of 'we just don't know yet' I can take."

I could tell today was different. Usually, we'd get an update from a squad commander or whoever they assigned to give the report. But today…today, the rebellion's leader, Falcon Feldstrom, had deigned to show up for this meeting. Chatter among the other rebels died down as they realize who exactly is in the room with them.

"We know where Aeron is hiding the children." Falcon announced once everyone had stopped talking. Liam elbowed me. A silent, "I told you so.", and a silent indicator that he was going to pretend yesterday didn't happen. My heart nearly stopped in my chest. My stomach dropped and voices erupted all around me. Did that mean, my brothers…?

"I know this information is long overdue but settle down!" Falcon commanded sternly. He couldn't have been older than 23 but he commanded the room with the ease of someone who had been doing it 20 years. The voices died down again. "The fortress is warded from the inside out and is guarded heavily by the Shadow Guard. We can only guess that since the children still live - he must have an ulterior motive for keeping them alive."

"What reason could he have for keeping them alive?" I lean and whispered to Liam, joining him in deciding to pretend that yesterday never happened. While a mildly amusing scenario played out in my head of Aeron running an evil daycare, I feared that the truth could be much more sinister. Liam's eyes darted to me, but he still faced the front of the room, "We've never known him to spare any lives - even children's." I continued, keeping my voice low as Falcon continued briefing us. "Something doesn't add up." I said, more to myself. Worry flashed in Liam's eyes, but he quickly turned his attention back to Falcon. I rolled my eyes - since coming here Liam has become such a perfect soldier.

"I'm posting your assignments for the foreseeable future here" He proclaimed, pinning 5 pages of names and assignments to the board behind him, "We are allocating all extra resources rescuing those kids. Anyone who does not request to be on kitchen duty will be investigating how to blast through those wards." He nodded to us in dismissal.

Adarra started talking to some girl on her other side. I turned to Liam as other rebels crowded the assignment list. I tried to hide my hope, schooling my face into pure boredom - though the fact that now we knew where my brothers were being kept had me doing cartwheels on the inside. I'd created sort of an alter ego for myself here - even if these people were all fighting for the same thing we were, there's a hierarchy. If you showed weakness - someone else would swoop in to try to claim your rank.

Determining that enough people had cleared from the crowd around the board, I turned to Liam and Adarra and tilted my head towards the list, "You want to go check it out?" Liam grinned at me, but suddenly his gaze turns dark as his eyes follow something behind me.

"Not eager to find your station, Foxglove?" Only one person called me Foxglove. I whirled around to see Falcon Feldstrom looming over me. His short, cropped chestnut brown hair looked like he just rolled out of bed - and yet somehow at the same time I could tell that's exactly how he wanted it to look. His gray eyes glinted as he raised an eyebrow, "For someone who's been harassing me for a year about finding the missing kids - you sure are slow to see how you can help." He crossed his arms as he all but glared at me. Oh, so now he wanted to start trouble.

I lifted my chin in defiance, "I don't see how-"

Liam stepped beside me, "We were just going now, Commander."

Falcon's eyes lingered on mine for a moment, then, as if concluding that I'm not worth the hassle, he gave Liam a nod and sauntered off. I whirled to Liam, "Why did you do that? I can handle myself just fine."

 Liam shook his head, "One of these days, Cass, you're going to push him too far."

I rolled my eyes and turned towards the assignment board. Since coming to Luminous Storm, mine and Liam's relationship had…changed, and not in the way that it seemed like it was going to right before we left Everloom. Sure, we had one emotional kiss the night we left, but the next day he acted like it never happened. Clearly to him, it had been a mistake.

Adarra and I trudged up the two small steps that separated the speaking platform from the rows of chairs all the rebels sat in during meetings, searching for my name along one of the five pages, "Brightwood, Brightwood, Cass Brightwood" I muttered to myself, trailing my finger down row after row. Nothing. That jerk - I wasn't even on here! My blood boiled. A year of following my own leads. A year of telling him to tail Captain Remus. A year of bringing every crumb of evidence I could to Falcon. A year of putting in the most hours towards this cause - telling pessimists that yes, I did think those kids are still alive - and for what? For this brute to leave me off the assignments that will finally rescue my brothers? My sweet, innocent, baby brothers who have suffered for a whole year.

I whirled around, my gaze pinpointing Feldstrom in the crowd - a mage's spell finding its target. The look on his face, the face of a cat who had just had the time of his life batting around a mouse, told me enough.

"Cass?" I thought I heard Adarra say - but my heart is pounding in my ears so hard I can't be sure. I felt murder in my veins as I marched up to him, pushing against some people - others practically leaped away, with my finger out and jammed it into his chest. The creep had the nerve to look amused.

"Cass!" Liam yelped in surprise.

"Don't even think about it!" I snapped at him - and he had the good sense to back away.

"You." I gritted my teeth, jamming my finger further into Falcon's chest. I met his eyes, letting him see every ounce of hatred and pain that I wished on his soul, "Are. Trash."

I heard murmurs around me, *"Can she talk to him like that?"* someone whispered. I didn't care.

"Foxglove-" He said, anger rising in his voice.

"No." I said sharply, and surprisingly he fell silent. Everyone was looking at us. I tried to calm down, "Do you think that I've spent the last year working myself ragged, trying to find information to save my brothers just so you could leave me off the assignment list to save them?" I asked.

I heard murmuring around me. I wasn't expecting an answer from him. Just more cruel laughter or condescending looks. I shook my head and turned to walk away.

"Your brothers?" He asked - almost softly, something like guilt briefly crossing his face.

I sighed and stopped, still facing away from him. I felt Liam's hand on my shoulder. "Yes. Kolby is 14 now and Bram is 5." My usual fight wasn't there anymore. I felt…broken. The last year my rage had been fueling me, pushing me to wake up every day. My emptiness from the day before returned to me. What was the point of it all?

"I…" I heard him say, and for the first time he sounded like he was unsure of himself, "I didn't know."

I shrugged, "You never asked." I kept walking.

LIAM

I couldn't believe she did that. I couldn't believe she just walked up to the leader of the rebellion, put a finger in his chest and declared him trash. In front of everyone. How many times had I told her to just leave things alone? It was like she *wanted* to be punished.

I was truly worried for her this time. There had to be some major repercussions for what she had just done. I pushed the door open to the library, trying not to think of what kind of punishment Cass would get. The word "library" was a generous term for this room. It must have been a conference room at some point, but now it was lined with tables stacked with old dusty volumes that had apparently been smuggled out of the castle before Aeron fully came into power.

I scanned the titles, searching for anything that related to glyphs or wards. I loved Bram and Kolby like they were my own brothers – I would do whatever I could to bring them home safely. And hopefully bring Cass back to who she had been before they were taken.

She had changed since that day. She was always sure of herself, that much was true. But she was also lighthearted, kind, and *warm*. Gods, she had been so warm. Not just to me, but to her brothers, her ma – anyone that she came across. Since leaving Everloom, though, she had frozen over. She was cold, calculated, and cocky. I knew part of it was a façade. I knew that some part of it – no matter how small - was a front so that she didn't have to feel the reality of what happened that day. But if this went on much longer, I was afraid that part would fall away, and she would never thaw out.

I picked up a dusty brick which read, *"Protective Wards: A Complete Study"*, sighing in resignation, I sat at a nearby table, and began to read.

CASS

I was curled into a ball on my bed - crying. There was a knock on the door. "Go away, Liam." I called - Liam would be the only one willing to talk to me after the spectacle I put on this morning. I rolled onto my back and stared at the ceiling. Did I really call Falcon Feldstrom *trash?* And in front of literally *everyone?* I groaned as another knock sounded. I trudged to the door, not bothering to check the redness of my eyes. I swung my door open "Liam, I said I wasn't-" I stopped. Looking at me through the door was not Liam, but Falcon Feldstrom. In both mortification and anger, I immediately tried to slam the door shut - but he'd already stuck his foot in the small opening.

"Ow." He said, wincing slightly - and it was the most human I'd ever seen him look. "Foxglove… Cass." He corrected himself. I kept my face down - I didn't need the embarrassment of him seeing me like this. "Can I come in?" He asked - almost politely. I kept the urge to check the temperature of the floor to see if Hell had in fact frozen over under control. I could only bring myself to silently open the door off his foot.

He stepped in, and it suddenly felt much smaller in my room. We stood there awkwardly for a minute until he thought to close the door behind him. "Look, Foxgl- Cass." He corrected himself again. 2 for 2, not bad. "I'm sorry." This time I couldn't stop myself. I put the back of my hand to my face, concentrating. He let out an exasperated sigh. "Do I want to know what you're doing?" He asked in his usual condescending tone.

"I just think I might have a fever to the point of delusion. Did the all great and powerful Falcon Feldstrom just apologize to a lowly woman?" I asked, moving my hand around my face. Yes, I knew that most likely, he didn't care that I was a woman. We had plenty of women in our ranks that he treated with dignity and respect. But he hadn't liked me since day 1 – and until I had an actual reason, that's what I was going to assume.

He rolled his eyes. "Ha ha." He looked down, "You know none of this was caused by you being a girl."

I snorted, "Yeah, okay, and I'm a complete ray of sunshine to be around."

"You're making it really hard to apologize here." I looked at his face and I could see it. He was really trying.

"You're right." I sighed and sat on the edge of my bed. Falcon sat on the chair that Liam had been sitting in just that morning.

Falcon clasped his hands, "Look - what I did - it wasn't cool. I just wanted to get under your skin. Your reaction under other circumstances would be grounds for punishment. But given that I abused my power as captain to make a point, I think I deserved it." He gave an almost sheepish grin.

"And what point was that?" I asked pointedly, "What point were you trying to make, exactly?"

He sighed, "This whole time - since you got here. Your arrogance - even if well deserved - and your attitude and insistence… I got the distinct impression you were in all of this for the glory. Which isn't necessarily bad in itself. But when there are other people whose siblings or kids were taken…it rubbed me the wrong way that you were treating it like a ticket to glory."

"But I wasn't!" I protested, "You didn't even bother to ask me if I had anyone that was taken, you just assumed the worst!"

He raised his hands in surrender, "That's on me." He admitted.

"But…" I started, a realization dawning on me, "You hated me before any of that happened."

"Hated you?" he asked quizzically, his almost grin turning to a frown, as if he genuinely had no idea what I was talking about.

"From the first day I got here." I explained, "You told me that from the way Liam spoke about my talent, that you assumed I was a man." He was silent. "And then, you made me spar you every day in hand-to-hand combat for a month - never giving me a break. And then, you gave me kitchen duty for a month - even though I beat you half the time." Ever since then I wondered what I did that he disliked me so much. My resentment of him grew every time he would look at me with those condescending eyes.

He sighed, rubbing his temple, "To be honest Cass, at the start I was hoping I could make you quit and go home."

What? Why would he want me to quit? "Why? There are plenty of other agents who are women-"

"I told you it had nothing to do with that-"

"Then why? Why try to make me go home? What is so awful about me that right off the bat you wanted me gone -"

"Because, Cass. You come here, you join the rebellion, that makes me responsible for your life. If you die or get injured…that's on me."

I was silent for a moment, "But that doesn't matter for anyone else." I said. It's not a question, not really. I said it as a statement. To let him know that I knew he wasn't telling me everything. If he cared so much about everyone's lives, there would be no members of Luminous Storm.

He sighed, and I had a feeling whatever he was about to say was the reason we had never had a real conversation until now, "Because not everyone is cherished by General Ren." My heart caught in my throat. General Ren? What did General Ren have to do with any of this?

There was a knock on the door, "Commander? Are you in there?"

"Come in," Falcon replies.

"Oh sure, make yourself at home." I muttered under my breath.

Falcon stared daggers at me as the door opens. I guess we're not all buddy-buddy now. "He's here." The man- I think his name is Randor - said.

Falcon glanced at me, "You're going to want to come with me."

Chapter 7

I trailed behind Falcon on the walk back to wherever he was taking us. The base was rumored to have been built back before the kingdoms unified - back when this city was in the Silverglade Kingdom. Some speculated that the rooms were carved with magic – others thought that degenerates and criminals carved the place out of the sewers, desperate for a place to do their illegal business away from prying eyes. Regardless of where this underground bunker originated from, we were lucky they made so many exits, and that one came out of La 'Bells.

We walked up to a door – unremarkable in every way, the same metal and frame as all the other doors in the hallway. Eyebrow raised, I peered past Falcon as he opened the door. Standing behind a giant wooden desk, rifling through some papers was-

"General Ren!" I cried, running to him. He turned from the desk just as I threw myself at him and wrapped my arms around him.

"Oof," He said, staggering back slightly in surprise, but less than a second later I felt his hand on the back of my hair. "Oh, my girl," He said, his deep, gravelly voice shaking slightly. He pulled back to look at me, to observe all that had changed in the last year, and I became aware of the tears that were now on my cheeks. He smiled sadly at me, "You look older." He said, studying me, "And you cut your hair." he added.

I smiled through my tears, "You always told me to take away their advantage in a fight."

He nodded firmly, "So I did."

"General Ren…" I started, not sure how to ask this without seeming rude, "I'm so glad you're here but…why are you here?"

General Ren smiled knowingly and gave Falcon a look over my shoulder. Crap, I forgot he was here as soon as I saw General Ren. I wouldn't hear the end of this now - so much for my reputation. "I figured I left my rebellion in the hands of my nephew long enough."

My head whipped back towards Falcon, "Your *nephew*?" Falcon smirked.

Then the other half of the sentence hit me, "*Your rebellion*?"

"How's Ma?" I asked, praying for good news. General Ren only shook his head in response. We were sitting in one of the 2 meeting rooms that had been furnished with comfortable furniture. Tea was a luxury we apparently indulged in when there were important guests. "Grand Elder Ira?"

General Ren looked at me with sorrow in his eyes and clasped a hand over mine, "She's still the same." I nodded. Of course. Why would anything have changed since the last time I dared to send a letter home?

Falcon was strewn across an armchair, one fist propping his face up. I was sure that seeing me display affection to anyone, let alone his uncle, was like seeing a dog walk on its hind legs. He looked between us, bewildered, "What happened with-?"

"Quiet, nephew." General Ren said sternly. I had to keep myself from grinning. The image of the big, strong, Falcon Feldstrom being put into his place by his grouchy uncle was more than a little amusing. Nevertheless, I appreciated General Ren sparing me having to talk about Ma. "Where's Liam?" General Ren asked, surely confused as to why we were no longer attached at the hip.

"Oh…" I faltered, realizing I didn't know where Liam was. When was the last time that happened?

"Probably in the library." Falcon answered for me. The library. Not really a library, but more like a room full of whatever books we could smuggle in, haphazardly stacked around a group of tables. "I'll…go get him." He said, and I could tell that he was just giving General Ren and I a moment to ourselves.

"You've changed." General Ren said abruptly, turning to me. "You can try to mask it to everyone else or pretend that you've always been this way. But I know you, and I know your heart, Cassie. What happened to you?"

"Besides my brothers being taken from right under my nose and not being able to do anything about it?" I laughed bitterly. What *hadn't* happened to me?

"Yes." Ren said, staring at me, demanding an answer. Fine. First time he'd seen me in a year, and he wanted answers? I'd give them.

"You weren't there." I said, meeting his eyes, knowing full well the impact the words would have on him. He flinched slightly, my words hitting him, and I knew he blamed himself as well. "I blamed you for them being taken. Because you were gone. If you had been there, maybe we could have done something. But…" I trailed off. "I don't blame you, not anymore." Relief flooded his features. "But now I don't have anyone to blame. Except Aeron, and he's been untouchable. And Captain Remus - don't know where *he's* gone off to-"

"Captain Remus?" General Ren said abruptly. Alarmed.

"He's the one who showed up and took everyone…the creep." I shivered, remembering the way he looked at me.

Just then, Falcon opened the door, followed by Liam.

"General Ren!" Liam greeted, shaking his hand.

General Ren whirled on Falcon, "Did you look into Captain Remus?"

Falcon glanced at me, brows furrowed, "Yeah, Foxglove said that he's the one that took the kids in that village, but we couldn't dig up anything of substance on him. Why?"

Pausing to raise an eyebrow at the nickname, General Ren shook his head and sat down, "Cass, Liam, do you know where I've been the last year?"

General Ren told us about how he started the rebellion 4 years ago, and how he enlisted his nephew and any of his old army buddies he could find. Placing Falcon at the head so there would be an unknown name to lead it meant less chance of attracting the attention of the Shadow Guard. Basing it in Everloom would put too many villagers at risk, so he located this underground bunker.

Every time he would leave to "attend to business" he would be coming here.

Apparently, shortly after the children were taken, General Ren returned to Everloom to find it in chaos, Liam and I gone. He fully entrusted the rebellion to Falcon at that point, ("And told me I would pay for it dearly if anything happened to her." Falcon added, jabbing a finger in my direction), and enlisted in the Shadow Guard undercover. For almost a year, he hid in their ranks, trying to find out more information about where the kids were hidden. "Because of the timing of the enlistment and my age, they were suspicious of me at first." He said, "So I was mostly cleaning barracks and bathrooms in General Remus's territory...About 6 months ago though, he deemed me worthy of cleaning *his* room."

A gasp escaped me, "*You're* how we found out where the children were taken!" I resisted the urge to throw my arms around him in gratitude. Couldn't have any more emotional outbursts in front of Falcon.

He nodded, "I was found out though, so I had to run. Stopped by Everloom to collect my things, and then came here."

Liam low whistled, "So all this time, Luminous Storm was *yours*?"

General Ren nodded, "Yes, and I had intended to run one more errand before coming back to claim it, but now they have wanted posters of me up everywhere." He looked around us, "It's too risky for me to go back out there right now."

"I'll go." I said, stepping forward, "After all, it's not like I have an assignment." I glared at Falcon.

"Hey, I apologized for that!" He protested, but I just stuck my tongue out at him.

"I'll go with you," Liam jumped in.

"No, you won't." Falcon and I said at the same time, then looked at each other quizzically.

"I don't need you to protect me." I spoke first, turning back to Liam.

"You already have an assignment." Falcon said.

"You can't just go alone!" He said to me, and then turned to Falcon, "And she's my-" His what?

"It doesn't matter," Falcon said sternly, "There's no room to break assignments because your childhood best friend that you never confessed your love for has a different objective."

My cheeks reddened, and Liam and I both blurted, "That's not-"

"You already have an assignment. End of story. We need people where they're assigned and that's that."

Liam, for the first time since getting here, talked back to Falcon, "You can't just-"

"Last time I checked, Holloway," Falcon interrupted, getting entirely too close to Liam's face, "I was the commander here. So, I can do whatever I want and the only person who can tell me otherwise is General Ren."

General Ren cleared his throat and stepped between the two men. "There, there." He said, "No use getting worked up over it, you two. Commander Feldstrom has proved himself a more than capable leader over the last couple of years. So, unless he tries to kill one of you." He looked from me to Liam, "I'm going to stay out of it."

I nodded, and so did Liam, though begrudgingly. "She still can't go alone though." Liam piped up.

"She's not." General Ren answered.

"She's not?" Falcon asked.

"I'm not?" I asked - was there an echo in here?

"Falcon, you're going with her." General Ren grinned. Did he know what he was doing?

"We'll murder each other." I pleaded, "Why not just send him on his own then?"

"Well, I hope not." General Ren replied, "And you have a special…expertise when it comes to getting what I'm looking for."

"Alright." Falcon sighed, "What *are* we looking for?"

Chapter 8

The next morning, I was coming back with a fresh pastry from La 'Bells when I passed by Mullins, Selby, and Grigsby- recruits that joined about 4 months ago. "Gentlemen," I nodded as I passed them, and they all turned to follow me, "Cass," Mullins said, pulling up to walk on one side of me, his mousy brown hair tied at the back of his head, "We heard something about you and the commander."

I rolled my eyes, "Oh yeah? What did you hear?"

Grigsby came up on my other side, "We heard you called him trash." He raised a black eyebrow in a way that reminded me entirely too much of Kolby.

Selby was behind me, "Yeah, and now, as punishment, you have to carry his bags for him on a mission that you're leaving for today." He ran a hand through his short golden hair.

I stopped in my tracks, turning on the three of them "You three," I took a pointed bite of my pastry, "Need to not believe everything you hear."

"So, you *didn't* call him trash?" Selby asked skeptically.

I swallowed, "No, I definitely did that."

"So, you aren't going on a mission today?" Grigsby added.

"No, I am." I said, suddenly not as confident in this conversation.

"So, what shouldn't we believe?" Mullins prodded.

"I'm not..." I trailed off, then rolled my eyes, "I'm not being...punished." I finished, not entirely sure that the sentence I said was true.

"So, you *want* to go on this mission?" Grigsby asked.

I looked between the three of them and shook my head, "I don't have time for this." I turned to walk away, but not before I heard Selby snicker to his friends, "I told you."

"That's it, recruits!" I stood at attention, pulling out my best drill sergeant voice, "You think it's funny to mock a superior? Drop and give me 20!"

They looked at each other as if they weren't quite sure if they were hearing right, "You want us to...?" Mullins trailed off.

I continued in a booming voice, "That's right, Recruit Mullins, 20 push-ups, let's go! Unless you want to add a week of latrine duty to the mix!"

Their faces went white as they each dropped to the floor and started doing push-ups. After watching them struggle for about 10 seconds I grinned and walked away, taking a bite of my pastry.

After I packed my bag and met Falcon by the kitchens, we headed out one of the more obscure base exits. It was one of the few that came out in the…less desirable part of the city. Footsteps crunched behind me as I sighed internally. "We could just go our separate ways now." I said hopefully, "General Ren never has to know. Take a break, live topside for a little. I'll be back before you know it."

He brushed past me, shouldering his pack, "Please. General Ren will skin me alive if so much as a hair on your head is out of place when we get back. I'm not risking it."

I followed him through the shadiest part of town, home to all of the less desirables. Petty thieves, arsonists, mercenaries…you name it, they got it. I would question the decision to base the rebellion here, but it had its perks. Shadow Guard presence was minimal – they preferred to focus their energy on the more affluent towns where they could drink, flirt with rich ladies, and rough up folk who wouldn't try to fight back.

MARK OF THE FALLEN

"I think General Ren knows better than anyone that I can take care of myself just fine." I huffed, stepping around the sprawled body of a homeless man sleeping in the path. "*You* know just as well." I added, not so subtly reminding him of all the times that I've bested him on the mat.

The problem with these men – the men I would come across in my travels…they thought if they just threw themselves at the problem they could squash it - completely ignoring the fact that their target is quicker than them - and was thinking through her moves strategically. They think I'll be shaking in my boots, which makes them overconfident. Once they do figure it out however, it's just a matter of being one step ahead of me. Let's face it - I'm half their size - they would never be as quick as I am with all their bulky muscles in the way.

Falcon underestimated me the first couple times we went to the mat. Once he figured out I knew how to use his strength against him, he switched up his tactics and the outcomes of our spars were more evenly spread.

He glanced at me from behind, "Yes, you're a formidable opponent one on one. But multiple Shadow Guard? No way, Foxglove. Not even you can pull that off." I guess he had a point. We walked in silence through the city, our hoods drawn tight, weapons hidden under the folds of our capes. It was the end of summer, so we opted for the ones that barely grazed the elbow over the full-length cloaks we wore in the winter. Nobody spared us a second glance as we went by.

There was a caravan waiting for us at the edge town. Falcon handed them more gold than was necessary, and we hopped in back with all the merchandise that was being transported. I sighed as I circled, looking for a place to sit.

"You're not a dog, just sit somewhere." Falcon snapped at me.

"If I'm not a dog then don't order me around like one." I shot back but found a spot in a corner. Just big enough for two. Well, wouldn't we be cozy. I scooted myself back into the corner and patted the spot next to me with a provocative grin, "Come on, Commander. Get comfortable."

His gaze hardened as he looked away, "I'll stand."

"The whole trip?" I scoffed, "Clearly you've never tried to stand in a moving caravan while it rides over dirt roads."

"Oh, how hard can it be-" He started, and is promptly thrown to the side once the caravan starts moving. I stifled a laugh. He caught himself on a stack of boxes, rights himself, only to lose his balance once again. Giving up, he dropped to all fours, and crawled over to the empty spot on the floor next to me. "You tell anyone about this," He growled, "and you'll be in kitchen duty for so long people will think we hired a head chef."

I couldn't help myself - I laughed. "What?" He snapped.

"You…" I laughed even harder, imagining it, "Liam tried to stand a lot longer" I almost choked on my laughter, imagining the two of them in one caravan, stubbornly trying to stand while being thrown side to side like ragdolls. I lost it even more.

"Well, I'm glad you think it's so funny." Falcon said, crossing his arms like a pouting child.

"You're such an oxymoron" I chuckled, shaking my head.

"Did you just call me a moron? We may be on assignment, Foxglove, but don't think that means-"

"Not a moron - an *oxy*moron," I said, elbowing his side, "A walking contradiction." He stared at me blankly. "You have this reputation. This tough, strong, flawless reputation. When you get thrown around like a ragdoll, or cross your arms like that, it contradicts your reputation. And it's funny." He started to protest "and it makes you seem a little more human, too." I said quietly. Falcon was silent.

"So, where are we going?" I asked, pulling my legs up to my chest and wrapping my arms around them. The space we were in was so tight our legs were almost touching.

Falcon shook his head, almost as if trying to clear it, and pulled some papers out of his pack. "We are going to General Ren's second residence in Hillsborough. He doesn't think Aeron knows about it, but just in case he does, we are the ones sneaking in. If we get caught, then we can have a cover story."

"Okay, what are we retrieving?" I asked inquisitively. Some locating devices or a special ward-breaker? Surely General Ren had something up his sleeve.

"I'm not sure." Falcon admitted.

"What?!" I was incredulous. He didn't tell us what we're looking for?

Falcon raised his hands in a placating gesture, "General Ren said that you would be able to find it, but he didn't want to give us too much information in case we get captured by the Shadow Guards." The hideout was warded so that if any mage peered into the mind of someone trying to find it, they would immediately forget what they were doing.

What was he talking about? I would be able to sense it? Has General Ren lost his mind? First he sends Falcon and I off together, and now this…?

"I hope you know that I have no idea what that means." I said truthfully.

He sighed, "Yeah I was afraid of that. I guess we'll just have to go and see."

I contemplated the rest of what he said for a moment, "Cover story? Like what?" I asked skeptically.

"Like we're a brother and sister who used to live in the home and we just really wanted to visit it?" Falcon said, clearly not thinking the idea through at all.

I scoffed, "Brother and sister? Who on earth would be stupid enough to think that we," I motioned between us, "are related, let alone siblings?" Between size, stature, facial features, hair, eyes, everything - we were completely different.

He brought a hand to chin in contemplation, "You're right. So, what else…married? Newlyweds looking for a new home?"

If I had been drinking anything at that moment I would have spit it out, "Married? You think *we* can pull off married?"

"Is that hard to pretend to like me for a couple of hours?" He asked dryly.

"Not if you gave me something to like." I smiled sweetly.

Suddenly his hand was on top of mine. He reached his other hand out slowly and tucked the gold strand of hair behind my ear and leaned towards me, "I've always been captivated by your eyes." He said, grazing his knuckles over my cheek in a way that sent shivers down my spine. "The way that they burn more gold when you're angry…it makes me want to push you harder just to see if I can set them on fire. I'm especially curious as to what color they are after I've kissed you." Had his eyes always been silver? I had thought they were more gray…

I loosed a breath I didn't realize I'd been holding. His gaze, though provocative, looked sincere…

"See, aren't I an excellent actor?" He said pompously, turning away from me.

He might as well have splashed cold water on me. "Yes." I said, clearing my throat, "A great actor. Do me a favor, and next time warn me before you go all suave on me - I was already thinking of how I was going to reject you."

"You liked it." He smirked.

"I was…momentarily taken by surprise." I admitted. "It's been a very long time since anyone has looked at me like that and I was caught off guard." I gave him a mocking salute, "It won't happen again sir. I'll be ready when we go undercover."

He shook his head, "Holloway looks at you like that every day. As well as half of the male cadets." He raised an eyebrow. "Don't tell me you haven't noticed. I might think your observation skills not up to par for this mission."

"I'm not…into dating anyone right now, so it doesn't even matter." I focused on my knees, "Not that it's any of your business, *Commander*. But since my brothers were taken from me the only thing I care about is getting them back. I don't have time to think about anything else. It would be irresponsible of me." I concluded.

Crossing my arms, I settled into my little corner, and tried to get some rest. It was going to be a long trip.

Chapter 9

I was sleeping…a warm soft bed. I fluttered my eyes open, but I wasn't at Luminous Storm Headquarters or even back in Everloom. I was in a house I had never seen before…something was calling to me. I hopped out of the bed and followed the call. The floorboards. I tried as hard as I could to pry up the floorboards but -

We jerked to a stop and my eyes flew open. It still felt like I was in a warm bed…I scrambled to my feet. Falcon. I had been sleeping in a sitting position, with the whole side of my body pressed against him. How embarrassing.

I checked through the flap of the caravan. We were just outside Hillsborough. "Commander!" I hissed, and he didn't move. "Falcon!" I whisper-yelled, tapping him with my boot. His eyes fluttered open. "We're here." I said. Hopefully he doesn't realize how we slept for who knew how long last night. I wouldn't hear the end of it. Although, I do have to say that despite the conditions - I felt more rested than I had in a long time.

"I slept better than I thought I would." Falcon said as he stepped from the caravan. My cheeks heated.

"Yeah, that's weird you looked super uncomfortable." I said quickly, turning away from him. The caravan set off to its actual destination. We looked over the hill to the town of Hillsborough. I could see from here that they had stone paved roads and shops everywhere. They even had streetlights - a luxury not many villages could afford.

Falcon let out a low whistle, "We are not going to fit in here."

I looked down at my clothes. A linen top with an armored corset around my middle, brown leather pants that were easy to move in, and two daggers sheathed on each side of my waist. The same clothes I had worn every day for the last year. Yeah, this wouldn't do.

"There's a small village about a mile the other way." He said, pointing behind me. "If I'm correct, they'll sell a lot of the same fashions."

Falcon was correct. We left the small shop in the village of Hillsclimb, 1 mile south of Hillsborough. I was wearing some ridiculous pale pink frilly top and skirt with my hair twisted up. I refused a dress, but I could keep my pants on under the skirt in case we had to make a quick getaway -the skirt was long enough to hid them. On top of it all, Falcon insisted that a "smart businessman like him wouldn't let his new bride walk around without any accessories like some sort of commoner." He *was* a really good actor. So here I was, with dangling earrings and a large, jeweled necklace adorning me. At least I could take it off and beat someone with it if I had to. I could probably stab the posts of the earrings into someone's eyes if the situation called for it. The shop lady had even helped me put on some cosmetics. Apparently, I was "too pale". Fortunately, the shop woman was sympathetic to our cause. Our fabricated cause of attending a family reunion but feeling self-conscious because we are not as well off financially as the rest of our family.

I forced myself to look in the mirror at the finished product. I had expected to be repulsed by what I saw – perhaps I might resemble a clown or look like a kid who had gotten into her mother's bag- but surprisingly, I wasn't. The subtle blush brought some color to my cheeks, and the black that lined my lids made my eyes pop. With the color on my lips, I could almost pass for a suitable lady. What would Liam think if he could see me now?

Falcon was wearing a dress shirt with a vest - a *vest* of all things. He also bought a pair of glasses that "make you look smart" - according to the saleswoman. Viewing ourselves in the mirror of the shop…we did look like a couple.

We made a show of hailing down a carriage taxi to take us into the town, stopping at the town square. On the ride over, Falcon had coached me on what etiquette the high-class women follow. He made sure to list out all my habits that a high-class woman does NOT do.

Falcon exited the carriage first, holding out his hand to assist me out of the carriage like I was some frail flower. We made the right call changing our appearance before coming here. The streets were bustling with people. "What was your uncle thinking, buying a secondary residence out here of all places." I whisper to Falcon, keeping a polite smile on my face. My unfamiliar skirts got bunched under my foot and I tripped just as I was stepping out of the carriage. I was falling - hands steadied me.

"Oh, my dear wife, I would be most devastated if you injured yourself." Falcon said loudly. His eyes saying *get it together.* I heard murmurs from the passersby.

I righted myself, and gracefully stepped down from the carriage, said loud enough for everyone to hear, "Oh husband, I apologize. You know I still get those butterflies whenever you look at me." I batted my eyelashes and looped my arm through his.

"Oh, how romantic." I heard someone whisper. Good.

"I'm starting to see what you meant about the oxymoron." He whispered to me as we made our way toward General Ren's secondary residence. We thought it might seem too suspicious if we just pulled right up to the house. Best to blend in. As we made our way through, arm in arm nobody even spared us a second look. Everything was going according to plan.

"Is it satisfying?" I whispered back, "Seeing me in a *skirt* of all things. Bet you're loving this…knocking me down a peg. Don't get me wrong, I love a pretty dress when the occasion calls for it – but not when lives are on the line."

We pass by a building with Shadow Guard standing watch outside. I hold my breath until we are clear past them – they glanced at us but looked away.

"Not at all," he said, patting my hand with his, successfully playing the role of a lovestruck newlywed. "Besides, the oxymoron I was referring to was you being nice to me. I much prefer how you looked before…the makeover."

I gazed at him, willing my features to turn loving, "I much prefer you with glasses." Knowing flashed across his stare and I knew Liam was right. One day, teasing or not, I was going to push him too far.

We walked up to the house General Ren specified, it was nestled in between two rather large houses, and General Ren clearly hadn't been keeping up on the maintenance. We went to open the gate, and a woman popped out of the house next door.

"Is someone finally going to do something about that eyesore-" Her eyes widened as she spotted us. Typical wannabe noblewoman, great poofy dress with an elaborate updo and feathers in her hair. Never mind that all the noble families in Trilithia died off years ago.

She eyed Falcon like a starving lion. "Oh." She said, noticing me on his arm. "What do we owe the pleasure?" She sneered at me.

"Good afternoon, good lady. My name is Barnabas Farkleberry, and this is my bride, Mrs. Eleanor Farkleberry." I almost burst out laughing at the names he picked out.

"Pleasure to meet you, my lady." I purred, tightening my grip on Falcon. He glanced at me, surprise filling his eyes. He turned back towards the woman, "My uncle, the owner of this home, has passed away." He pulled out a key, "We were just going to look it over and see if we would sell it or possibly move in."

"Our first home together." I said, gagging internally at the sappiness in my voice. But if that's what it took to get this woman to back off then so be it.

"You can never be too careful." The woman said, "There was a burglary in Laires just a few days ago. The Chancellor himself was tied to a chair and robbed blind. The woman called herself 'The Red Fox'." I suppressed a grin. It was satisfying that I had made such an impact.

Falcon stiffened, but continued speaking casually, "Oh, how horrid. We will certainly keep an eye out."

The woman just nodded and went back inside.

"You can loosen your grip now." Falcon said out of the corner of his mouth.

Releasing him casually, I held my hand out for the key to the house. Falcon gave me a look that said, *no way am I handing over this key and letting you take charge.*

"My love?" I asked through gritted teeth, feigning a smile as my eyes pointed towards the window of the house next door, where our lovely neighbor was peeking her nosy head through the curtains. One suspicious move and she could call the Shadow Guard in the name of a disturbance - and he knew it.

He plastered a grin on his face and handed me the key. We walked through the front door and quickly shut the door behind us. Falcon whirled on me, "Any particular reason why you felt so inclined to put our cover on the line for a lousy key?"

I shrugged, "If it's such a lousy key why didn't you just hand it over?" It was petty. I didn't care. If I'm the one who can supposedly find whatever it is we're looking for, why can't I open the stupid door?

He took another step toward me, backing me up against the wall, "*You* were in Laires a few days ago."

My breath caught in my throat, as I braced myself on the wall behind me, "*And?*"

"And," He grit out, staring me down, "You have a habit of trying to take things into your own hands and blatantly ignore orders."

I held his gaze, and raised an eyebrow, "You think I'm a burglar?"

He stared at me, his brow still furrowed. Sizing me up. I held my breath. He shook his head, sighing, "You're right." He said, "I'm just…on edge." He backed up and looked around, "Do you…feel anything? Or…sense anything I guess?"

I let out an internal sigh of relief. I was safe for now. Turning my attention to the task at hand, I concentrated for a moment, reaching out with my senses for anything…weird. I wasn't sure what I was looking for, but I'd know it when I felt it, right?

"Let's spread out." I suggested. I took the upstairs, Falcon stayed downstairs. I wandered down a hallway, something familiar tugged at me. I followed the tug, almost like I was following a thread…I found myself in a bedroom. Why did this bedroom look so familiar…?

"Falcon!" I called, scanning the room. It only took him a few moments to find me.

"What is it?" He sounded almost concerned.

"It's in here somewhere."

"How do you know?"

"I don't know, I just do."

"Well, do you know *where* in here?"

I shook my head, trying to remember my dream from the night before. I felt my cheeks heat at the memory of the soft, warm bed. What did I do after that?

I breathed, "The floorboards." I reached into my belt for - I cursed under my breath. This wretched skirt was keeping me from accessing any of my weapons. I went to rip the cursed thing off when Falcon held up a hand to me.

"Wait." he felt a hand around under the bed and pulled out a sword that had been secured to the underside of the mattress. "I know my uncle," he explained, handing the sword over.

I nodded and settled the tip of the blade in the crack between 2 of the floorboards. It lifted easily, as if it had been done many times before. I peered inside and found…an amulet? What was so special about this? It was a circle amulet on a silver chain, and upon closer inspection, there was a symbol on it…3 circles overlapping each other, two on the top, one on the bottom, and an intersection of all 3 in the middle. Hmm… The pull I felt earlier was…gone.

"This isn't it." I declared, carelessly tossing the amulet to Falcon, who had been observing me silently.

"What do you mean?" He caught the amulet with unsurprising ease. He took a close look at it, "I've seen this symbol before." He said, lost in thought. "We need to contact General Ren."

Suddenly, there was a shuffling sound from under the bed, making us both jump. We backed up, me holding the sword Falcon handed me in a ready position, prepared to take down whatever threat -

Two vibrant amber eyes blinked up at us from under the bed, followed by two black paws stretching out in front, and finally, the rest of the creature emerged from its hiding place under General Ren's bed,

"A fox?" Falcon questioned, eyebrows raised.

The fox blinked up at us, it's head tilting in a question as if to ask, "What are you doing here?" It seemed small, for a fox, probably the size of a large cat. The fox was black, which was unusual enough, but its paws, the tips of its ears, and the tip of its tail was white. Though there was one other thing that stood out. There was a round white patch of fur its chest, surrounded by lines that started right next to the round patch and moved outward – almost like sun rays.

"Hi sweetie." I said, leaning down, and holding my hand out to it. It took a tentative step toward me.

Falcon started., "Cass, that thing could be rabid-"

"Just like me then?" I asked, raising a brow. I shook my head and ignored him, continuing to hold my hand out to the fox. After shooting a wary glance at Falcon, the fox continued to move toward me, and gingerly sniffed my hand. Its eyes moved from my hand to my face, its head tilting again. This time it nudged my hand with its nose. I reached to scratch behind its ears, "Is that what you wanted?" I asked, giggling as it flopped over on onto – it seemed like *her* back, "Belly rubs it is."

"Do you think she's been here very long?" Falcon asked, crossing his arms.

"I'm not sure..." I trail off, further inspecting the mark on her chest. If I didn't know any better, I'd think-

MARK OF THE FALLEN

I was shaken from my internal thoughts by Falcon sighing and pulling a chain out from under his shirt, and speaking into the pendant attached, "General Ren, can you hear me?"

Suddenly, the pendant started to glow, and I heard General Ren's voice coming from it, "Falcon, I hear you, did Cass find it?"

At the suddenness of General Ren's voice, the fox sprang up, and darted from the room with her tail puffed. I looked after and frowned.

"No, but we found something else." Falcon explained how I knew to come to this room, but that there was something else under the floorboards.

"An amulet?" General Ren's voice reverberates through the room, "What kind of amulet?"

"It has this symbol on it-"

"Symbol? Is it 3 overlapping circles?"

"It is, how did you-"

He cursed, "That Callum Abernathy just doesn't know when to leave well enough alone." I could hear the irritation in his voice.

"Callum Abernathy, sir?" I chime in…had I heard that name somewhere before?

"He was the Grand Mage of the Royal Court. He, the royal spymaster, and I were all bestowed those amulets by the King to represent our loyalty and our standing with him. The spymaster was in the castle the night that everyone died so it couldn't have been him."

"Where is this Callum Abernathy? Will he be on our side?" Falcon questioned.

"His loyalty has always been to the king. I can only guess that he felt my hiding place too…unprotected. You're going to have to go retrieve it from him. Head to Kleidis, the locals should be able to point you the way."

"But Sir," I interject again, "What if he doesn't believe who we are? How will he know you sent us?"

The pendant was silent for a moment… "Sir?" Falcon asked tentatively.

"Tell him, 'The Mark Lives On,'" He finally said. The pendant went dark.

FALCON

My back was killing me. I shifted uncomfortably on the couch, my legs hanging off the end of it. Leave it to my uncle to not have a spare bed in a house with four bedrooms. Maybe I would be better off on the floor.

MARK OF THE FALLEN

I wasn't sure why my uncle thought Foxglove would be able to lead us to…whatever he had sent us here for. He more cryptic than usual in his instructions, which was irritating. The fact that he sent the two of us alone only irritated me more.

She was infuriating. Constantly trying to push my buttons, shoving in my face the fact that she could handle a weapon – she acted as if I would be mortally offended that she could find her way around a blade. As if my uncle wasn't the one who trained her. I'm sure that she just thought of me as some kind of misogynistic brute. Whatever. Let her think what she wants.

Though, it had been oddly satisfying to see her out of her element today in that ridiculous frilly skirt – so impractical. The fashions here were ridiculous. Nothing like the clothing nobility would wear before the fall of the royal family. I had vague memories of balls my uncle would attend before the they fell…he brought my mother to one and seeing her dressed up like that - I had thought she was a princess. I smiled at the memory. Suddenly an image of Cass in one of *those* dresses entered my mind. She would need hidden pockets or straps for her daggers of course, but…my cheeks heated involuntarily. I shook my head and lifted myself from the couch. Perhaps I would be more comfortable in one of the upstairs bedrooms.

CASS

I was laying in the bed in the room we found the amulet, staring at the ceiling. Falcon was on the couch downstairs. It was strange, being in the same space as him in a such a…domestic setting.

We were to get a good night's sleep and set out first thing in the morning. Unfortunately for me…I couldn't sleep. I eyed the frilly top and skirt I had discarded on the floor in disgust, I would die if I had to wear that again. Falcon had rummaged through some of the rooms and brought me some very roomy men's pajamas to wear for the night.

Sighing, I threw my legs over the side of the bed and padded to closet. Throwing the doors open, I stepped inside. It was mostly empty, save for a few jackets hanging at the end and a spare blanket folded on the floor. It looked especially cozy, so I grabbed it, wrapping it around my shoulders and over my head like a hood. Something caught my eye - there was a slightly raised floorboard where the blanket had been. I shook my head. General Ren needed to find better hiding places for things. Lifting the board, still wrapped in the blanket, I reached down and found…paper?

I pulled out a stack of papers and sifted through them. I settled in, sitting cross-legged. I felt a little guilty snooping, but it's not like he's being exactly forthright with us. It was more than a little annoying that he wouldn't tell me why he thought I would be able to find what we were looking for without actually knowing what it is.

A small square of paper fell out of one of the letters. I read the back, scrawled in hurried writing, "Falcon, 1st birthday." I flipped it over and grinned. It was a bit blurry- the moment clearly captured by an older magical image device. But it was Falcon, at just a year old, smiling a two toothed smile at a young woman – who I would guess to be his mother.

I skimmed the letter, there was no information pertaining to our situation. Something about Falcon finally taking his first steps and a disbelief at the cost of meat increasing. I picked up another letter, this one written in a different script than the first.

R,

    I am at a loss. Please hear my plea. Father will not bless the marriage, but I am already with child. We have married in secret, but I am afraid for my child's future. I know that you warned me all of this would happen, but I am desperate.

    Please speak with him if you can. You're the only one I can trust.

    Lovingly,

        E

Scandalous. A child out of wedlock… could this letter be from the woman in the picture of Falcon as a baby? R…I assumed that was General Ren, but I had no idea who "E" was. I shook my head, as juicy as this gossip is, it still has nothing to do why we're here. I heard a creak in the doorway.

"Do you often make a habit of sitting in closets?" Falcon asked, leaning in the doorway. His hair was unintentionally disheveled, his shirt was only half buttoned, like he had thrown it on hastily to come up here. He had obviously been asleep. There was a hint of a tattoo peeking out on his chest…

"Probably about as often as you sneak into women's rooms uninvited." I retorted, hastily stuffing the second letter into my blanket. I stood up, and walked past him, shoving his baby picture into his chest. "Cute baby." I raised an eyebrow and sat on the bed.

"I wasn't sneaking-" He paused, looking at the picture and reading the back, his eyebrows knitting together in confusion, "Where did you get this?"

I shrugged, "The closet. I was looking for a blanket. Are surprised that your uncle has a picture of you as a baby?"

He tilted his head, "My uncle isn't the sentimental type. Except with you, apparently."

I ignored the comment, "Why are you up here?"

"I heard rustling, and wanted to make sure everything was okay." He said, rubbing a hand on the back of his neck.

I rolled my eyes, "Don't worry. The monster in the closet didn't get me."

He rolled his eyes right back at me and turned to go out of the room, "Okay, fine. Next time I'll just-"

"Falcon." I called out before I could stop myself. He stopped and turned to me, a questioning look on his face. "Thank you." I said, the words burning in my throat. Then I hurriedly turned around and laid on the bed, facing away from him. I swear I heard a low chuckle before he walked back downstairs.

Chapter 10

I tried to find our new fox friend before we headed out, but she had disappeared entirely. It was the next day, and though we *had* set up for the same caravan that brought us to take us back home, the change of our destination had us scrambling for other means of transportation. Because we blew most of our money on useless fashions the day before, we had to spend over half of our remaining money on one horse. We tried to get our money back but the shopkeeper all but laughed in our faces when we trudged back in asking to return the clothing for a refund.

Kleidis was a two-day trip on horseback. That meant two days on a horse…with Falcon. I wasn't too used to horseback riding to begin with, but now sharing with another person? Let's just say the urgency of this mission was the only reason I didn't insist on walking behind the horse every step of the way. Not to mention the last time I had shared a horse with someone was the night Liam and I left Everloom.

We were on a dirt path in the middle of the Forest of Gilea - a forest that was once sacred, but now just mostly serves as an intersection of roads for merchants, travelers, or mercenaries. Our chestnut mare, Nera, was timid enough, and I had a feeling she didn't appreciate my constant nagging either. Regardless, I continued - maybe he would be annoyed enough to steal us another horse from some bandits.

"Your knee is digging into my leg," I complained, trying to adjust myself without falling off Nera.

"No, it's not." he said, not moving an inch. I huffed. Rolling my shoulders. "Stop that." He snapped at me, like I was a child annoying their babysitter.

"I'm just so *uncomfortable*." I all but whined.

I heard him sigh in frustration, "Stop being such a princess."

"Princess?!" I asked indignantly. He really just called me a princess? "How many princesses do you know that can beat you on the sparring mat?" I asked with a smug smile.

"Just one, apparently." He said, suddenly unbothered. I was content to sit for a moment, trying to come up with the next thing I could complain about, when an uneasy silence took over. "Do you feel that?" I said quietly.

"Oh, what is now-" He started, but suddenly stopped, his eyes scanning the trees. He sensed it too.

Without warning, he whipped the reins, causing the horse to take off in a gallop. The sudden movement jolted me back against his chest, the wind whipping through my hair. Before I could ask him what we were running from, a large black horse ran out of the forest and into our path, causing our horse to rear back, dumping both of us off the back of the horse.

Falcon groaned beneath my weight. I quickly rolled off him and righted myself, who would go into our path like that?

"Well, well, well. What do we have here?" A massive, muscled, tattooed man stepped from around the horse in our path. Nera whinnied nervously behind me. Falcon slowly got up and casually stepped in front of me. I shot the back of his head a look - what was up with the sudden protectiveness?

The man was bald and had a handlebar mustache. I rolled my eyes. Typical mercenary. "Looks like we got a couple of young ones here!" He exclaimed, raising his arms. Chills went down my spine as I witnessed a dozen other men step out of the woods from around us. All tattooed, most of them missing a couple of teeth, and all of them sneering at us. The one who threw us off our horse was clearly the leader. I almost shrank back behind Falcon before I stopped myself. What was I thinking? I could take down any one of these men in a fair fight. Key word - fair.

"Look, we don't want any trouble." Falcon said, raising his hands. "Let us pass without a fuss, we'll be out of your hair. What's your toll fee? Five, ten gold?" The leader of the mercenaries chuckled and started circling us. "Try 50 gold, boy."

I nearly choked, "50 gold, that's-" Falcon jabbed an elbow back into me.

The leader's eyes flickered to me, something dark lit within them. "Interesting…" He said quietly, and side-stepped Falcon, focusing in on me. I could feel myself fight the urge to shrink back in fear. Falcon tried to step back in front of him, but one of the other men grabbed him by the arm with a sword in his side.

"We don't have 50 gold." Falcon said all too calmly despite the fact there was a sword poking into his ribs. "But we can give you everything we have."

The leader lifted the pale gold strand of my hair with his blade. I refused to break his stare - let him see my hatred. He gave a wicked grin and turned back toward Falcon, "My price has just gone up, boy."

Pure rage consumed Falcon's features, "Don't you touch her." He said through gritted teeth.

There was a rustle in the bushes nearby, nobody seemed to notice but me. Imagine my surprise when a fox started to step out of the bushes. My eyes shot to its chest, searching for that mark– it was the same one from General Ren's house. Her ears were back, her teeth bared, and she was staring at the leader of this mercenary gang. Sensing my gaze, her eyes shot to me. I shook my head, hoping beyond all reason that this little creature could decipher the meaning of the movement. Who knew what these cretins would do for a fox pelt that beautiful?

Falcon, following my gaze, had his eyebrows shoot up so far they nearly disappeared into his hair. At his sudden change in demeanor, the leader started to turn towards the source of our distraction.

Uh-oh. I needed to change tactics - fast. "So much trouble just for me?" I purred, batting my eyelashes sweetly at the leader. His head snapped to me, completely forgetting to investigate what had caught Falcon's attention. "All you had to do was ask, stud." I dared to touch a hand to his shoulder. Falcon's jaw nearly dropped. "I was getting so bored of this…man." I said, waving my hand nonchalantly towards Falcon, who seemed to finally catch on to what I was up to. Now I had the attention of all the men around us. Good. "What's your name?" I asked innocently. My eyes shot behind him, the fox was still staring tentatively, but I willed all my emotion and thoughts into a glance at the fox. Surprisingly, it almost seemed like she nodded, and scampered away back into the bushes.

I let out an internal sigh of relief. "You can call me Ryker." He said, practically puffing out his chest.

"Ryker." I said, the sound rolling off my tongue as if I was testing the name out. "Do you know why I'm so much fun to be around?" Now that I'm able to focus entirely on distracting him, I'm a little more confident in the outcome of this battle.

He smiled stupidly at me, "Are you gonna tell me?" This was too easy.

"Because…" I trailed off, walking my fingers up his arm, "I keep things exciting. You never know what I'm going to do" I winked at him… "next."

At that moment, the man who had Falcon collapsed with a grunt, a dagger in his throat. He turned his head toward the commotion and in a split second, I took my dagger and jammed it into Ryker's side. "You little-!" But he couldn't get out whatever he was about to call me, because that's the moment that my fist connected with his face, and he fell to the floor.

Absolute chaos ensued. There were about 10 men against the two of us. I had two daggers and a short sword on me but Falcon…Falcon was fighting with one dagger - the one he pulled out of the dead mercenary's neck. Where were his weapons? Three men slowly came towards me, backing me into a corner.

"You're going to regret that, hag." One of them spat in my direction. I kept backing up, trying to come up with a plan to get both of us out of here alive.

Before long, I backed right into Nera, who had been nervously whining off to the side. Ow. Something prodded into my back. That had to be Falcon's sword.

"Now, now boys…You can't really blame me for not wanting to be manhandled." I uselessly tried to reason with them. I sighed dramatically. "Men. They never learn." I unsheathed Falcon's sword from behind me.

"Oho don't hurt yourself, girly." One of them laughed. I didn't dignify it with a response. I was done. I'd let the blade do the talking now.

I started by ramming into the one directly in front of me with my shoulder, the suddenness of the move catching him off guard enough to knock him on his back. The man on the left tried to strike from behind, but I whirled and blocked his attack, and cut him down with my second blade. The last one was slightly more cautious - he eyed me warily.

I heard a familiar voice groan behind me. I chanced a glance - Falcon wasn't doing too well. He was surrounded. As well trained as we may be…it was still 4 against one for him. I scanned my surroundings. I only had two to deal with now… I should be able to handle it. "Falcon!" I shouted. His eyes whipped toward me. I flung his sword as hard as I could in his direction. Time slowed. My eyes stayed on the sword…Falcon rolled out of his mess of opponents, caught the sword, and turned just in time to cut down the one who had been ready to strike him down right behind him.

Suddenly, I was knocked to the ground. I cursed - I let myself get distracted and gave my two men the opportunity to get the jump on me.

"That don't feel too good, does it?" The first mercenary I knocked down jeered at me. Well, he didn't take very long to get up.

I made a show of rolling over and putting my hands under my aching back, "Owww!" I cried. The two mercenaries exchanged a glance. They took steps towards me, to try to yank me up from the ground. "That's. Not. Fair!" I flung my arms out from under my back, flinging my two daggers at them. I jumped up quickly.

One hit in the throat of the mercenary I had knocked down previously, the second went into the shoulder of the more cautious one. Fast as lightning, I removed my dagger from the neck of the dead mercenary and cut down the last one, pulling my second dagger from his shoulder.

I turned to see where Falcon was fighting. He truly was a sight to behold. Whirling, and blocking, and slashing…Did he even need my help? I shook my head and chuckled. Of course he needed my help.

Falcon still had two men on him. I ran towards them, but instead of running into the battle, I aimed behind them, sliding in last second and running my daggers along the back of their calves. They both dropped to the ground in agony.

"There." I said, standing up, brushing the dirt off my pants as Falcon finished them off. I turned to him, "Don't say I never do anything for you-"

"Cass!" I was wrapped in an unfamiliar embrace. He pulled back, hands on either side of my face, turning it side to side, "Are you hurt?" Oddly enough, there was worry in his eyes.

Cass.

Not Foxglove.

Ignoring the pounding in my chest, I stepped back from him, "I'm fine. I saved *your* ass, remember? Don't worry. General Ren has no reason to skin you alive. I'm completely fine. Not that I can say the same thing about you." I observed. He was covered in small cuts from where the mercenaries nicked him - but luckily there didn't seem to be any major injuries.

He shook his head, "I'm fine. They're just cuts."

I grabbed his arm to examine it. For some reason the thought of him in any sort of pain made my stomach turn. "Yeah but if enough of these get infected you could be down for a while. Let's find a nearby town and call it a day." He nodded, his jaw set in a hard line. Did I say something to upset him?

"Did that fox...follow us?" He asked suddenly, a hand rubbing his neck.

"Must have..." I trailed off, scanning the trees surrounding us, heart dropping when I didn't see her, "She looked about ready to attack Ryker."

"I wonder if she...imprinted on you or something." He said thoughtfully.

"Well, she's not a newborn fox," I scoffed, even though I myself have no knowledge of how animals imprint, "I don't think that could have happened."

I trudged past Ryker. He was still breathing. "Should we...?" I asked.

Falcon shook his head. "No. Without his mercenary band, he won't be a threat."

"What if he just builds another one?" I asked.

Falcon just shrugged, "I'm not a huge fan of killing unconscious people. It's bad enough having to do it when they're actively threatening you."

I spied the brown bag at Ryker's hip and started to untie it.

"What are you doing?" Falcon asked sharply.

"We need gold." I said flatly. It's not like this guy would use it for good anyway.

He was quiet a moment. "Fine." He conceded and started walking again.

We padded back toward Nera, and I noticed something. "Hey, Falcon." I grinned.

"What?" He asked, following my gaze.

"We got another horse."

Chapter 11

After calming down the second horse the mercenaries had brought in as a blockade, we set back on the road, Falcon made sure to leave his sword on his back this time. We came up to the small village of Halover and checked in at an Inn. Of course, they only had one room. "I'll sleep on the floor." Falcon said, turning his back to me.

I went to a nearby general store and got some potions and ointments with some of the coins I took off Ryker. No use in stopping if we didn't get him healed up.

I used the key to our room, and was met with the sight of Falcon, with his back to me, shirtless. "Falcon!" I exclaimed, rushing to him.

"What are you-" He whirled on me in surprise.

"Your back!" I said, turning him back around. There was a deep cut spanning across his back. How did he *not* feel that? I saw his shirt on the floor. Of course, it was a dark shirt, so I didn't even notice he was bleeding. I tenderly touch around the sides.

He hissed in pain "Is it bad?" He asked.

"It looks pretty bad." I admitted. "Lay down." I commanded him.

"What-" He started to protest.

"Lay. Down." I commanded again, and he begrudgingly complied, laying belly down on the bed. I sat next to him, dumping my shoulder bag out on the bed. I pulled out the salve I just bought from the general store and handed him a vial of potion. "For the pain." I explain.

"It doesn't hurt." He grumbled but downs it anyway.

"Probably from the adrenaline." I said, "But when it wears off, you'll need it. Plus, this probably needs stitches."

"It's probably never going to hurt then." He mumbled into a pillow, "I'm always running off adrenaline when I'm with you, Foxglove."

What did he just say? I shook my head. "Whatever. I make rash decisions. Well guess what, we're still alive aren't we? Where would we be if I hadn't pretended to seduce old Ryker back there?"

He snored. I quickly realized that the potion I gave him for the pain was almost instantly in effect. So, he was just delirious then. Cool.

MARK OF THE FALLEN

I continued muttering to myself, as I readied the equipment for stitching together the gash on his back with equipment I brought from home. I started the stitching, praying that the potion was strong enough to keep him knocked out. As I continued, I got lost in thought.

All Luminous Storm recruits were required to learn how to do basic wound stitching and first aid. Liam and I took the classes together.

Liam… for the first time since leaving Luminous Storm with Falcon, I wondered what Liam was doing. The sun was setting, he was probably eating dinner with everyone, finally free of me and my attitude.

I knew I changed after leaving Everloom. But I had to. How would I survive losing my brothers, what happened to Ma, if I didn't?

A glow filled the room. I wasn't stitching up the wound anymore. It was dark outside, and I was holding the amulet that we found in General Ren's house, and it was…glowing. More specifically, the symbol on the amulet was glowing with white light. How did I end up holding this? In shock, I dropped it, and it landed on Falcon's back. Which…was healed. What?

Even the stitches I already put in were gone, like his back was never injured to begin with. What was the meaning of this?

Was I going crazy? I checked my pocket watch. 2:45am. How did I lose so many hours?

I threw the amulet back into my bag, along with the rest of my things. I caught a flash of something in the corner of my eye. A blur of white, walking along the ledge outside the window. I threw the window open, leaning out to look on either side...nothing.

I shut the window and sighed, shaking my head. I must have been seeing things. I was overcome with exhaustion, but…I lifted my arm and sniffed. I needed to bathe. I entered the washroom, shutting the door behind me, and let out a deep breath. I reached into the well attached to the wall filled with magically kept hot water, and filled the tub. Undressing, I climbed in, and let the hot water wash away the blood and dirt on me that I hadn't even noticed.

I washed my hair and contemplated the meaning of what had just happened. Why did the amulet glow? And did it actually heal Falcon's back, or was it just a really strong healing potion I gave him? That had to be it. I must have blacked out from exhaustion and the glowing amulet had to be a trick of the light or a reflection or something.

After finishing my bath, I threw on the loose night clothes from General Ren's house, and too tired to care about sleeping arrangements, I climbed into bed on top of the covers and fell into a fitful sleep.

FALCON

I woke up face down on a mattress and groaned internally. My head was so foggy – had I been drugged? The events of the afternoon came rushing back to me. Right. The mercenaries. My heart clenched at the memory of being held by one of the brutes and watching helplessly as their leader leered down at Cass. For a moment there I really thought they were going to…I clenched my eyes shut. I couldn't think about that. Thank goodness Foxglove created the opening we needed to get out of there.

Something else stirred in my gut. I had never felt such rage as when Ryker approached her. Like she was his for the taking. I let out a shaky sigh. This was… I would feel this way about any of my subordinates if they were approached like that….right? I turned my head and was met face to face with Cass's sleeping form. For a moment, I was transfixed. To see her so…at peace. Without the normal mask of calculated indifference. Without her mouth being perpetually set in a tight line. She looked almost innocent – and I never would guess that she could cut me down as easily as any man.

I froze as realization hit me. I was staring at Cass's face. Which meant…I cursed, all but jumping out of the bed. I was supposed to sleep on the floor. I allowed her to get too comfortable with me. I needed to put some space between us.

CASS

"The mark is stirring, Master." The voice came from a hooded figure. I recognized them. "It should appear on one of the children soon."

"Good." a deep voice rolled out of the shadows. "Begin the preparations."

I awoke in a cold sweat, jolting up, "The mark!" I could hear myself crying out. My breathing was jagged, and terror filled my soul. "Falcon!" I shouted.

He came out of the washroom fully dressed, "What is it? Are you ok?"

"I…" I stopped, my heartbeat settling. Should I tell him? Could I trust him?

MARK OF THE FALLEN

"What is it?" He asked, sitting on the edge of the bed. His hair was wet - ugh I can't believe I dragged him from the bath for this.

He was the only one here - I had to trust him. "I had a dream." I said finally.

His shoulders loosened, "Oh is that it-"

"No, that's not it." I cut in. He looked at me, expectantly. "It's not the first time I've had a dream like this."

His eyebrows furrowed, "What do you mean?"

"About a year ago," I said, "I had a dream about a man…who I think was Aeron. He was talking to someone…some*thing* about a child being alive. He demanded that they bring the children to him. The next day…my brothers were taken."

He was stony faced, "And what was this dream?"

"In this dream, it was the same person…thing. Saying that the 'mark' was starting to manifest itself."

"Anything else?" He said, turning away from me, studying the floor. I contemplated telling him about the amulet, and how it glowed-but it might have been a trick of the light. And how his back was suddenly healed.

I found myself shaking my head instead, "No. That's it."

He stood, walking back towards the washroom, "Did you ever tell anyone else about this?" He didn't even turn to look at me.

"No." I said quietly.

"Good." And then he shut the door.

We still had a day and a half to travel due to our detour. But at least I had my own horse. We rode in an uncomfortable silence. I stared at the back of his head as he rode the mercenary's horse in front of me. Falcon still hadn't asked about his back, and I wasn't about to volunteer the information. Any warmth he had come to show me the last two days had vanished since I told him about my dreams. I suppose I was right not to tell him about the amulet.

"There's one thing I still can't figure out." I said, breaking the silence. He didn't even spare me a glance backwards, just kept riding, determined to ignore me. "Why did Aeron even take the children to begin with?" I mused, determined to fill the silence even if it was only my prattling.

"He makes no secret of his Seer, so it's possible one of the children could grow up to be a threat to him."

Still no answer. "But then why keep them alive after all this time? He's not exactly known for his benevolence and mercy, it would not be outside the realm of his skewed moral compass to just kill them all." His shoulder slightly tensed at my last sentence.

At least I knew he hadn't gone deaf.

Tired of talking to myself, I slightly spurred Nera on to catch up to Falcon. Pulling up next to him, I made a show of staring. He didn't deign to turn his head. "So, are you just going to ignore me for the rest of this mission? Or have you taken a temporary vow of silence?"

I could have sworn his cheeks reddened as he determinedly stared ahead. "I'm just putting some necessary distance between us."

"Necessary distance?" I questioned, "I didn't think we could fit any more distance between us while still being on the same continent."

He huffed a sarcastic laugh, "I'm just saying I woke up this morning and there was very little distance between us."

"So?" I asked indignantly, "You passed out after taking that healing potion and I graciously didn't roll you off the bed and onto the floor."

He cleared his throat, "Well thanks for that. Still, I'm your superior officer and that kind of situation shouldn't happen again. I don't want anyone to think I'm taking advantage of you."

I scoffed, "Ha. As if you *could* ever take advantage of me."

He shook his and chuckled, "I'll give you that. I'm sure your father rests easy at night knowing you can handle yourself." The sentiment was nice enough that I didn't bother correcting him.

"Still," I said as we meandered along, "Please don't just stop talking to me like that."

He studied me for a moment, as if I was a puzzle he couldn't quite figure out.

"Alright, Foxglove, I won't." He nodded finally. We continued our trek in comfortable silence.

Chapter 12

Kleidis was a beautiful town perched on a set of green rolling hills. The town square was bustling with people and there was a lively market happening on one of the fields. We were walking our horses down the road when we came across an inn. "You stay here." Falcon said, "I'm going to go inside and see if I can find out where this Callum Abernathy lives." He hurried off. I tied Nera next to the black stallion and observed my surroundings. No children over the age of 1, but life had seemed to resume here. It made me angry. How could they all just go about with their lives without trying to do something?

My anger was short lived though, as it was quickly replaced by fear. A group of Shadow Guard passed by, luckily not paying me any attention. A flash of red caught my eye as I slunk behind my horse, not eager for that to change. Suddenly, I felt a hand on my shoulder turn me around. I was met face to face with that polished armor, slicked back hair, and manicured beard. Captain Remus.

"Oh look, a stray cat." He sneered, "You're a long way from Everloom, Red."

Oh, the things I had imagined I would do when I saw his stupid face again. Unfortunately, I was not in a position to do any of those things - I had to wait and pray that Falcon would find me soon.

"You remember me?" I asked, feigning innocence, "and my small village?"

"I've received many death threats in my life, Red, but yours was by far the most memorable." He admitted and reached out to touch that cursed white-gold strand of hair, "You're not that easy to forget." If it was anyone else saying this, I might have been flattered.

Instead, I stepped back out of his reach before he could touch me, "Why are you bothering talking to me?" I asked, "Aren't there some kids somewhere that need kidnapping?"

He let out a feral grin, "Not today. What brings you all the way to Kleidis?"

Remembering our ruse from Hillsborough, I blurted, "My husband and I are here on our honeymoon."

At that moment, as if summoned by my lie, Falcon appeared next to me and put his arm around my shoulders, "Well, my dear, are you ready to get settled?" He feigned surprise at the Captain in front of me, "Oh, and it seems you've caught the attention of the Shadow Guard. Hopefully, she didn't cause any trouble." He faked a laugh, "She has quite the rebellious streak."

The Captain's eyes darted between the two of us, as if scanning for the validity of our claim. "Quite." he nodded to Falcon, "She threatened to kill me a year ago. Quite rebellious."

Falcon faked another laugh and I tried to look embarrassed, "She threatened to kill me this morning. Oh, she couldn't harm a fly if she tried. Her bark is worse than her bite."

Captain Remus gave a tight smile, "Noted." he said curtly, "Enjoy yourselves." With that, he left, and I breathed a sigh of relief.

Falcon grabbed my arm and led me to the side of the building, "I leave you alone for 5 minutes and you somehow attract the attention of the Captain of the Shadow Guard? What the hell did you do?"

I wrenched my arm from his grip, "I didn't *do* anything. He recognized me from when he took my brothers away. Although I actually did threaten to kill him. And may or may not have told him to go to hell."

Falcon shook his head, "I don't like it. Why did he remember you? This is not good for us."

I frustratedly grabbed at the gold strand in my hair, "It's this cursed hair. I hated it growing up but now it's causing me even more problems than I thought possible."

"You hate it? I always thought you did this to your hair on purpose." He genuinely thought that I would do this to my own hair?

"No," I said, "I was born with it, and it's resistant to all dyes. I've tried. Brick dust, berries, even blood doesn't stain it." He gave me a look, and I rolled my eyes, "I've never intentionally put blood on it."

"Is it magic?" He asked, suddenly studying my head.

I shrugged, "Must be some kind of magic, but my ma and pa could never tell me."

"Maybe the Archmage will know." Falcon said with a rare smile, pulling a piece of paper with an address out of his pocket.

We walked up to the house sitting atop the farthest hill from the town square. We were almost to the top when a black blur sprang out of the nearby bushes. Surprised, Falcon and I jumped, hands on our weapons. I sighed when I realized that it was just the fox...again. Falcon rolled his eyes and muttered something that sounded a lot like "That cursed fox."

"What is it, girl?" I ask, and the fox chittered in response. She moved to stand next to me, leaning her body against my leg. I kneeled down next to her, and she put her front paws on my knee, pushing her face into mine.

I scratched behind her ears, and said thoughtfully to Falcon, "I think we should take her with us."

He just rolled his eyes again and said, "You're going to bring her either way, I might as well save the argument."

I grinned, looking back at the fox, "Is that what you want, girl?" She chittered again in response, hiking her back legs onto my knee as well, so she was essentially in my lap. I looked at her thoughtfully as I stood up, fox in my arms, "What should we call her?"

"You mean what should you call her, as I will not be calling her anything." Falcon stated haughtily.

I looked into her bright amber eyes thoughtfully, and a name came to mind, "How about...Ayla?" Her ears perked in recognition, and she hopped down from my arms, circling me, and chittering again.

"Ayla it is." I couldn't help but smile, she was so cute.

Falcon sniffed, "Are we done now? Let's go."

I motioned my arms to Falcon in a way that said, "Lead the way," and followed behind him, Ayla at my heels.

Falcon knocked on the door. We heard some rustling around on the other side, "He sure moves quickly for an old guy." I whispered to Falcon, he elbowed me in response.

The door swung open "Yes?" A young man answered the door, no more than 20 years old. He had brown hair, and freckles. His eyes were green, like the forest. He was slightly thin in stature, almost like he had been ill as a child. And yet, I felt like I had seen him somewhere before. "Can I help you?" The man asked, clearly puzzled by our presence.

"Yes, um…" I realized I had been staring, "Sorry. Yes, we're looking for Callum Abernathy?"

"I'm Callum. Does someone need healing?"

"The man we're looking for…he'd be much older than you." Falcon interjected.

"Ah…" the man said, understanding flashing across his face "You're looking for my grandfather. I was named after him."

"That makes more sense!" I said, "Would you be able to go get him then? We have some very important business to discuss with him."

Callum shook his head, "Sorry, Miss." he said sadly, "I'm afraid that's impossible. We buried him three summers ago."

I gaped, turning to Falcon. What do we do now? "I-I'm sorry." I stammered, turning back to Callum.

Falcon reached into his jacket and pulled out the amulet we found at General Ren's house. "We're here about this." Callum's brows furrowed as he reached out for the amulet. Falcon allowed him to take it, and Callum studied it for a moment. Then he shook his head and let out a low chuckle.

Arching an eyebrow, I shot Falcon a questioning look. Falcon only shrugged and turned back toward Callum. "My grandfather..." Callum shook his head and chuckled again. "I thought my grandfather had gone near mad by the end. But it looks like he knew at least a little bit of what he was doing. Please come in."

Falcon glanced at me and nodded. We stepped in, looking around the house. "Is that a... a fox?" Callum asked as I passed through the doorway. I smiled as Ayla sniffed Callum's pant leg and pawed his boot. "Yep!" I said, walking the rest of the way inside, Ayla following closely at my heels.

"...Alright." He said and locked the door behind us.

Falcon whirled on him, "What are you-"

"The Shadow Guard don't knock." Callum explained.

The room in which we sat had bookshelves lining the walls filled with what had to be hundreds of books. The only spots on the wall that was spared a bookshelf was the space that housed a desk, which was piled with papers and other volumes of work. Callum led us to a set of plush chairs, "Please excuse the mess." He said, motioning for us to sit.

Falcon's eyes checked mine as we sat down. I know we were sent here by General Ren, but Falcon seemed uneasy about this whole situation. Callum disappeared into another room, and I heard papers rifling around. Ayla made herself comfortable at my feet.

"Foxglove, if anything goes south, you get out." Falcon whispered to me.

"What? Why? He's harmless." I whispered back, "There's something about him…" I shook my head, "He doesn't mean us any harm. I can tell."

Falcon looked skeptical but surprisingly settled into his chair. A moment later, Callum came out holding a long bundle of fabric. "Near the end," Callum began, perching himself on one of the comfortable chairs, "Grandfather became obsessed with this item. He was constantly running experiments on it. He wouldn't even share with me what he was doing. Which was odd because I was his assistant in everything he did. Before he passed, he stored it away and told me if anyone ever showed up with his amulet, to give them this." Callum pushed the bundle into my arms. Falcon did little to hide his bristling at the fact that Callum handed me the bundle, and not him.

"Are you a mage as well?" I asked Callum. Magic was passed through bloodlines, but that didn't mean that every single offspring would be gifted with magic - especially if only one of their parents was a mage.

Callum nodded and settled back into his chair, "Yes, the gene skipped my dad, but according to my grandfather, magic always skipped a generation in our family." I nodded as I started to unbundle the fabric, Callum continued, "I've studied it multiple times over the last 3 years to try to figure out what had Grandfather so intrigued, but it's just a sword."

"A sword?" I asked, my fingers singing in confirmation when it made contact with the metal. Running my fingers along the smoothness, I held it up. Beautiful as it was, it did seem like just an ordinary sword. Its hilt was covered in metal vines and leaves that wrapped around the cross guard. The bottom of the hilt, as well as either side of the cross guard, had a half moon shape attached to it. It was odd though, the rest of the sword was so detailed and ornate, but these half-moon shapes were not adorned at all. As if they were not merely for decoration but were there for some other purpose.

Falcon eyed me carefully, "General Ren must have had some reason for wanting us to find it. Though I do wonder why he thought you'd be able to locate it."

"General Ren?" Callum asked, sounding intrigued, "Grandfather did mention him a couple of times. He was the General of the King's army before the plague, right?"

I nodded, "Yes, he's the one who sent us to find this. He says he had it hidden in his house, but when we went there we only found this amulet." Falcon glared at me. "What?" I asked.

"Listen." Falcon said, "Callum? Right? I know that you're the grandson of the previous Archmage but forgive me if we can't just trust you right away." He was right. I couldn't believe I had just blurted that out to a complete stranger. I was strangely at ease here. Maybe it was my lack of proper sleep the last couple of nights.

Callum shrugged, "I'm not asking you to trust me. I'm just passing along the information I was supposed to."

Falcon nodded "Glad we understand each other. Now if you'll excuse us-" He stood, and turned to me, "Let's get out of here." I shoot Callum an apologetic look, and we move towards the front door. I'm not sure why I feel the need to act so polite to him, but I lift my hand in a wave as Falcon all but drags me out the door.

MARK OF THE FALLEN

Before we reach out to unlock the door, however, there was shaking at the door, as if someone was trying to rip the door off its hinges, followed by a BAM BAM BAM of someone pounding at the door. Ayla jumped up and bared her teeth at the door, ears flat against her head.

"Shadow Guard, OPEN UP." I looked up toward Falcon, his face had gone white. This was not in the plan. Did Captain Remus follow us up here?

Callum cleared his throat, "One moment please!" He turned toward us and said quietly, "Sit back down, as far as they know, you're just here for a healing session."

Falcon stared for a moment, but after releasing a breath, nodded. We sat back down and tried to look confused, not scared. I schooled my features into mild curiosity. I was a newly married woman whose husband is having back pain. "You're having back pain." I whispered to Falcon. He nodded, his mouth in a tight line.

Callum slowly opened the door, "What can I do for you gentlemen? Is someone in need of a healer?" His voice was calm and collected. I wondered how many times he's faced off with the Shadow Guard?

"Shut it, Abernathy," one of them barked. A few times, then. "We saw a suspicious couple come up this way."

"I'm afraid I haven't seen any suspicious people come up this way." He said lightly. I heard some mumbling behind the door and suddenly Callum cried out in pain, and there was a thump on the floor. I shot up from my seat, Falcon grabbing a hold of my arm. Callum was laying on the floor, one of the Shadow Guard soldiers had rammed the door open. There were 4 of them standing there, looking at Falcon and I triumphantly.

"I think we got 'em boss." One said to someone behind him. The 4 soldiers step to the side, some tracking footprints on Callum's jacket as he lay on the floor. Anger seethed in my bones as I watched them. Captain Remus stepped into the room, his arrogance wafting around him like an overwhelming cologne. One of the guards yanked Callum up by the arm. Ayla growled, as if sensing my anger.

"What, might I inquire, have we done that makes you so suspicious of us?" I asked politely, my rage boiling just beneath the surface of my skin.

Captain Remus clicked his tongue, "Did you really think that I would let someone who threatened my life go free?"

"Yes, to be honest," I answered sharply, "considering I'm sure at least half the continent has reason to wish you dead and I don't see them all locked up." Falcon's fingers dug into my arm.

"They may wish me dead but very few have the courage to voice it directly to me." He said, no shame in his eyes whatsoever.

"Imagine my surprise when I returned to Everloom for you a year ago to find out you had run away from home."

Returned to Everloom for me? Just because I threatened him? "So, what? Did you go around killing anyone who makes a threat in the throes of justifiable rage?" I asked indignantly.

"No," He said slowly, something dark in his eyes, "You rejected my offer to come with me, and I didn't like that. So, I came back to take you by force." A shiver ran down my spine.

"You're sick." Falcon said quietly behind me.

"That might be true," Remus conceded, "However, I've grown tired of this conversation." He turned towards his soldiers, "Kill the men. I'm taking the girl."

Suddenly a burst of energy erupted from by the door - Callum. I had forgotten, he was not only a healer - he was a mage. The blast of energy took everyone by surprise, the man holding on to Callum was blasted away, and the other three stumbled back at the force of the impact.

Without thinking I readied the sword in my hand - the blade we had come all this way for. Hopping over a chair, Falcon charged a guard by the door. My eyes locked on my target - Captain Remus. This would end here, even if it killed me.

I barreled towards him, swinging the sword down as hard as I could. Remus was ready for me though, and met my sword with his, our blades scraping against each other in an unholy symphony of metal on metal. "Did you really think that your little escapades as 'The Red Fox' would go unnoticed?" He sneered as we pushed against each other, "The minute I heard the description of your hair, I knew it was you." I cursed to myself. The first couple of times I targeted someone close to Aeron, I was less careful. I could almost feel Falcon's stare drilling into the back of my head. Had he heard? We locked cross guards, Remus's eyes darted down to my sword.

Shock registered in his face. "Now where did you get that?" He asked coldly. Oh no. He knew about the sword. Would feigning interest in him work now? I didn't think so. Before I had a chance to even think of an answer, Ayla bit into Remus's leg, his face contorting into one of shock and pain. A cry started in his throat, but then just...stopped. His face was frozen in place.

"Go!" Callum yelled. He was holding something tight in both his hands, a light emanating inside his clasped fists. Everything else around us had paused. General Remus's face was frozen in one of cold anger and the guards were mid-action as if time itself - "Hurry! Upstairs! I can only hold it a few more moments!" I didn't have time to question anything. How this was possible, or if we should trust Callum.

For some reason beyond my understanding, I did trust him. I nodded and scooped Ayla up in one arm, grabbed Falcon, who had been standing shocked, by the hand to run upstairs. Callum backed up slowly, his strength to hold the spell weakening by the second. We reached the top right as the guards burst back into motion and heard the commotion as they responded to their prey disappearing from underneath them. Surprised shouts filled the air as Callum slammed and locked the door behind us.

In this room there was almost nothing. It was bare except for a bed and nightstand. On the floor, in the middle of the room, a large circle was drawn in white chalk, big enough to fit about 6 people, with runes and wards scribbled around it.

"What-" Falcon started, but then there was shouting and pounding on the door. Ayla scrambled out of my arm and managed to bury herself in my bag on my back.

Callum went to the nightstand and opened the drawer, pulling out a blue crystal. He moved to the middle of the circle. He looked at us. The door shook as the guards continued to throw themselves against it. He looked towards both of us, "That last spell took a lot out of me. I might pass out after we get out here. There is a vial in my pocket, I need you to give it to me after we land." Falcon gaped as Callum held out his hand to me. Stepping into the circle, I took his hand in mine, still grasping Falcon's in my other hand.

"We'll take care of you." I nodded.

"But we don't-" Falcon started, but I was having none of it.

"We. Will. Take. Care. Of. Him." I said again, punctuating each word with my determination.

Falcon's nostrils flared, but he nodded, "Do it." He said.

Callum began to quietly chant words in an unfamiliar language. As he did, the blue stone in his hand began to glow, as well as the chalk that made up the circle around us. The pounding on the door became more intense, the wood starting to splinter. As Callum continued, his words became more forceful, the stone growing brighter and brighter until-

The door burst open right as the light swallowed us whole. I only got a glimpse of Captain Remus' enraged face before we were sucked into a vacuum so bright I couldn't tell left from right or up from down, my stomach felt like it was being sucked out through my throat and into my ears. Just as quickly as we were picked up, we landed in a forest, and the world stilled. I was on my back, blinking as I looked up at the fading sky.

Chapter 13

I heard a groan somewhere near me. It sounded like Falcon. My body had stopped spinning, but my mind still felt dizzy. I sat up slowly, "What…was that?" I asked, trying not to vomit. I looked around, careful not to move my head too fast. My pack had ended up on the floor next to me, Ayla crawled out of it as if the whole ordeal had been just a simple walk. Callum was on his back on my left and Falcon was on my right, trying to stand up.

"Where are we?" Falcon said, looking around. We were surrounded by forest. As my mind settled, I could hear the small trickle of running water. My eyes shot to Callum again - he was passed out. I scrambled to my feet and crouched by him. He said there was a vial in his pocket to give him.

I fished around in his pockets, the sound of leaves crunching under Falcon's boots as he paced irritating me. Finally, I pulled out a small glass vial of purple liquid. Tearing the stopper off, I squeezed Callum's cheeks together and gently poured it down his throat.

Nothing happened. His skin was even paler than before - was he breathing? I quickly put my fingers to his throat to try to find a pulse. I couldn't feel anything. Ayla came over and sniffed him, then laid on his chest.

Panic was setting in, "Falcon!" I called, trying to find a pulse on Callum's wrist next. I felt Falcon kneel down next to me, "He's not-" I started, the tears stinging my eyes. I pressed my ear to his chest, much to the displeasure of Ayla, - desperate enough to hear something that I didn't care what Falcon thought of me. This couldn't happen. Callum had risked his life to save us when he didn't have to, and now he was close to death. My ear settled to Callum's chest, and I heard it. Quiet, and weak, but it was there. I lifted my head, breathing a sigh of relief. Ayla was looking at me in a way that said, *See? I told you.* I couldn't quite place the look Falcon was giving me.

"What?" I snapped, wiping a tear that had spilled onto my cheek.

Falcon shook his head, "That was quick."

"What are you getting at?" I asked sharply.

"You just met the guy. I just don't know why you care so much."

I blinked. "Are you asking me why I care if an innocent - one who helped us, nonetheless, - dies?"

Falcon turned away, "Forget it."

"You…helped me." Callum's voice rasped behind me.

Afraid of how much he heard, I whirled back toward him, a smile on my lips, "Of course we did."

"I was half sure you wouldn't" Callum admitted, motioning to Falcon, who had his back to us.

"Don't pay him too much mind." I said quietly, helping Callum to his feet as Ayla hopped off his chest, "His uncle is my mentor, so he feels responsible for me."

"I thought-" He started, but then seemingly thought better of it, "Your fox was laying on me like she was trying to lay an egg."

"I think she was trying to comfort you. Her name is Ayla." I smiled at her as she trotted happily next to me.

"And what's *your* name?" He asked, brushing himself off.

"Cass." I answered him, "My name is Cass."

The place we had been transported to was on the outskirts of a property that Callum's parents would take him to when he was a child. We were on the northwestern border of the old Kingdom of Silverglade, the central territory of the old Kingdoms of Trilithia. It didn't take us long to trek to the cabin and get settled in for the evening.

Callum had explained to us that since his Grandfather died, he had kept that circle drawn upstairs just in case he ever needed to make an escape like this one. I had never even known that traveling like that was possible. According to Callum, the stone used in the spell breaks after the spell is completed, meaning the spell is a one-time use unless you have more stones - which he doesn't. Unfortunately, we needed to travel back to the base on foot.

Callum and I were in the sitting area, sipping on some hot tea, Ayla curled up in my lap, when Falcon came back into the cabin from outside. As he stomped the dirt off his boots, he turned to us. "I spoke with General Ren through the pendant. He says you should come with us, Callum."

"To where?" He asked, brows furrowed.

"I'm afraid we haven't been properly introduced," Falcon said, reaching out his hand, "I'm Falcon Feldstrom, leader of Luminous Storm." In awe, Callum shook Falcon's outstretched hand, "General Ren said that we could fully trust any family of Callum Abernathy Sr." He added reluctantly.

"Luminous Storm? THE Luminous Storm?" Callum asked, his eyes lighting up, "I've wanted to join them for ages, but felt guilty leaving Kleidis - I'm one of the only two healers in town."

Falcon chuckled, "Remember when you were that excited to join, Foxglove?" He asked me.

I rolled my eyes, "Yeah, you beat that out of me real quick."

His eyes turned serious, and if I wasn't mistaken, some regret was there too. I regretted my words, but before I could say anything else, Callum jumped up. "Okay, when do we go?" He asked, looking between the two of us like an excited puppy.

Falcon and I looked at each other, "Um, tomorrow?" I asked hopefully, in desperate need of a good night's sleep.

Falcon nodded, "Yes, General Ren is expecting us to leave first thing in the morning. Based on the location you gave us, Callum, it should be about a week's journey."

"A week?!" I ask incredulously, "What about our-" horses...our horses we had to leave behind in Kleidis. I palmed my forehead in frustration, "We left our horses behind."

Falcon gave a grim nod, "It would have been 5 days otherwise" Laying out a map, he continued, "We're on the northwestern border. If we take this road that leads south, it will take us past the old castle of Silverglade, as well as past the Trilithia Castle. It's risky, but any other route adds at least 3 days onto our journey. We don't have time for that." I nodded in agreement. Shadow Guard activity was always heavier around the old kingdoms and castles, but the risk was worth getting back to base sooner. "Besides," Falcon continued with a grin, "It'll give us time to get to know our new recruit."

Callum grinned then, changing the subject, he said, "Are you guys hungry? I think we have some dried jerky and fruit somewhere around here, I'll see if I can scrounge up enough for dinner."

Callum disappeared into the kitchen, Falcon and I stayed in the sitting area. He flopped down next to me on the couch, causing Ayla to get up from my lap and follow Callum into the kitchen, "Why does she like him more than me?" He asked.

"Are you jealous because of a fox?" I asked teasingly.

He shook his head, "This is not how I thought this trip was going to go." He said, throwing his head back, his arm over his eyes. I had never seen him so…disheveled before. His hair and clothes were rumpled, and stubble had started to appear on his face. I had only ever seen him clean shaven. It was…disconcerting.

"Are we…okay?" I asked, hating at how tentative my voice sounded. Maybe it was the guilt at keeping The Red Fox a secret. "I'm sorry I brought up how things were when I first joined…"

He lowered his arm from his closed eyes and sighed. He opened them slowly, the silver gleam in stark contrast against his tan skin. He looked tired. "Cass…you didn't say anything except the truth." He wasn't wrong, I didn't lie about anything but… "Do I wish I could go back and do things over? Yeah, probably. But we're here now, I'm not going to pretend like what I did didn't happen, I can only move forward and hope you forgive me one day."

Forgive him? Falcon Feldstrom didn't get forgiven. He didn't *need* forgiveness. If you asked anyone at Luminous Storm, especially Liam, Falcon never did anything that didn't need to be done. And if you didn't understand why he did it, then that was your loss because he obviously had some greater plan in mind. To hear him admit this…I couldn't help but chuckle.

"Is it that laughable?" he asked, shaking his head.

"No," I said, sitting up a little straighter, "The almighty Falcon Feldstrom asking for forgiveness- if I told anyone back home, they wouldn't believe me. You can do no wrong in their eyes."

Falcon looked down, "I mean it though. I shouldn't have been so hard on you. Especially now that I know you had just lost your brothers…" Did I daresay he looked…remorseful? My gut turned again in guilt. He was laying it all out before me, and I still kept secrets.

"It probably wasn't easy, having General Ren breathe down your neck about me…suddenly being personally responsible for one more person" I said. Was I trying to comfort him? I suppose I was, considering my hand found its way to his shoulder.

He looked at my hand, then to me, "Are you trying to console me because I feel bad about how poorly I treated you? That's ridiculous." Cheeks burning, I snatched my hand back from his shoulder. Fine. He didn't need me to feel sorry for him. *I* was the wounded party here. His hand reached out and caught mine before I could fully withdraw. He chuckled and shook his head, "You never cease to surprise me, Foxglove."

"Can I surprise you one more time?" I asked, my instincts raging against me sharing this information. Before I could change my mind, I blurted out, "You were right before. About me being The Red Fox." He stared at me blinking. Was he in shock? "Before you say anything," I rambled on, and to my surprise, he *didn't* say anything, "I didn't actually steal anything. I would knock out the guards through poisoned coins that they would share amongst themselves after they stole from me. If they had servants, I would forge notes telling them that they had been given the night off, so they wouldn't be in the castle. Then I would climb into my targets room while they were sleeping and…" I trailed off, "Get information."

Falcon shook his head, "I- I don't even know- why do they call you a burglar then?"

"Because that's what I would tell them to tell their guards when they woke up. And if Aeron found out I was there or if they told the guards the truth, I knew where they lived." I gulped. Saying it out loud sounded a lot more…. extreme than actually doing it. "The first couple of times I didn't even think to hide my face." Falcon cursed under his breath. "But after that, I was really careful. It just must have been one of those first few that got a description of me."

He sighed, resignation in his features, "Did you get any good intel?"

I grinned, "Just that Aeron doesn't tell anyone where they are, and that he thinks one of the kids has something he wants."

"Hmm." He looked pensive, then shook his head again, "Look. The Red Fox is officially retiring, got it?" I nodded. Now that we knew where the kids were, I didn't need to anyway. I couldn't tell what he was thinking. On the surface he looked frustrated, but underneath, it was almost like there was a glimmer of pride in his eyes.

His eyes caught something just to the left of my head, "You have…" He reached over with his other hand and my breath caught in my throat as he reached his hand to the side of my hair, "a leaf." He held it up triumphantly. It must have been in my hair since we landed here from Callum's transportation spell.

Just then, Callum walked into the room. "I found about a half pound of jerky and some dried fruits and nuts…" He trailed off when he noticed Falcon and I jump apart - I hadn't even noticed how close we had gotten. "I'm sorry, did I interrupt something?" He asked awkwardly.

"No!" We said at the same time, and I jumped up from the couch, and passed by Callum to go to the kitchen. My cheeks heated at the memory of my heart skipping a beat when he reached for my hair. This could not happen. Whatever I was feeling for Falcon- it was not good, and it would not last. I didn't have time for any of this. Ayla walked past me, scratching at the front door. Whether to hunt or relieve herself, who knew, but I was all too happy to occupy myself with letting her outside.

A few minutes later, Callum and Falcon found me sitting at a table in the kitchen munching on the jerky and nuts. They settled around the table with me, putting some food on their plates.

"So, what was that?" Falcon asked, ripping off a piece of jerky with his teeth. What was what? Was he seriously asking about our 'moment' in the other room right now?

"What was what?" I choked out, mid bite.

He turned to Callum, "That whole time-stopping spell you did. I've never heard of - or seen - anything like that."

"Oh," Callum's face reddened, making his freckles almost disappear into his skin. "I'm not…I'm not really supposed to do that. I just couldn't think of any other way to save us."

I blinked, "Not supposed to? Said who?"

"My grandfather." He said, "I did it once when I was younger by accident, and it nearly killed me. I was sick for a long time after." He looked down, "It's why I passed out once we got here. It takes an exorbitant amount of energy to generate a time-stop spell, let alone hold it."

Falcon contemplated for a moment, "But you risked your life to save us? You could have just let the Shadow Guard take us and be done with it."

"I-" For just a second, his eyes were on mine. As quickly as he looked at me, he was looking back down at his food, "I couldn't let two innocent people be taken by the Shadow Guard. Especially when they were led here because of something my grandfather did."

Falcon looked between Callum and I, his eyes narrowing.

Callum cleared his throat. "So…why do you call her Foxglove?" He asked, trying to change the subject.

"Yes, Cass," Falcon said, serious demeanor vanishing, propping a cheek on his hand, "why *do* I call you Foxglove?"

My cheeks burned. It was a stupid mistake I made months ago. I turned to Callum, "I was telling my friend, Adarra, about these beautiful red bell-shaped flowers I had seen in the glen just outside the city. I decided to go out and pick some for her as a surprise on her birthday. The Commander here," I said, jerking my head towards Falcon, "was hunting some game nearby and managed to stop me before I poisoned myself. He thinks it's funny to remind me that I almost got myself killed by some flowers 6 months into joining the rebellion." I arched an eyebrow at him.

Falcon shrugged, "It just kind of stuck after that."

Callum had a pensive look on his face like he was going to say something, but then stopped himself. Shaking his head, he said "If you guys want to get an early start tomorrow, we should probably get to bed. There are two rooms down the hall, I'll take the couch."

"You don't have to-" I started, but he stopped me.

"My grandfather taught me to be a gracious host." He said with a small smile.

FALCON

The immediate connection between Callum and Cass had…bugged me. Though I didn't want to admit it. We were finally getting to a point where we weren't constantly bickering, and this guy just shows up and she's instantly nice to him? I bristled at the fact that it bothered me at all.

I paced my room. Being on good terms with Cass would make life easier for me back at base. That's why I cared. Smooth relations with General Ren's prodigy? I would be stupid to not want that. And once General Ren took the rebellion back over completely, maybe… I shook my head and rubbed my temples.

I thought about our confrontation with the Shadow Guard back in Kleidis. Captain Remus had recognized the sword that my uncle had sent us to find. That couldn't be good for us. The fact that he *went back* to her village…and the way that he looked at Cass, if I ever saw that guard again I'd… I shivered. She was bringing out emotions in me I didn't think I had. Especially when she admitted to being the Red Fox. I hated to admit it, but I was a bit impressed. Staging the interrogations as burglaries was genius, even if the overall scheme was reckless. If anything, I wish she had come to me with the idea so we could have better backup in place in case anything went wrong. But…I would have said no.

Was this what it was like to throw logical reason out the window? To care about someone outside of the causes of the rebellion? I found myself chuckling, and said quietly to myself, "Foxglove, what are you doing to me?"

CASS

I stepped out of the washroom and was padding back to my room, wearing some of Callum's mom's pajamas he scrounged up for me. Ayla had shown up at the window shortly after we finished eating dinner, and since letting her in, she had stayed in my room of her own volition.

The room Falcon was staying in was adjacent to mine, and the door creaked as he opened the door and leaned against the doorframe.

"Commander." I acknowledged him with a nod of my head, toweling my wet hair, moving to walk past him.

"Foxglove." He answered, the corner of his mouth tugging upwards. Suddenly feeling very vulnerable with wet hair and pajamas, I tried to hurry past him. "Wait." He breathed, grabbing my arm.

My brows furrowed as I looked down at his hand on my arm. Tilting my head up, my eyes searching his face, I was drawn to a faint scar going across his left eyebrow. Strange, I hadn't noticed it before- "That's not why I call you Foxglove." He continued, hand still gripping my arm. I didn't pull away.

I arched an eyebrow, "That's how it happened though-"

He shook his head, "The name stuck, yes. But the similarities…"

"So…I'm a poisonous flower." I stated, not sure if I should be offended or not.

He smiled, his eyes softening - not an expression I had seen on his face before. And somehow, I found myself closer to him. "Foxglove is deceivingly beautiful. It comes in a variety of colors, red being my favorite. Misused or handled carelessly, it's poisonous- it can kill you. But treated correctly, used in a precise way, it can be used to cure the heart."

My throat went dry. His eyes darted to my mouth for just a second. I could have sworn he leaned in slightly. Before anything could happen, I found myself pulling back, gently pulling his hand from my arm. This wasn't…whatever was happening, it was just a result of being forced in the same space for too long. It had to be. I let out a shuddering breath.

"Goodnight, Foxglove." He said quietly and shuts his door.

Chapter 14

CALLUM

We were at my parents' cabin. I hadn't been here in…years. I shifted on the couch, tucking my arm under my head. This morning when I woke up, I never would have guessed at the circumstances that brought me here.

3 years. I had been holding on, studying, trying to figure out what was so special about that sword. And then Cass showed up and the world turned upside down. I should be angry. I should be seething that they led the Shadow Guard to my home, my grandfather's home, and caused me to have to flee. But I wasn't. I was…glad. I had longed to find and join the rebellion, to make a difference. But Kleidis needed me. Now though, I had no choice. I could leave with not guilt…well, almost no guilt.

There was something about her…about Cass. I could not say what it was but there was a compulsion to protect. To trust. To tell her anything she wished. The fact that she saved my life after less than an hour of knowing me…

She was a force to be reckoned with, that much was clear. The relationship between her and the commander though…less clear.

CASS

I was being shaken, "Cass. Cass!" My eyes flew open. It was dark. Where was I? Who was calling my name? "Cass, it's me, Callum." Callum? Who is- right, Callum.

"Callum? I asked groggily, reaching over to switch on the bedside lantern. "What are you doing in here?"

"Ayla came and got me." He said, and I noticed that the indent on the pillow next to my head was empty. "I was really confused when I woke up to her pawing at my face but I when I got up she led me back here. You were having a nightmare." He said quietly. He was kneeling next to the bed, his hair disheveled and his eyes were tired. "You were calling out names… Bram, and Kolby? And you said something about a 'mark'."

I shook my head and rubbed my eyes, "I'm sorry, I didn't mean to wake you. What time is it?"

His brows furrowed, "It's about 2. Are you alright? Who are Bram and Kolby if you don't mind me asking?"

"My brothers." I swallowed, "They were taken by Aeron last year."

"Oh, I'm sorry…" Callum said quietly. "And the mark?"

"I…" Could I trust him with this? General Ren said we could fully trust him. Plus, he was a mage. It was possible he could have some information on what Aeron was talking about. "A year ago, I had a dream where Aeron ordered children to be taken away. The next day my brothers were taken. Then, on our journey to Hillsborough, I had a dream that I was in a bedroom and started to pull up the floorboards. We found your grandfather's amulet in a bedroom identical to the one in my dream, under the floorboards. A few days later, I had a dream that someone told Aeron that a 'mark' would manifest itself on one of the children." I shook my head, "I just don't know what it means. Everything else has come true, so what am I missing? What could it mean?"

Callum looked serious, "The only mark I know of is the Mark of Alistair…"

Something panged in my chest. "What is the Mark of Alistair?"

"It's a mark that would reveal itself on the next heir of the kingdom. The royal family paid no mind to who was the eldest in terms of succession. If the Mark of Alistair appeared on someone in the royal family, it was the gods appointing them as the next ruler of the kingdom. It's the same symbol as the one on Grandfather's amulet."

"Could that mean…" I swallowed, "Aeron thinks there's a child of the royal bloodline, and that's why he kidnapped the children?" If this was true, it was huge. But then a thought struck me, "But wait. The whole family was wiped out by plague that was centralized to the castle. How could there be a survivor, a child no less?"

Callum looked serious, "Maybe someone escaped? Or was out the night everyone died, and then had a baby? I'm not sure. It doesn't make much sense."

I nodded, "We have to tell General Ren. He'll know what to do."

Suddenly my mind flashed back to the night I was stitching up Falcon's back… "Did your grandfather ever mention anything about the amulet…glowing?" I asked tentatively. After all, I didn't know if it actually did glow or if it was a trick of the light. I felt silly even asking, but it had been bothering me.

"No, he didn't." Callum said, "But…"

"But what?" I asked, sitting up.

"It has glowed for me before. When I was a child, I found it in Grandfather's study. I was wearing it while I was practicing my healing magic and it started to glow." I swallowed. It might make some kind of sense for that to happen to Callum - he was a mage. I, however, wasn't.

"Why?" He asked, his brow furrowing, "Have you seen it glow?"

I shook my head, "I thought maybe one time, but I also wasn't sure if maybe a light reflected off it or something. I'm not a mage, so it wouldn't make any sense anyway." I settled back down into bed and turned on my side, facing him. We were quiet for a moment, he had his arms crossed on the edge of the bed, his chin resting on his arms. His eyes were fluttering, as if he was trying not to fall asleep. "Thank you for waking me up." I said sleepily, "Normally Bram or Kolby would wake me up if I was having a nightmare. But since leaving…" I trailed off. "Can I ask you something?" I said, changing the subject.

Callum nodded, "Sure."

"Do you know why a blood curse would become impossible to lift?"

"A blood curse?" He asked, concern edging his voice.

"My Ma." I said, taking a deep breath, "When my brothers were taken, the mage assisting Captain Remus put a curse on her because she put up too much of a fight. The highest-ranking mage in our village, Grand Elder Ira, said it was a blood curse. But my blood wouldn't lift it." After the boys were taken, I found my Mama in front of our home, unconscious. Grand Elder Ira was kneeling next to her. He told me it was a curse so powerful, the only way to lift it was with a spell using the blood of a direct relative. But when he tried to perform the spell, it didn't work. She's been asleep since. Grand Elder Ira had written to me occasionally on her status. Mostly unchanged, though he says he's been researching.

Callum finally spoke, "I suppose if the mage was adept enough, they could have modified the curse so that even a blood relative couldn't lift it."

"How would he modify it?" I asked.

"I'm not sure. I know that very skilled mages can rewrite the spells and curses to close any loopholes, but closing one loophole will always open another. The magic needs balance."

"So, I just need to find the mage that put the curse on her and figure out what he did." I said, letting out a bitter laugh. "Great. I'll put it on my to-do list."

MARK OF THE FALLEN

"I'm sorry about your Mama." Callum said quietly, "I lost both my parents when I was young, so though I know your pain is fresher than mine, I'm here if you need to talk."

I nodded. "You can stay here…if you want. But I know it's probably less comfortable than the couch." Something about him here…it brought me back to when I lived in Everloom, and I shared a room with Kolby and Bram. It was comforting.

Callum gave a grin, "I'll stay a little longer."

We started bright and early, packing what we could carry into packs found in the closets of the cabin. Most of the space in my pack was taken up by Ayla – foxes were mostly active at night, so she seemed to be catching up on her sleep.

Callum was gone when I woke up in the morning, I assumed he only stayed long enough for me to fall asleep. I was in the kitchen, rubbing my eyes, and stretched my arms out behind me. My left elbow made contact with something hard.

"Hey!" A voice said to my left. Falcon had been trying to get to the cabinet next to me when I threw my hands behind me in a stretch. He rubbed his shoulder where my elbow had made contact, "Your elbows are sharper than your daggers."

"You'll probably do something to deserve it later." I shrugged, a wicked grin on my lips. He raised his eyebrows at me. I whirl around and walk to the sitting area, passing Callum. "Good morning." I smiled, standing on my tiptoes to ruffle his hair as I passed. A look of confusion crossed his face as he continued into the kitchen.

I was in a good mood. We had escaped Captain Remus, we had what General Ren had sent us to find. Hell, I even had more of a lead on what to do for Mama than I've had the last year. If I ignored the weird moment with Falcon the night before, things were good.

I had told Falcon about mine and Callum's conversation about my dream- well, about the mark. After his initial anger at me telling Callum about my dreams after he told me not to tell anyone had subsided, he did agree that Callum had valuable insight on what the mark could mean - if it was indeed the same one that my dreams were about.

I had gathered a bag with supplies I found around the cabin and was hiking it on my shoulder when Falcon snatched it from me, "I'll take that." He said gruffly.

I rolled my eyes, "Oh thank you, my strong male companion." Though I wasn't complaining about not having to carry the bag, it rubbed me the wrong way that Falcon thought I would slow us down.

He was fastening the buckles of the bag across his chest as he said, "Your advantage in a fight is your speed. If we run into any trouble you don't need any extra weight slowing you down."

I crossed my arms and stared at him. I guess if it was for the sake of our survival, I could deal with it. I still kept my bag with my personal belongings on my back though.

Callum came back into the room. "Are we ready?"

"Let's do it." I answered, and headed for the door.

LIAM

General Ren clapped me tightly on the back. I looked at him, and back to what was in front of us – Everloom. Home. I hadn't been back since we left a year ago. Everything looked…the same. The same, except there was no laughter in fields, no little ones scampering through the town square. It was quiet – unsettlingly so.

General Ren had filled me in on our objective shortly after Cass and the commander left. My gut clenched at the thought of what trouble she must be getting into. She never learned when to stop talking. General Ren took the lead, horse's reigns in hand, and made his way to the infirmary. I followed close behind, trying not to focus too hard on the silence.

"Ira?" General Ren called out, stepping through the front door.

"Ah, Ren, you made it." An old, wizened voice spoke. Grand Elder Ira was standing, slightly hunched from old age. He had almost no hair on his head – what he did have was stark white. His brown robe nearly swallowed him as he shuffled towards us, "I was afraid you might meet trouble on the road."

General Ren chuckled and clapped me on the shoulder, "Not with this young buck to protect me." I raised an eyebrow and reached out my hand.

"Grand Elder Ira, it's good to see you again." I said, smiling.

He smiled as he took my hand, clasping his other hand on top of it, "Now, now, no need for pleasantries, my boy. My how you look so much like your father." A mix of sorrow and pride filled my chest as he let go and turned to General Ren.

"She is ready for you." He motioned towards one of the beds. I followed his gaze and sucked in a breath. Helena. Her eyes were closed, and her blonde curls rested around her face. She could have been asleep. But we knew better.

"Have the men readied the cart I requested?" General Ren asked gruffly, not staring too long at Helena. No doubt he felt some measure of guilt for what happened, regardless of the fact that he would have been powerless to stop it.

I looked at the woman who acted as a mother to me when I had none, who fed me and made sure I had enough during the winter. My heart ached. But we would bring her back to her family. We had to. Maybe, just maybe, Cass could be a little bit of her old self again.

CASS

We walked all day, trekking up and down hills and through forests. It wasn't until the sun set that we finally let up.

"Alright." Falcon said, coming to a large clearing off the side of the road, "We'll camp here."

I stretched my arms out behind me and looked around. We were surrounded by dense trees, the grass was green and lush. This seemed to be a common spot to stop at because where was a round spot of dirt in the middle of the grass perfect for building a fire.

"It'll do." I shrugged, and gently put my bag on the ground.

After we set up camp, built a fire, and ate some rations from the cabin, we all laid out our bed rolls around the put-out fire.

After tossing and turning for a good hour, I exhaled a frustrated sigh.

"Can't sleep?" Falcon called from the other side of the fire, slight amusement in his voice.

"No." Callum and I said at the same time. My lips pressed together to keep from laughing.

"What's it like – being in Luminous Storm?" Callum asked. I glanced at him, rolling onto my side.

"Up until recently it was…frustrating." I concluded, "There weren't any real leads on where they were keeping the kids, but now-"

"Now we know where they are and we're working on how to get them back." Falcon cut in.

It was silent a moment, "Callum?" I called out.

His answering "Hmmm?" told me he had almost fallen asleep.

"What was your grandfather like? Callum Abernathy Senior."

He let out a low chuckle, "Grandfather was…a character." He said, "He raised me after my parents died ten years ago. He was very insistent that I learn healing magic. And him with that sword…"

My interest piqued, "What?"

"Near the end – he spent all his time locked up in his office with that sword. He wouldn't tell me what he was doing or why it was important. Sometimes…sometimes I would press my ear against the door and all I could hear was shuffling papers and him mumbling something about 'the blood. It all comes back to the blood'."

"That's disturbing." Falcon stated.

"That's what I said." Callum said nonchalantly, "So Commander Feldstrom – what's the famed General Ren like?"

"Just about as stoic as you would expect him to be." Falcon sighed, "except for with *that* one." I assumed he was talking about me.

"What can I say?" I said dryly, "My personality is magnetic."

Callum choked on a laugh.

I could almost *hear* Falcon roll his eyes, "In all truth, I didn't see him much when I was younger. It was only when I was about ten years old he started visiting my mom and I again."

"Not your dad?" Callum asked, prodding perhaps a little too far.

"No." Falcon said tightly, "No… he died when I was eight."

"Aren't we a group of lucky ducks?" I said sarcastically, "We have dead dads, dead grandparents, brothers who have been kidnapped by our country's evil overlord…" I trailed off, my voice having gone a bit bitter.

"Tell me, Cass." Callum said, "What was your favorite thing about your brothers?"

"I…" I trailed off. What was my favorite part? I had spent so long focusing on finding them I realized it had been too long since I thought about *them*. "Bram – he'll be 5 now. He had this mop of curly blonde hair – same as my Mama. He made me a crown of flowers for my birthday…the day everything happened." I smiled to myself, "He didn't care that flowers were falling off or that they were wilting – the whole day I wore the darn thing he would just gaze at me with those big brown eyes and tell me that I looked just like a princess…he was just so sweet."

"And Kolby?" Callum pressed.

"Kolby…Kolby will be 14 now. He looks just like our Pa did - he was so funny. He told Liam that he should write a book on how *not* to play King's Diamond." I giggled at the memory. "My Mama, she was just sunshine personified. She lit up any room she walked into and always knew how to make us feel loved and special," I got quieter, "even when times were tough, or money was tight…" I suddenly felt a tear drop down my face. "Thanks Callum, now I'm a wreck."

"You needed to remember." He said, a familiar self-satisfied tone in his voice.

"Remember what?" I bit out, still annoyed at him for making me...*feel*.

"What you're fighting for." He said simply.

FALCON

I had never heard Cass talk about something for more than 2 minutes without some kind of sarcastic comment. She sounded...happy. How could I have never asked her about her family before? I never even knew that she *could* giggle. The sound brought a broad smile to my face, and I was thankful they couldn't see my face in the darkness. That fox...Ayla, she had also brought out another side of Cass that I hadn't seen before. She still had that hard edge to her, but I was beginning to see who she had been before her life was changed.

CASS

Two days later, we were trekking through a dense forest on a narrow path. My feet were killing me, my hair was a mess, and I could smell myself sweating. Extreme combat I could do for hours on end without losing my breath. But walking? For three straight days? I was dying.

The sun was just starting to set when we finally made it to another clearing. Falcon dropped the pack next to a large boulder and then sat on it, wiping his brow. I took off my pack, unintentionally jostling Ayla, and set it on the ground. Then I let myself fall to the ground in a heap. I heard Callum chuckle behind me as I let out a groan. "You must have some magical anti-tiredness spell going or something." I complained.

"Nope." He said, sitting on the grass beside me and pulling off his pack. "I made countless trips - on foot - with my grandfather to nearby villages that were days away. I'll probably start feeling it in a day or two, but for now, I'm used to it."

I could almost hear Falcon's eyes roll at my dramatization, "I don't think I've ever heard someone complain as much as you, Cass."

"You say, as you complain about me." I smirked. Suddenly, a sound caught my attention. I snapped up to a sitting position, causing Callum to raise his brows at me, "Is that?"

"What?" Falcon said, reaching for his sword.

MARK OF THE FALLEN

There it was again. I felt a grin plaster onto my face as I hopped up and grabbed my pack, ran in the direction of the sound, into the forest, "Running water!" I yelled behind my shoulder, running as the sound of water got louder. I heard Falcon sigh, and then their footsteps followed after me. I came across another, smaller clearing, and a river- the source of the sound.

The crystal-clear water rushed over opalescent rocks and pebbles, leading into a shallow looking pool of water that then ran into a smaller stream that disappeared into the forest. I turned around, facing Callum and Falcon as they came through the trees to the newly discovered clearing, "This looks like a good place to set up camp." I grinned triumphantly.

I was getting used to Falcon's sighs by now, but this one seemed to be the most exasperated. "Fine," he said, "we can all get cleaned up and sleep here but we leave at first light. We should pass the old Silverglade Castle tomorrow."

Ayla peaked her head out of my pack and yawned, hopping out entirely and stretching out on the ground. She lazily walked over and started to drink from the stream.

She had taken care of hunting for herself while we'd been travelling – she would disappear for about an hour in the evening, coming back with a rabbit or two. Callum and Falcon would get this disgusted look on their faces when she would eat – but what was she supposed to do – pull out a knife and fork and eat with a napkin around her neck? I would pet Ayla and look pointedly at them, "Oh, you caught a big rabbit, didn't you girl? My little hunter."

Chapter 15

It was completely dark by the time we all took our turns getting washed up, and Falcon had gotten a roaring fire going. Fastening the warm wool coat that I snagged from the cabin, I nestled into the spot between Callum and Falcon. "You boys have been busy." I said, eyeing, the 3 skewers roasting over the fire. "What is that - rabbit?"

Falcon nodded, "Shot by me, prepared by Callum."

Callum grinned sheepishly, "Hopefully it won't be too bland, I had to use some herbs growing in the area for seasoning."

"At this point, I don't care if you seasoned it with dirt." I said, my mouth watering. I was starving.

"Maybe we'll just do that next time." Falcon quipped, raising an eyebrow at me.

I could almost feel my eyes rolling in the back of my head already. "Yeah, yeah." I said, waving a hand at him in dismissal and further inspecting the roasting meat. It looked mouth-watering, and smelled even better, "Looks about ready to me." I said, leaning back.

Callum carefully lifted the meat off the makeshift spit and placed it on a flat stone by the fire. We all silently ate for a moment, the quiet contemplation a welcome reprieve from being on the move all day. Falcon held some of the meat out to Ayla – and she gingerly took it from him, laying down next to me and pulling the food apart with her teeth.

Falcon mentioned that we would pass by Silverglade Castle tomorrow. Something panged in my chest at the thought of the Old Silverglade Castle. I wondered if it would be empty since there were no longer any nobles to inhabit it.

"Falcon." I said, slightly turning towards him "You said we will pass by the old Silverglade castle tomorrow?"

Falcon took a bite of meat and nodded. I waited for further information, or for him to question why I wanted to know, but then Callum spoke up as he picked a piece of meat off a skewer, "Do either of you…know what happened?"

I swallowed, "What happened to what?"

"What happened to the royal family…to the rest of the nobles after." He answered, the fire reflecting dangerously in his eyes. "Silverglade castle will be empty."

So, it would be empty. I don't know why that gave me a sinking feeling in the pit of my stomach - or how that was related to the plague that overtook the royal family.

"A plague. That's what they've always said. A plague - that thanks to Aeron's magic - stayed localized in the castle. About the only good thing he's ever done." I said, drawing lazy circles in the dirt by my feet with my now empty skewer.

"That's not what happened." Callum said, shaking his head, "My grandfather…he wouldn't speak of it. Refused. One day he let slip that he had returned to the castle shortly after the fall of the family. I wanted more details. He would turn as white as a freshly washed sheet whenever I would bring it up. Which I would, often. It just seems too...convenient for Aeron. To be a savior and have everyone that might ever oppose him taken care of by a…plague."

"Then what do *you* think happened?" I challenged.

"I can tell you what happened." Falcon said, speaking for the first time in a while.

"Something actually happened?" I asked, my mouth practically hanging open.

Falcon stabbed his skewer into the ground next to him. "Aeron happened." He said angrily, "He didn't 'keep the plague localized to the castle'. He attacked with an army of undead in secret in the dead of night and killed everyone in the castle. He put a sleeping spell on the surrounding town so nobody would wake up and slaughtered them all."

Slaughtered? I swallowed despite the lump in my throat. "How-?"

"My uncle." Falcon said, "He said he had been requested by name by a high-ranking noble, and the king allowed him to leave. My uncle sent word about a day ahead that he would be there soon…but the family responded saying that they were not expecting him. Uncle Ren knew something was wrong and raced back to the castle, but it was too late. He arrived shortly before dawn - and saw the carnage left behind before Aeron sent in his clean-up crew.

He made it look like everyone died of a plague and the citizens were none the wiser. They were all so grateful that he 'saved everyone else' they didn't push back when he took power."

I felt tears stinging my eyes, "All those people…" I didn't know why it was different now. They've all been dead for years. But now, knowing it was intentional, and not just some tragic accident…every time I think I hit the ceiling for my level of rage towards Aeron…well, I keep proving myself wrong.

"Then what about the nobles and the old kingdoms?" Callum asked, voice wavering slightly. This was a lot of information to take in.

Falcon shrugged, "That one is a little more unclear. It seems that Aeron waited about 5 years, then when it seemed like they were going to turn against him, used assassins and spies to wipe them out slowly so it all looked unrelated. At least, that's all my uncle and I can think of."

"Callum." I turned to him, "Where was your grandfather that night? Why wasn't he in the castle?"

"Oh. Um-" he stammered, his cheeks turning slightly red, "That was the night that I was born. He was visiting my parents."

"Aw, baby Callum saving his grandfather from a horrible fate." I smiled, elbowing him gently.

Falcon cleared his throat ,"So, Foxglove," he said, motioning to the sword that I now kept on my back at all times, "How is that sword treating you? I know you're used to carrying daggers and a short sword."

I arched a brow, surprised that he knew that about me. "It's taking a little bit of getting used to, but I'm getting there."

We stayed up for only an hour or so after eating, then rolled our packs out around the dwindling fire. It was handy having a mage around - Callum supplied us with enchanted blankets that kept us at optimal body temperature. No matter how hot or cold it could get, we wouldn't go cold or get too hot. I found myself stirring to the sound of hushed voices. Falcon and Callum were whispering to each other. Keeping my back turned, I listened intently.

"I told you already, I don't think she has any magic." Callum said lowly, "Mages can sense each other's magic, but I don't sense anything from her." I couldn't see his face, but he sounded more aggravated than I have ever heard him.

I also heard the edge in Falcon's voice, "Then why does she have these visions? Why did General Ren think that she would be able to find that sword? He didn't even know about her visions as far as I'm aware. It must be all connected."

I decided now was as good of a time as any to announce my growing consciousness. Making a show of rolling over, I stretched my arms out over my head and sat up. Falcon and Callum abruptly stopped talking. "Why are you guys up? What time is it?" I asked groggily. Sensing my motion, Ayla groggily moved from her position under my sleeping pack and into my bag.

"It's 5, Foxglove." Falcon said gently, "We were just about to wake you. We should probably get an early start." I nodded and stood.

"I'm going to go splash some water on my face." I walked over to the stream and gasped at the sting of the cold water. Yes, I was suddenly very much more awake. I wondered why Falcon was so concerned about whether I had magic. It wouldn't change anything if I did. If I did have magic, I would have used it to stop Captain Remus from taking my brothers in the first place. Or I would have died trying, anyway.

"Did you sleep okay?" Callum's voice asked behind me.

I turned and gave a weak smile, "Perfectly. Those blankets are genius. We'll have to tell General Ren about them." Truly, Callum seemed to be an untapped source of creative and innovative spell work. My eyes searched behind him, it seemed that Falcon had gone into the woods. I lowered my voice and said to him, "You really don't think I have any magic?"

He shook his head, "Sorry you had to hear that. I think there's too many missing puzzle pieces for Falcon to feel confident of our course of action. Hopefully General Ren will have some insight into your…situation. But no, I don't sense anything within you that would be considered magic."

"How does that even work?" I asked, my curiosity getting the best of me.

"It's not a conscious thing we do. It's kind of like seeing the color blue. Or smelling something, if that makes any sense. It's like…a 6th sense almost."

I roughly raked my fingers through my hair in an attempt to detangle it, "Did you say anything to him about the amulet glowing?" I nervously chewed my bottom lip.

"Not my information to share." Callum shrugged, his green eyes flashed conspiratorially.

Relief settled in my chest, "I knew I liked you for a reason." I teased, playfully shoving his shoulder as I passed him to go back to the campsite.

Falcon looked up from his compass as he heard my steps approaching, "You guys ready?"

I got on my knees and started rolling up my bed pack, "Ready to torture myself another 4 days before we get home? No." Standing up and securing the Sword to my back I continued, "Ready to get home and never travel by foot ever again? Yes."

Falcon snorted and shook his head, "Will I ever get a straight answer from you on anything?"

"Not if I can help it." I grinned.

The sun was high in the sky when we came into the vicinity of the old Silverglade Castle. An eerie feeling overtook me as we passed through the surrounding town. The town was…lifeless. Compared to Kleidis, it had no color, no vibrancy. There was barely anyone in the street, and it was near noon - it should have been bustling with people. Not to mention the fact that the town should have been crawling with Shadow Guard, but I only saw one, and he was asleep at his post.

"What happened here?" I whispered behind me to Falcon, who was following close behind.

"I'm not sure," he said quietly, "but I want to get out of here as soon as we can."

I glanced at Callum, and he nodded. We steered carefully through the town, attempting to avoid any attention. Pointlessly, seeing as nobody paid us any mind anyway. We took a sharp right turn down an alleyway. We stopped, looking at each other, wide-eyed. "There's some sort of magic at play here." Callum said quietly. "Something that's keeping everyone…sedated."

"I-" I started, but suddenly, the sword on my back…vibrated? No, not vibrated, but sort of…reverberated. There was a sharp, high-pitched echo that answered the ringing of the sword. It was pulling me - "-the sword-"

"What is that?" Callum asked sharply.

"What is what?" Falcon asked, looking between us.

"You don't hear that?" I asked, and my feet started walking. Towards what, I wasn't sure. It was as if the sword was leading me somewhere. Through the alleyway I floated - no not floated. My feet were carrying me, but I wasn't in control of them.

"Wait, Cass!" I heard Falcon yell behind me - but I couldn't answer them. Not when I heard the song calling out. A song that called out to my soul - or was it the sword's soul? Could swords even have souls? Callum and Falcon's footsteps echoed behind me as I made turn after turn. Darkened houses flashed by as I ran through the belly of the sedated town. I don't know how long I ran until I pushed through a set of large hedges and found myself-

"Silverglade Castle." Callum breathed behind me, all of us out of breath.

"Cass, what the hell was that?" Falcon choked out, hands on his knees, trying to catch his breath. "So much for not drawing any attention."

I turned back to them, the ringing had stopped - it was like the siren's song had been extinguished.. "I don't know. Something was calling the sword-"

"Calling the sword? Do you know how crazy you sound?" Falcon all but shouted, "You just take off in the middle of a town that we just agreed seemed dangerous-"

"Falcon. I heard it too." Callum said, stepping in front of me. "It was - it was almost like the sword shouted out and something answered. There's a magical signature as well - it seems…ancient."

"I thought you said it was just an ordinary sword." Falcon said, narrowing his eyes, no doubt noticing how close behind Callum I was.

"It is…it was. Something about being in the town…awoke it, as ridiculous as that sounds. It has to be whatever was 'calling' to it." He shook his head, "I mean if you think about it, if it *was* just an ordinary sword, would General Ren have sent you two to get it?"

I stepped out from behind Callum, "We need to go in there. We-"

Falcon scoffed, "We don't know what's in-"

"The sword is incomplete, I can feel it." I said. "It has this…feeling-"

"You're going off of a feeling?" Falcon asked incredulously.

"I know this feeling!" I shouted, tears stinging my eyes, "It's incomplete, and it needs to be whole again!" I couldn't tell you how I knew, except- "It's the same feeling that I had in my chest the day my brothers were taken from me." I said quietly, looking down. "It would do anything to be whole again. With this level of desperation, Falcon…I feel that whatever this sword is…it won't work without whatever it's missing."

I felt a hand on my shoulder. Looking up, I wiped my eyes as Falcon stared at me. Was that understanding in his eyes?

"One hour, Foxglove." He relented, his expression softening, "One hour to find whatever is 'calling' to the sword. But then, we need to keep moving."

Chapter 16

I moved slowly across the stone bridge that connected the village to the castle, carefully reaching out with my senses to see if I could recapture that feeling that had been emanating from the sword. Falcon and Callum's footsteps echoed behind me - a quiet reassurance. The further along the bridge we went, the more apparent it became that this castle had been neglected for years. Vines laden with white flowers snaked up and around the castle walls, covering windows and partially obscuring doorways. The flowers were closed, not quite in bloom, their soft petals meeting above the bud in a point. My steps slowed as I neared the castle wall. Upon further inspection, the flowers weren't entirely white. They had an almost metallic sheen to them…

"The Silverdrop flower." Callum said next to me, making me jump. He reached out a hand to touch one of the flowers. "They only bloom for about an hour before they wither away, so for the majority of their lives they look like this - like silver teardrops."

Silverdrop flower… fitting name for a flower that looked as it did. I wondered if the flowers had anything to do with the name of the old kingdom as well. Ayla peaked her head out of my pack, her nose sniffing in the air, then hopped out, using my shoulder as a launching pad to land on the floor, stretching herself out.

I stepped around Callum and pushed on the large wooden door behind the vines. It swung open with surprising ease, giving way to a large outdoor courtyard. The three of us stepped in cautiously, Falcon with a readied hand on the sword at his hip, Callum scanning the area for any dangers.

A quick scan of the courtyard showed it was pretty much in the same condition as the outside of the castle. Overgrown vines with Silverdrop buds, dirt and leaves collected in the corners, and…the front door of the Castle was broken in.

"What could have done that?" I asked quietly, drawing Callum and Falcon's attention. Ayla walked next to me, her ears back again.

Suddenly, I noticed the sword on my back…pulsating. Pulling it out in front of me, I observed it. It didn't look any different…you couldn't tell it was pulsating by sight, but I could tell. I could feel it. Not with my hands, but something different. Deeper.

Turning slowly, I adjusted my grip. Two-handed swords were not my weapon of choice, but I could adjust.

"Feel anything?" Falcon whispered to my left.

"Yeah." I answered, my voice at regular volume. "Why are you whispering?"

"Oh," He cleared his throat, "I didn't want to scare the sword if you were…feeling something from it."

Callum's short burst of laughter mirrored my own. Falcon's cheeks reddened slightly, "Hey I don't know how any of this works and I'm *trying* to be supportive."

I chuckled again and shook my head as I took a step towards the castle, "Thank you, Falcon. I-" I stopped, a shift in the pulsating catching my attention. "Hold on." Taking a step back, I paid extra attention to the sword. Just as I thought.

I looked back and forth between Callum and Falcon's confused faces, "When I step toward the castle-" I said, illustrating my point with a step forward, "the pulsing quickens." I walked a few more steps towards the front door of the castle. Again, there was an increase in the speed of the pulsating of the sword. "I think this is going to lead us to whatever the sword is looking for." I continued my steps towards the castle.

"Wait." Falcon said, quickly stepping around me, "Let me check to make sure this isn't a trap."

I rolled my eyes. Sure, a trap. Somehow Captain Remus knows where we are, caught up to us, and managed to hide out in a castle that I didn't even plan on going in 10 minutes ago. But, if it makes him feel better… "Sure." I said, planting my feet with a hand on my hip. I watched him as he quickly advanced to the door, sword drawn. He looked so ridiculous I couldn't help but grin.

"Is he always like this?" Callum asked, coming up next to me.

"No." I said pensively, "He's only started resembling a mother hen since we left the cabin."

He nodded and kept an eye on where Falcon had disappeared through the crack in the doors. "I don't want to overstep, but…" He trailed off, a look in his brown eyes telling me that even though he didn't *want* to overstep, he would.

"You clearly do." I laughed, "What is it?"

"Just be careful." He said, with a glance in my direction, "He's your commanding officer, and I doubt that the leader of a rebellion would put himself in harm's way like his for every recruit he has. The last thing Luminous Storm needs is their rebellion leader getting himself killed because he…treasured one soldier too much."

As much as I wanted to argue with him, I couldn't. It's not like Falcon did treasure me – but let's say there *was* a trap in the castle like Falcon was worried about. We would no longer have a rebellion leader and who knew what that would do to the cause.

"And here I thought it was *me* you were worried about." I clicked my tongue, deflecting his concern. "You've wounded me." I said, a mocking hand over my heart.

"Please, Cass. You're the last one I'm worried about." Callum sighed, shaking his head in resignation.

Just then, Falcon poked his head out of the crack in the door, "Bottom floor is clear." He said, waving an arm to us. Ayla trotted up to Falcon and chittered at him. Perhaps she was warming up to him after all.

Callum walked ahead of me, stepping into the castle first. On my way past I said to Falcon, "Next time, Commander, leave the scouting to us disposable soldiers." Before I could continue all the way into the castle, he caught my arm.

Caught off guard, I could only stare at his silver eyes as his brow furrowed and he quietly said, "You are *not* disposable."

I tilted my head, eyebrows raised, "You know what I mean, Falcon. If you die, the whole rebellion could unravel."

His face fell slightly for just a moment, but he quickly schooled his features, "I don't want you worrying about that." He said, dismissal in his voice.

I shook my arm free of his grasp, "*Someone* has to." I shot back. He held my eyes for a moment, but I broke eye contact when I felt the sword continue to pulse.

I didn't need to tell him what was happening - he could tell as soon as my eyes caught the blade of the sword. I quickly scanned my surroundings - the castle had been abandoned for years, but the inside still gleamed like it had been polished yesterday. True to its name, Silverglade castle had an overabundance of silver-sheened staircases, wall sconces, and statues.

Before I could even wonder what sort of magic could make that possible, the strength of the pulsing of the sword increased so dramatically I had to stop and see what could have caused it. The speed had stayed the same, but the intensity was stronger than anything I had felt up until this point. Ayla had turned back to face me, her ears perked straight up. Could she sense this too?

I focused my mind back on the sword, and almost immediately the pulsing lowered its' intensity - almost like it was upset I had stopped paying attention to it. I raised an eyebrow - cheeky thing.

"Okay, okay, I'm listening." I said to the sword, and Falcon looked at me for the second time today like was crazy. Ignoring him and stepping further into the castle, the swords reverberation picks up in frequency again. There was enough natural light from the windows that we didn't have any trouble seeing - but I wouldn't want to be caught in here after dark without a light. I follow the sword, continuing through the room, down a hall, and end up in a throne room when the pulsing stops completely.

I stop in the entryway, Falcon and Callum close behind me. One of them lets out a low whistle. The walls are gilded with silver, the throne an extravagant, bourgeoisie chair that reaches halfway up to the ceiling in a gruesome display of wealth.

I shake my head, "How has no one melted any of this down yet? I'm surprised The Shadow Guard haven't ransacked the place."

"That *is* odd…" Falcon admitted, suddenly more alert.

"Why do you think it stopped?" Callum asked, his curiosity piqued.

I'm not sure." I shrugged, walking further into the room. Suddenly, I heard the song again. The same song that had guided my footsteps through town and brought us to the end of that stone bridge.

I crossed the room, completely bypassing in the throne and instead focusing on the wall behind it. Curtains. There were curtains in front of the wall, and I couldn't get the blasted things out of the way. Struggling with the curtains, I didn't even notice Falcon come up next to me, sword drawn. He grabbed them from my hands, and cut the curtains clean across.

I shot him a look of appreciation. But when I turned back to the wall I could feel my face fall. It was just a brick wall. A very rugged, out of place brick wall. In frustration, I placed a hand on the brick in front of my face and closed my eyes. Our one hour was almost up.

"Cass…" There was warning in Callum's voice - my eyes shot open. Under my hand…was glowing. Shocked, I quickly withdrew it, and saw the fading symbol glowing on the brick underneath.

The same symbol on the amulet we found under the floorboards at General Ren's house. Three circles - two on top, one on the bottom, with an intersection in the middle.

"I think this is it." I said quietly, and the sword in my hand sang in response. Following instinct, I reached back out to the brick and rested my hand. The glowing resumed, and I pressed against the brick slowly.

It slowly gave way, pushing all the way into the wall until we heard a fateful "click". With a collective gasp, we all watched as the wall - which was actually a door - swung open in front of us.

"After you." Callum swallowed. I nodded and stepped through the doorway, followed quickly by Falcon and Callum, who lit a wall sconce with his magic. Immediately the room was illuminated. It was empty. There was absolutely nothing in here and we came all this way…

"What do you think-" Falcon started but was interrupted by a voice. I couldn't see anyone in the room, the voice seemed to come from everywhere at once.

"Holder of the Blade of Strattera." The deep voice boomed, "Are you worthy to wield the power you seek?" What was this? The Blade of Strattera? Is that what this sword was called?

I felt a nudge in my back "This is ancient magic, Cass. Answer carefully." Callum whispered. Answer carefully? Was this a test? How was I supposed to know if I was worthy? Surely I had to say that I *was* worthy - why would the disembodied voice allow someone who was unworthy to carry the sword? What would happen if I wasn't?

I felt Falcon's arm push into mine. His presence grounded me. I took a deep breath and said into the void, "Yes, I am worthy." The room seemed to rumble in response.

"We shall see." The voice answered…it sounded skeptical.

Materializing out of thin air, a pedestal appeared in the middle of the room. Sitting on the pedestal there was a small gem, no larger than a marble. It was silver, but at different angles reflected all sorts of different colors. It was breathtakingly beautiful.

Slowly, I approached the pedestal. Reaching out my hand to grab the gem, I hesitated. This seemed too easy. I didn't know what *this* was, but the hidden entrance, the disembodied voice, and pedestals appearing out of nowhere really gave the impression that this was an important gem.

Important gems aren't supposed to be easy to get. But here it was, presenting itself to me on a silver platter…er, pedestal. "I am worthy." I said again to myself this time.

I reached my hand out, but before I could grab it, I was met by an invisible barrier, keeping the gem protected. The barrier started to glow, just as the symbol on the brick did. "I *am* worthy." I said again, a plea, and close my eyes tight as I pushed against the barrier, feeling the warmth of the glow. But, just as quickly as the barrier started to glow, it faded.

"You cannot be worthy until you know what it is to be worthy." The voice boomed out. My heart dropped in my chest, just the same as the pedestal dropped back into the ground, swallowing the gem with it.

Chapter 17

You cannot be worthy until you know
what it is to be worthy.

The words echoed numbly in my head like nonsense shouted into a void. I cannot be worthy until I know what it is to be worthy? I would never be worthy then, apparently.

It had been two days since we left Silverglade Castle, and I'd barely said a word. I could tell my silence was worrying Callum and Falcon. They continued speaking to each other and me like nothing was wrong, but I saw the glances they shot towards one another when they thought I wasn't looking. Heard the hushed conversations suddenly stop when I would come near.

There was a gaping hole in my chest, one that I had previously spackled over with sarcasm and deflection. It had been ripped open with the call of that cursed sword. For a swift moment, it felt as though I might be able to heal the sword in a way that I hadn't been able to heal myself yet.

Since leaving the castle, an occasional call came from the sword, but it was different than before. It was less urgent, melancholy even. The further we got from the castle, the less frequently the calls came, like it was slowly giving up. If Callum heard the call as he did before, he made no mention of it, and I didn't ask. Now the sword hung on my back; heavy, lifeless, and empty.

We were walking adjacent to a small river, no wider than a wagon's length across. I found myself staring into it as I walked, at the iridescent stones that paved the bottom.

"Cass." Nearly stumbling into the body in front of me, I came to a sudden stop. Falcon had turned around and was looking at me like he had been trying to get my attention for a while.

"What is it?" I asked, looking around.

"We're going to stop here for the night." Falcon said to me, his brow furrowed in what one might mistake as concern.

I blinked and looked for the sun. It was almost set…odd that I didn't realize that.

"We made good time, so we should be reaching the base tomorrow - one day ahead of schedule."

"I, for one," Callum piped up behind me, "will be glad to sleep in a real bed this time tomorrow."

Falcon scoffed, "New recruits sleep on the floor, didn't I tell you, Abernathy?" But a grin appeared on his face a moment later.

"Ha ha." Callum threw back, throwing his pack on the ground.

Ayla had gone out for her evening hunt, and we set to work fixing up our campsite - me, silent, as Falcon and Callum continued their banter around me. I was coming back from gathering firewood when I heard Callum and Falcon speaking in hushed whispers again. Without thinking, I hid behind a large tree by the campsite.

"We need to do something." Callum was saying, his voice low, "We need something to snap her out of it."

"She'll be fine when we get back to base." Falcon answered, his voice equally low. "She has a friend - Liam. They joined together. He'll be able to get through to her."

Snap out of it? Get through to me? Is that what they think I needed?

"Are they...?" Callum started, but quickly stopped his line of questioning, "Never mind. It's none of my business."

Falcon let out a low chuckle, "No, I don't think they are, but I know they've been friends since they were toddlers, and their parents were very close. He's the closest thing to family she has. I'm sure he'll know what to say."

Was Liam the closest thing to family I had right now? I would have said General Ren was - before he sent us on this wild goose chase that ended up with my heart shattered all over again.

Not needing to hear anymore, I made my presence known. I stepped out from behind the tree, carrying my pile of firewood, and clumsily tossed it by the circle of stones one of them had constructed while I was away.

"Liam *was* the closest thing to family I had." I clarified, wiping my hands on my trousers, "But I've treated him so poorly the last year that I'm sure by now he's realized how much better it is without me at base and wishes for me to never return." Callum's cheeks reddened slightly- no doubt embarrassed that he was caught asking about me. "I-" He started, but I turned on my heel and walked down the river a ways, putting some more distance between myself and my two male companions. Let them talk. Let them devise ways to fix me. Let them waste their time.

Because there was no fixing me. We were taking an incomplete sword back to General Ren, which would be useless in getting my brothers back. Without my brothers, I would never be whole again, that I knew for certain.

I sat on a large boulder that jutted out over the river, crossing my legs in front of me. Whenever I was alone the last two days, I found myself holding the sword - the Blade of Strattera, as the voice in the castle had called it - running my fingers along the beautiful vines, the smooth blade, the crescent shaped pieces on the hilt and cross guards.

I couldn't tell you why this sword called to me - how it spoke to my soul. But the more I held it, caressed it, the more it seemed like a part of me - even if it was incomplete.

I heard footsteps behind me come to a stop. I made no motion to turn to see who it was - I already knew. Callum wasn't one that could leave someone upset. Though I wasn't necessarily upset, just thinking.

"Cass." Callum's voice called gently.

I turned my head and smiled, "Hey, Cal."

He sighed with relief, walked over to me, and patted the boulder I was sitting on, "Can I sit?" He asked meekly, his freckles crinkling slightly with his forehead.

I nodded and scooted over a bit to make room. He climbed up the boulder, joining me in my cross-legged position. We both just stared out at the river for a moment, and then Callum spoke.

"I want you to know, Cass, I didn't ask about you and Liam because I-"

"I know, Callum." I interrupted him. He didn't need to say it. I knew that wasn't what he felt for me, nor I for him.

"I know you can take care of yourself. Obviously you're better in a fight than I am - I just feel…protective of you." He admitted. "Is that weird?" He asked hesitantly.

I shook my head and felt the corners of my mouth turn slightly, "I got so angry that first day we met you - when the Shadow guard barged in and knocked you over. Falcon looked at me like I had grown two heads with how much information I gave away to you."

Callum shifted, "So you…you feel it too? This sense of - familiarity?"

I nodded, "I don't know what it is, but yes. It made me want to thrash that guard who took a shot at you."

Callum laughed heartily at that, "You really wanted to thrash that guard because of me?"

I elbowed his side, "Yeah, yeah. I like you just fine." He grinned at me - I couldn't help but smile back.

Just like Falcon said, we were a day early coming back, so nobody was expecting us when we walked back into the base. I felt a little better after my talk with Callum, but there was still something off - something missing.

Falcon was showing Callum around the base as I went to drop my pack off at my room.

I was coming out of my door – Ayla snug on my bed - when I was surrounded by three bodies, "Cass, you're back!" Selby said excitedly. I blinked in surprise at the three first-year recruits around me.

"Yeah, we weren't expecting you until tomorrow!" Mullins said.

"We can get you back for those push-ups you made us do – we know you couldn't make us do those." Grigsby announced.

"Okay, okay, give her some room you three." Liam came out of nowhere, gently shoving the first years aside to get to me.

He threw an arm around my shoulder, "Hey Cass." He said, pressing a kiss into my hair, his cedarwood and citrus scent flooding my senses yet again. I let him hold me close, closing my eyes against his chest.

"Liam." I said quietly, taking a shuddering breath. All the tension I had been holding in the last few days slowly escaped me as I settled into him. Coming back to Liam was like pulling on a favorite jacket. Comforting, and reminded me of home.

"Bye guys." I said, effectively dismissing the three of them. They continued down the hallway, roughhousing and pushing each other around like a trio of golden retriever puppies.

Liam pulled back and held me by my arms, looking me over intently, "Are you okay? How was your trip? I'm so glad you're safe." His hair had grown a bit in the time we were away, it almost flopped into his eyes.

I nodded numbly, not wanting to talk about the sword, "It was fine, I'm fine, everything is fine." I gave a weak smile.

His eyebrows furrowed in concern, "Cass-"

"I don't want to talk about it." I said abruptly, stepping out of his grasp. Hurt flashed across his eyes before he spoke.

"I think I have something that will cheer you up."

"H-How?" My voice shook disbelief. One year. It had a whole year since I had seen my Mama's face…but there she was. She was settled in the infirmary, her eyes closed peacefully, a pillow tucked under her head and a blanket pulled up to her shoulders. If I didn't know any better, I would have guessed that she was merely sleeping. My heart ached at the sight of her.

"General Ren and I left for Everloom not long after you and Falcon went to Hillsborough." Liam said, putting an arm around my shoulder. I leaned into his touch. Liam was the only one here who knew how much my Mama meant to me and how much it gutted me when my blood wouldn't break the blood curse. "General Ren thought we might have better luck waking her with a greater number of mages at our disposal." I nodded, my heart lifting slightly. My Ma. How peaceful she looked. Her shallow breathing slightly lifted and lowered the sheet covering her. I gently pushed a blonde curl from off her face and clasped her hand in mine.

"Mama." I choked out, tears threatening to surface, "I'm so sorry." I whispered, bringing her hand to my lips, and pressing a kiss against it. "I'm sorry I never came to see you." I felt Liam's hand grip my shoulder. My Ma was the closest thing to a mother Liam had as well - he had tried so many times over the last year to get me to go back home and visit my Ma.

But I... I wouldn't. Couldn't. The thought of traveling back to see my Mama like… like this put a knot in my chest. I preferred to put my head in the sand and pretend it wasn't happening. That Mama was just happily waiting for me back home, and not withering away in her bed at our empty house, with Grand Elder Ira keeping her body supplied with enough nutrients that she didn't starve to death.

Liam didn't say anything, he didn't need to. As much as I had pushed him away this year, there he was, my rock. My constant.

I climbed into bed next to my Mama, clasping the hand at her side, and rested my head on her shoulder. Without really knowing what I was trying to accomplish, I softly sang the song I had sung to Bram the night before they were taken. A song my mother had so often sung to me, that perhaps it might permeate her sleeping mind and provide her some comfort.

There once were three that became one,
Its power was compared to none,
A weapon so fine it turned to fame,
But no one yet recalls its name.
What is the name of this long-lost treasure?
Its name will soon be gone forever
But we remain these kingdoms three,
For one day soon we will be free.

As the ancient lullaby ended, I realized just how tired I was. The last week and a half caught up to me, and I allowed myself to drift to sleep.

Chapter 18

I couldn't find the will to open my eyes as the voices started talking around me. The comfort of my mother's presence, even if she wasn't conscious, had lulled me into a deeper sleep than I had had in weeks.

"How long has she been like that?" A deep gravelly voice asked - General Ren.

"Probably about two hours." Liam answered, voice low.

"Is that...is that a fox?" General Ren's voice sounded incredulous, and I became mildly aware of a warm presence pressed against my back. How Ayla had found her way here, I couldn't even think about.

"It took a liking to her." Falcon's voice ground out, "What's wrong with her? She's even paler than… who is that in the bed?"

"It's her Ma." This time it was Callum who answered.

"How do you know that?" Liam's voice asked sharply.

"She told me what happened to her Ma when her brothers were taken…seemed like a logical conclusion." Callum brushed off, voice unusually brusque. "As for what's wrong with her…" I felt a hand on my brow "She's burning up. We should get her to her own bed."

I couldn't even attempt to open my eyes before I felt strong arms lift me, one behind my neck, and one under my knees. I distantly heard Ayla chitter in annoyance at being moved. Whoever it was lifted me gently, effortlessly, as if I weighed nothing at all.

General Ren's voice startled, "Falcon-"

"I've got her." Falcon's voice rumbled in his chest against me. Falcon Feldstrom was carrying me to a sick bed. I willed my eyes to open blearily. My vision was filled with the side profile of Falcon's face, my face nestled against his chest. I sighed, delirious with fever, so happy that Falcon was the one carrying me..

"Commander." I greeted him, as if this was the most normal thing in the world.

His eyes darted down to me as he gently laid me on the bed next to my Mama's, "Foxglove." he answered easily.

My hand seemed to move on its own, I reached out and patted his cheek, "Such a pretty face." I said sloppily, my voice sounding distant from my ears.

His facial expression flashed confusion, then an easy, beautiful grin spread on his lips, "There, there Foxglove. You're clearly delirious from your fever."

I wasn't sure what he was talking about, but I must have said something wrong, based on the redness of Liam's face. Though Callum looked like he was holding in a laugh, and General Ren's eyebrow arched in a way I couldn't decipher.

"I'm not delirious." I heard myself explain, "I just really like looking at your face." I said, as if that's all the explanation necessary.

Falcon leaned down next to my ear, "As much as I enjoy hearing that, Cass, let's see how you feel about my face when your fever comes down."

He patted my head and backed away, and someone spooned something sweet and cool into my mouth. "That should bring the fever down." I heard Callum say distantly, and I sunk into black oblivion once again.

It was two days later, I was finally awake, and sitting up in the infirmary bed, "I said WHAT?!" Ayla was curled up in my lap, she apparently hadn't left my side since I passed out.

Callum was laughing so hard he couldn't sit up straight, "You said that Falcon had a pretty face." He gasped, holding onto the sides of the chair he brought to the side of my bed, "Then, you said you just loved looking at it." He wiped a tear from his eye.

I covered my face with both my hands as I felt my face heat up - this time with embarrassment. "No no no, I cannot believe I did that." I mean it wasn't incorrect, I *did* enjoy looking at Falcon's face, but he wasn't supposed to *know* that.

"It's okay Cass, we know it was the fever making you hysterical, but that doesn't make it any less amusing." Callum grinned.

I took a deep breath and swung my legs off the bed. Ayla gently grabbed my sleeve in her mouth and tried to pull me back towards my pillow. I pulled my sleeve, but she held firm. Shooting Callum a look, I turned back to Ayla, "I don't need to go back to bed." I tried as gently as I could to remove her clamped jaw from my sleeve - she nipped my hand when I tried to stand, and I shot a surprised look at her. I could have *sworn* she motioned her head back towards my pillow, as if she was saying *lay back down right now.* "I'm fine." I found myself muttering to her, rubbing my hand where she nipped me. She let out what sounded like a short growl, and hopped off the bed, stalking out of the room. I shook my head and stood, my eyes lingering on my Mama, her form still breathing gently.

Callum was staring at the fox, mouth silently agape, before he followed my line of sight, all traces of laughter gone. "I don't think it's a blood curse, Cass."

My heart dropped, "It's not? But Grand Elder Ira said-"

"It presents just like a blood curse. But there's one symptom missing." Callum walked over to my Mama's bedside, "Normally, with a blood curse, there's a…trace of some sort. I've seen it present as reddened streaks coming up the neck, or some mages prefer to leave their own *brand*" He said the last word with disgust in his voice, "But your Mama…she has no mark to speak of. For all intents and purposes, she could simply be sleeping."

"Then what's…" My voice broke, "Then what's wrong with her?"

"I'm not sure, Cass." He said, sadness in his voice, "I've been examining her the last two days, but I can't find anything that's actually wrong with her."

My heart panged, but I reached for Callum's hand, "It's okay." I said, squeezing his hand tightly, "Thank you for trying. We'll figure it out."

"You're up." A voice said from the doorway. I turned, my hand still in Callum's. Liam was standing in the doorway, jaw clenched, eyes locked on our intertwined hands. I didn't drop it.

Whatever Callum and I had wasn't like that, and I didn't need to prove anything to anyone, least of all Liam. He had a whole year to confess all – if any - feelings he had for me - he did not get to play the jealous man now.

"I am." I nodded, giving Callum a reaffirming pat to his hand before I let go. "Thank you." I said, "I can't remember if I said it before - everything is kind of fuzzy. But thank you, Liam, for bringing her here." His eyes softened as he looked at me.

"You're welcome." He said gently. Seeing Liam made me realize how much I missed him while I was away. Romantic feelings or not, he was still my best friend.

Shaking his head as if remembering why he came in the first place, he quickly spoke, "I was coming to fetch Callum, General Ren wanted to see all of us. But Cass - since you're up, you should come too, if you're feeling up for it."

"I do." I said. I didn't - I felt like I had been hit by a carriage, but I wasn't about to tell anyone that.

"You should really eat something first-" Callum jumped in.

"I'm fine," I cut in, stepping towards Liam, "I have a bone to pick with General Ren about the Blade of Strattera."

Chapter 19

I barged into General Ren's office, not bothering to knock. He and Falcon turned their heads towards me, eyes glancing at Liam and Callum behind me.

"You're awake." General Ren said, matter-of-factly.

"I am." I said, pulling out a chair and sitting down with purpose. "And I want to know what the hell is going on with this sword." I demanded, motioning to the sword laying on General Ren's desk. "Why were you convinced that I would be able to find it, and why did you send us off without giving us any real information?" I tried to keep myself calm, but I could hear the edge slipping into my voice. His brows furrowed deeper the longer I spoke, "Why do I have a…connection to it, and why am I dreaming about things happening that come true the next day?" My voice grew more calmer with each word. "And how," I took a deep breath, tired of keeping secrets, tired of denying what was so clearly in front of my eyes, and pulled the amulet out of my pocket, holding it up "does this glow when I hold it too long?"

Nobody said anything for a moment, the silence was palpable. As if on cue, the amulet started glowing in my hand, it's image a twin to the symbol on the hidden wall in Silverglade Castle. "Do you see this?" I asked, practically shoving the amulet in General Ren's face.

"What on earth-" He started, eyes glued to the amulet. I hear Callum and Liam gasp behind me. Falcon's eyes widened in surprise.

"I hold it longer than a minute, it starts to glow." I practically spat, tossing it down on the desk. The light immediately left it once it broke contact from my hand.

"I suppose I do owe you some sort of explanation." General Ren said, rubbing the back of his neck. "I don't know anything about why the amulet is glowing or your dreams -but…" He looked around the room to Liam and Callum, "Please, gentlemen, come in, get comfortable."

Falcon moved around the desk to stand behind General Ren, arms crossed. Liam and Callum took the two other available seats across from General Ren.

"Aeron is holding the children in the old Castle of Dragorah." General Ren informed us. Falcon nodded - of course he knew, he was the one who informed us that we had found where the children were being held.

"I thought we searched there already?" Liam asked, brows furrowed.

"We did." It was Falcon who answered, pushing himself off the wall he was leaning against. He paced back and forth behind General Ren, "He must have moved them there after the fact. Now he has the place surrounded by so many wards, we can't even get in to check on the situation."

"I've sent some mages ahead to watch from the shadows - see what they can glean from it. We should be getting word any day now." General Ren explained, "In the meantime, we have teams doing research here on the different types of wards and how to break them. Once we have that information we can come up with a plan to get them out."

I nodded. It made sense - what it takes to break the ward depends entirely on who made it and what symbols it's composed of. Even someone with the barest knowledge of wards knows that.

"Now onto the sword." General Ren said, placing a hand on the hilt, "As you've gathered Cass, this is the Blade of Strattera. It is not as complete as it was when I hid it." He said, his face pained, "We can thank Callum Abernathy Sr. for that...may he rest in peace." Callum grimaced next to me.

"There are 3 stones that power the sword." General Ren continued, "one goes into each half-moon shape here-" he pointed to the pommel of the sword where the empty half-moon shape was, "here, and here." He said, pointing to each end of the cross guard. So, I was right - the half-moon shapes weren't just for decoration.

"Stones?" I asked, my breath catching in my throat, "I think we found one."

General Ren looked at me, his eyes softening, "Yes, I was informed. That was one of the stones. I was also informed that Captain Remus is aware that Cass has the sword, but he doesn't know her connection to Luminous Storm, so we'll keep an eye on the situation. In the coming weeks, we'll need to travel to each of the old kingdom's castles, Dragorah, Silverglade, and Eldoria."

I nearly choked, "Dragorah? That's where you just said they're keeping the kids, and we can't get in."

Falcon grimaced, "That one's going to be complicated. We're going to figure out how to break the wards first, then somehow get the stone while also trying to free the children and fight off the Shadow guard."

Not to mention the fact we already went to Silverglade castle, and it did not find me worthy.

Callum jumped in, "If you don't mind me asking, General Ren, what does the sword *do*? What makes it so special? My grandfather, after he took it, spent the better part of a year researching that sword, but I -" he swallowed, "I can't find anything special or abnormal about it. Besides the calling it exhibited when we got close to one of the stones-"

"A call that I couldn't hear." Falcon interjected, looking back and forth between Callum and me.

"Other than that." Callum continued, eyes still fixed on General Ren, "It truly just seems like an ordinary sword."

"I carried this sword, before the Royal Family was wiped out." General Ren said quietly. "I cannot say as to why you could hear the call, Callum, but based on all the other information given it would seem that…the sword has chosen Cass to carry it."

My throat goes dry, and I meet General Ren's eyes, "…Why?" I asked quietly.

He chuckled softly, "Cassie." He was the only one who could get away with calling me that, "Perhaps it found a kindred spirit in you - three pieces of itself were wrenched from its' world - perhaps you two have more in common than you think."

It was strange, the way he was referring to the blade as if it was sentient somehow, but…based on my experiences with it so far, it seemed more true than not. He offered the sword to me, and I took it, the metal sang when I touched it - as if it was relieved to have me hold it again.

Something like pride shined in General Ren's eyes, "Yes, yes. It *does* respond to you."

"Okay…" I said, "But that doesn't tell me why it's important to begin with."

"The Blade of Strattera," General Ren said, leaning forward in his chair, "is the only weapon that can destroy the Amulet of Vilin - the source of Aeron's power."

"So, why has it been stored away this whole time?" I asked, standing in rage, "Why did you store it in the floorboards under your house instead of using it?!" How could he do this? How could he have the key to defeating Aeron, but not use it? Why did he leave my brothers stranded for an entire year while he sat on this information?

"The blade, it…it didn't respond to me." General Ren explained, his face pained. "I was not chosen by the sword after the royal family was wiped out."

There was that silence again. I hated that silence. I looked between Callum, Liam, and Falcon. I wondered if they were all just as confused as I was as to why the sword chose me.

"When I first moved to Everloom," He said finally, eyes only on me, "I had the sword with me." He smiled, his eyes crinkling, "I felt a tug on my pant leg. I looked down, and there you were, a little firecracker. You looked up at me and asked me why my sword was so sad -that it was singing a sad song. Your Pa told you to stop letting your imagination get the better of you. But I knew then, Cass, that the sword had chosen you."

I swallowed dryly and shook my head, "I don't remember that."

He sighed, "No I suppose you wouldn't. You were only around five."

Callum spoke up, "Cass, if you don't mind, I'd like to study the sword while it's in your proximity. All those years I studied it, it seemed like an ordinary sword, but it sort of shifts in your presence." he said.

I nodded, my head swimming with the new information, "That's fine."

Liam spoke up, "So is that why you trained her?" His voice was surprisingly angry, "You've known from the beginning that she would be the one to defeat him?"

I shook my head, "Liam, what-?"

"He's been raising you like a lamb for slaughter!" He said to me, his eyes full of rage, "You could die, Cass!"

Falcon stalked over from behind Genera Ren, "Now hold on just a minute-"

"No, he's right." General Ren said. My heart dropped a little. "When all of this started, my goal was to train you up to be able to wield the sword to defeat Aeron. But you know how much you mean to me, Cassie." He said lowly, "I never settled down or had children of my own, but-"

"I know." I said, nodding at him, saving him from having to make a confession in front of everyone, "I know, General Ren." I turned to Liam and put a hand on his arm, "Liam." He met my eyes, his brow furrowed, "Yes, I could die. But there were also about 10 other times over the last two weeks that I could have died. This is the business we're in. You can't afford to get all sappy on me now." I gave him a weak smile.

"I still don't like it," he all but grumbled, clasping his hand over mine.

"You don't have to," I stated, matter-of-factly, "but if I have even the slightest chance of being able to bring Aeron down, I have to take it. This sword is the only thing that can defeat him. I'll gladly be the sacrificial lamb if that means I get to be the one to plunge the sword into his blackened heart."

Callum choked on a cough, "Geez, Cass, thanks for the visual." There was a slight chuckle around the room, the mood lightening slightly.

"Not even *you* will be able to heal him when I'm done with him." I winked, and Falcon laughed.
"Feeling back to your old self then, Foxglove?" He asked, a twinkle in his eye.

My cheeks heated at the knowledge that everyone in this room knew what I said to him while I had my fever, "Yes, I'm feeling much more…lucid."

It felt like I finally made a step forward in finding my brothers. Having some answers - especially answers on how to put an end to Aeron once and for all, gave me some hope.

"We'll discuss retrieving the gemstones after you've all had a night's rest." General Ren said, getting up from his seat. "You're all dismissed." I thought about staying behind and telling him about the dream I had – the one where the hooded figure was talking about a mark...but now wasn't the time.

"Cass!" Adarra flung herself at me as I walked into the mess hall with Liam and Callum.

"Oof." I grunted on impact, as she wrapped her arms around me in a tight embrace.

"Are you okay?" She asked, pulling back, and taking my face in her hands, looking me over like a mother hen, "I can't believe you went through what you did and made it out only to fall to a fever so soon after getting back."

I let her fuss over me for a minute, "I'm fine, Adarra, really. Nothing to note except for some minor embarrassment. Callum took care of me." I said, jerking a thumb in his direction.

Adarra's eyes darted to Callum, who waved sheepishly at her. She looked back and forth between us for a moment, her brows furrowing and a look of confusion glancing over her features. "His grandfather was the Archmage for the royal family…?" I trailed off, not knowing what was going through her mind.

She shook her head, "Right, General Ren told us about you," she said, and reached out her hand, "I'm Adarra."

Callum reached out to shake her hand, "Callum - as Cass said." He smiled.

Adarra got that look on her face again, "I'm sorry, have we met somewhere before? You just look so familiar."

"Not unless you've ever come to Kleidis for a healer." He said, "But I don't think so - I would definitely remember someone who looks like you."

I whipped my head around to reprimand him, but he was looking at her with softness, not with the harsh glare of judgment. Ohhhhh. So, he didn't mean her eyebrow piercing or her ornate tattoos on each arm, he meant-

Liam let out a low whistle, "Real smooth, Abernathy."

Callum turned beet red, "No, I didn't mean-"

I shoved an elbow into Liam's side, "It's more offensive if you *didn't* mean it that way." I winked, and before Adarra could answer, I whisked her away, linking her elbow with mine and leading her to the line for food. Liam tried to keep pace with us, but I waved him away, "I've been surrounded by men for two weeks, I need some girl time." He sighed, and turned around.

"Now, Adarra Nassar, was that a line?" I inquired, a smile teasing at my lips.

"What? No!" She protested, her voice going uncharacteristically squeaky. "I swear I really have seen him before somewhere, I just can't put my finger on it."

I raised an eyebrow, "Sure, sure." I teased.

Adarra and I took our plates and sat at an empty table. I observed my plate with growing hunger. I couldn't remember the last time I ate and it was taking all my self-control to not just inhale the plate of food on site.

Samuel Eric Cooke III, or Cook, as everyone called him, was the grumbly older man who prepared all the meals and headed up the kitchen. He had been the preferred cook for the soldiers back in the Royal Family's heyday and came from a long line of cooks who had served the royal family. He was a little gruff, but had a twinkle in his eye that showed he liked the company more than he let on. He had a soft spot for me and had given me an extra helping of the chicken, with a pat on my cheek he said I didn't look "bloodthirsty as usual" so the extra protein should remedy that. Between that, the potatoes and savory vegetables on my plate, my mouth was watering.

"So." Adarra said, taking a bite of potatoes. "Nearly two weeks - alone - with the commander." She raised her eyebrows suggestively.

"Oh, stop it." I said, helping myself to the chicken. I had to keep myself from groaning out loud. There was a reason why Cook was the preferred cook for the royal family. "Nothing weird. As usual, we nearly killed each other, but after the debacle in the briefing room-"

"Where you oh-so-eloquently called the commander *trash* in front of everyone." Adarra grinned.

"-Yes, thanks for the reminder." I give her a pointed look, "Ever since then, we have a sort of…understanding." I didn't tell her about what he said in the hallway that night at Callum's family cabin. No, talking about it would make it real, and I wasn't ready to face that yet.

"Ooo I *bet* there's an understanding." She said again, wiggling her eyebrows.

I couldn't help myself, I laughed, "Probably the same understanding you wish you had with Callum."

She looked around as if trying to spot him in the room before saying anything, "He's cute, I'll give you that. Can't tell you until I know him better though."

Adarra wanted to act like she was a player, but in reality, all she wanted to find was "true love" - or whatever variation of that existed in this world. I didn't know what true love would look like if it did exist…but if it did, Adarra definitely deserved it.

"He's a great guy." I said, "Actually…" and then I told her about our…connection. Familiarity, whatever it is and our protectiveness over one another. How it was an instantaneous thing, and how neither of us know why. "It's not romantic in the slightest." I said, "I just instantly knew that I could trust him with my life."

"Hmmm…" she said thoughtfully, chewing slowly. "I wonder if that's why he looked familiar. Maybe I could sense the bond between the two of you?"

"Or you just want him." I teased. We both dissolved into a fit of giggles.

Chapter 20

LIAM

I couldn't sleep. Cass was back. She was safe. And I still couldn't sleep. I hadn't been able to sleep properly since. I laid in bed and stared at the ceiling. I waited and waited for her to get back so I could show her what we did for her – what I did for her. She comes down with a fever immediately after getting home. And then I come to check on her, and she's holding *that guy's* hand. I didn't like him-didn't trust him. I didn't like how quickly Cass had become close to him that she let him past walls she didn't let me even touch.

He had to be influencing her somehow…I just didn't know how. I would have to keep an eye on him. I turned and stared at the wall.

Cass. How many times did I have a nightmare where she didn't come back? Before I knew it, I was standing, my legs carrying me out my door.

CASS

I woke up to the sound of a knock on my door. It was heavenly sleeping in my bed after two weeks of sleeping outside on the floor. After introducing Adarra to my Mama after dinner, she and I stayed up talking and catching up. I told her everything that happened, how Ayla came to be with us, and about the Blade of Strattera.

She was on one of the teams researching the wards surrounding the Dragorah Castle. She complained that I got to have "all the fun" while she was stuck studying. Ha. She went back to her room around midnight, and I tried to get some sleep. Ayla hadn't come back to me yet - if I didn't know any better, I'd think she was mad at me for getting out of bed before I was fully healed.

I sleepily switched on my bedside lantern and checked my pocket watch. It was 3 in the morning. Thinking something must be wrong with Ma if someone is getting me this late, I threw open the door, expecting the worst.

"Liam, what-" I started, but he brushed past me into my room. He looked a mess, his hair was disheveled, and his clothes were rumpled, as if he had spent the last several hours tossing and turning in bed, which he very well might have. "Is everything okay with Ma-"

"I…I couldn't sleep," He said, as if that was the only explanation I needed for him showing up at my door at 3 in the morning.

"Okay…" I spoke slowly, not sure what I could do to help with that, "I doubt my floor is more comfortable, but-"

"I couldn't sleep, because of *you*," He said, desperation lining his voice.

"Because of me?" I echoed, searching my brain for anything I've done to him that would cost him sleep. "What did I do?"

He let out a bitter laugh, and started pacing around my room as I watched helplessly, "What *haven't* you done to me, Cass?"

I shook my head, "I-"

"You could be talking about how you made me fall in love with you while we were growing up? Or maybe how you kissed me the night everything happened, and we came here?" I blinked in surprise at his frankness, "Or could you possibly be talking about how you left with Commander Feldstrom, and almost got yourself killed multiple times, leaving me a stressed out mess every time I saw General Ren for fear he would give me another update."

"I didn't-"

"And then-" He interrupted yet again.

"Listen to me!" I grabbed his arm, "None of this is fair." He looked like he was going to try to say something else, but I beat him to it, "You can't act like you were the only one affected. I fell in love with you too, just as much. I kissed you, yes, and then *you never did anything about it..*" I rambled, trying to hit each of his points, "Then, I had literally no choice in going with Falcon. You know that as well as I do. This is the nature of the job, Liam, that we both knew going in. I can't control bandits or Shadow Guard ambushing us any more than I can control the wind or rain,"

"I didn't do anything…?" He shook his head, "Cass, you had just lost the only family you had. You came to my house in the dead of night with bags packed. I didn't know if it was grief, or even real. I wanted to see if you would still feel the same way after all the dust settled."

"I…" My thoughts raced back to that night. After my brothers were taken, I had sat in the house by myself, staring at the wall until something snapped in me. Grand Elder Ira had carted my

Mama out to Everloom's infirmary that he ran out of his home. The first thing I did after the children were taken, after I had gathered my wits, was ask after Mama.

Grand Elder Ira had witnessed the incantation and said that he believed it to be a blood curse. The antidote - a counter spell cast with a family member's blood - had failed. I sat there ever since. I didn't know where Liam was.

Goodness knew if he ever even spoke to me again, the way I screamed at him after the Shadow Guard left. It wasn't fair of me to blame him, I knew. But if I hadn't been sparring with him, I could have been *there* - I could have protected them. He argued that I would have been in those caravans right along with them and I'm lucky I wasn't there. I said a few more choice words to him that I was sure I would regret later, but I needed someone to blame.

I had to get out of the house. I had to *do* something. I didn't know what time it was, and I didn't care. I wandered around the empty house, gathering anything that could be useful. I pulled a bag from my mama's closet, and shoved everything into it. I went into our room and gathered my clothes from my drawer of the dresser. I didn't dare make eye contact with the empty beds on the adjacent walls.

Before I exited the room, my eyes involuntarily darted to Bram's bed. Sweet, thoughtful Bram. His bed was half-made, his loved and worn small stuffed bear sitting against the pillow. I picked it up gingerly, tears pricking my eyes. Before I could change my mind, I put the bear in my bag.

Before I knew it, I was in front of Liam's house. It had to be at least 4 in the morning. I raised my hand hesitantly, shifting under the weight of the two bags I had packed, but knocked anyway. Liam answered fairly quickly - he must not have been able to sleep either. His expression changed from relief to concern when he saw the bags on my back, "Cass, what are you-"

"Let's go." I said, pushing past him into the house, "We can leave, tonight."

He shook his head, "I thought you wanted to wait-"

"I wanted to wait because I had to take care of Bram, Kolby, and Mama." I said, my voice wavering slightly.

Understanding flashed across his face. "Do you want to take a couple of days and think about it?"

"No," I fervently shook my head, "I can't go back to that house. I can't go back and look at their empty beds. I need to leave, and I need to leave now. Are you coming with me?" I searched his eyes for something…anything.

He reached out, holding each one of my arms at my sides, "Cass, are you sure?"

The hurt was raw in his eyes, and I knew that he felt the loss almost as much as I did. I wished that I could convey to him that it wasn't about being sure. There was no other option.

I don't know if it was love, or desperation, or needing to feel something other than heartbreak, but I crossed that line that he and I only toed from time to time.

I reached up, and taking him by surprise, wrapped my arms around his neck and kissed him. I kissed him with all of the longing of our unsaid words over the last 10 years. He kissed me like he had been waiting just as long.

I pulled back, and placing a hand on his chest, searching his eyes, I repeated, "Are you coming with me?"

I was snapped back to reality, Liam was staring at me with an indecipherable look in his eyes. Maybe he had been thinking about that night too.

"First, I was giving you space to go through whatever you were going through." He said, his face soft, "Then, we met Adarra. And she asked us if we were together - you said no *so quickly*…"

I shook my head, "I said no because I had just served my heart to you on a silver platter, and you never said another word about it."

"So, all this time," He ran a hand through his hair, "all this…was due to *miscommunication*? Why didn't you try to talk to me about it?"

"I felt rejected, Liam." I whispered, tears stinging my eyes at the memory, "You completely withdrew from me. I couldn't even lean on you anymore. You only came back to me after I told Adarra we weren't together." I folded my arms over my chest as if it might protect me from the pain of the memory, "I had just lost my family and then I lost you too. I thought things would never be the same between us, so I made sure you thought I didn't feel that way about you anymore."

"I…I'm so sorry Cass." Liam said, drawing me into an embrace. I begrudgingly let him, resting my head on his shoulder, but kept my arms folded across my chest as his wrapped around me. "I…I didn't want to come off like I expected anything from you. I was trying to give you a way out in case you thought it was all a mistake - a lapse in judgment brought on by grief."

I huffed a pained laugh, "Yeah, telling me that would have been nice."

"I know. I was an idiot." He said quietly, resting his head on mine.

I pulled back and raised an eyebrow? "Was?" I tease, trying to lighten the mood. He smirked at me, and something raw flashed in his eyes. His stare darted down to my mouth, then back up to my eyes. This was a bad idea. Such a bad, horrible, no-good idea. But I wanted to see what would happen.

"I've missed you, Cass." He said roughly…and I knew he didn't just mean the two weeks I was gone. Then, before I knew what was happening, one hand that had been wrapped around me came up to my chin and lifted it slightly.

He leaned down, resting his forehead against mine. He closed his eyes, letting out a shuddering sigh. Then, he turned his head, his stubble lightly brushing my cheek as his lips met mine. Tentative, testing, seeing if I would let him. I did.

I waited for the spark, for the same feeling that I felt that night a year ago. I waited for my chest to flutter with butterflies. I hoped that my heart would race. None of those things happened. I pulled away. "Liam." I said, my eyes still closed, "I-"

"I never stopped loving you." He said, as if he was trying to beat me to whatever I was going to say.

I opened my eyes, "I'm a different person now. You're a different person. I don't think… I don't know-"

"You need time to think." He said, a small smile playing on his lips. I nodded tightly. I did need time. I mean, this was Liam. My best friend, confidant, my rock. Did I want him to be more than that?

"Is it Falcon?" He asked, and I could tell just by the look on his face that he hated that he had asked.

I shook my head, despite the pang in my heart, "No, that's ridiculous. I just…so much has changed Liam. We're on the cusp of finding my brothers. I just need you to wait."

Chapter 21

It was two days later, and I was sitting in Callum's room, strewn over his couch with an arm thrown over my eyes while Adarra sat cross legged in the armed chair in the corner, book in her lap. Callum was across the room sat at his desk with the Blade of Strattera laid across it, carefully studying and making notes. How he got a room with a couch was beyond me, but I wasn't complaining - it was almost more comfortable than my bed. Ayla was still gone – I had come to accept that she had decided to move on from us. She *was* a wild animal, after all. I did my due diligence of calling out for her in the forest surrounding the city, but she was nowhere to be found. I was sad, but I couldn't force her to stay.

Liam hadn't approached me since that night - nor I him. But at least this time we actually talked about it. We would work together when necessary, but not seek each other out until I got my brothers back. Then we could evaluate with clear heads whatever…this was. I only told Adarra what happened because she hounded me relentlessly when he didn't eat breakfast with us for the first time in a year.

"So, you felt...nothing?" She had asked me, her eyes wide, "No spark, no butterflies or anything?"

I had shaken my head, "No. But maybe all this battle and life-threatening danger has desensitized me to any sort of nervous reaction." She just rolled her eyes at me.

I didn't tell her that I suspected that being with Falcon these last few weeks might have had something to do with it. I would never hear the end of it.

"Okay, it's ready." Callum announced, I heard him step from his chair.. "I think it's been away from you long enough to…reset itself. Now, when you hold it, it should respond to you anew and I can see if anything shifts in it."

I yawned, opening my eyes "Wouldn't you have noticed already if that were the case? I had the cursed thing on my back the whole way here."

Callum sighed, "No, Cass, I wasn't focused on the sword. I was too busy trying to figure out why I suddenly trusted a stranger with my life." I lifted my arm slightly above my eyes and let out a wolfish grin. Callum was staring at me, holding the blade with an exasperated look on his face.

"Alright, alright." I said, swinging my legs down to the floor. The action caused that cursed amulet to fall from my pocket. General Ren had left it with me, and I forgot I even had it to give it back to Callum. I quickly picked it up, "Here, I forgot to give this to you-" The darned thing started glowing again and this time it *tingles*. I dropped it in shock. Adarra looks at me like, *"What is wrong with you?"*

Callum was looking at me with awe. Without breaking his stare, he picked up the amulet and held it out to me. "Can you do that again?"

Adarra looked between us like we'd both gone mad, "Do *what* again?"

I shook my head, clutching my hands to my chest, "No. I can't." I couldn't even describe what feeling it gave me, but I didn't like it.

"Cass…" Callum shook his head in disbelief, "Please, trust me. One more time."

I looked at Callum. His sandy brown hair, his freckles, his kind eyes. I did trust him. I knew he wouldn't tell me to do anything that would hurt me. Make me wildly uncomfortable perhaps, but never hurt me. Despite everything in me screaming not to, I nodded, and took the amulet again.

Immediately the glowing resumed, and the tingling came back. Everything in me wanted to drop it like it was burning me. But I held on. Callum gasped, "Gods, Cass…you…" Everything went black.

A dark, rainy night. There is a hooded figure, fleeing a village at the foot of a castle. The village is quiet…too quiet for comfort. A guttural cry…something is chasing the figure out of the village. It moves unnaturally. By the moonlight, its face is illuminated - or at least what's left of its face. There's only one eye and the cheek has been ripped open, giving a clear view of the rancid tongue inside its mouth. The skin has a green tinge but other than that, it could be human. The undead.

The sound of a baby crying seems to spur it on. "Shh. Shh little one." The figure hushes. She hurries into the surrounding woods. She's made it far ahead, she might actually make it - distracted by shushing the distressed child, she trips over a fallen log in the path. Twisting to avoid crushing the babe, she lands on her back in a burst of pain. She cries out, further spurring on the undead monster. She tries to get up, but putting weight on the leg she tripped over causes her to cry out yet again. She looks at the babe in her arms and smiles despite the tears welling in her eyes.

She yanks a chain off from around her neck, and as the undead moves closer to her, she starts chanting. A prayer to the gods or spell, it is unclear. But she places the chain around the babe and leans close, whispering words too quiet to hear. The undead is gaining on them. Without another word, she lays the baby on the floor as close to the edge of the path as she can manage and uses all her strength and might to stand up. Not able to hold in the cry of pain, she starts to hobble in the opposite direction of the baby. An attempt to lead the monster away, give the baby a chance at life.

She is too slow - before she even makes it to the other side of the path, the undead catches up to her and strikes her down. The last thing she sees before she dies is the monster moving toward the baby.

The baby cries - never once has the baby stopped crying. The undead reaches down, and - there is a blinding flash of white light.

"Cass! Cass!" It's Adarra's face looming over me that I see when I come to. I looked around – I was lying on Callum's bed, my head is pounding.

"The baby - what happened to the baby-" I asked frantically, trying to sit up.

"Baby? Wha-" She shakes her head, "Cass what are you talking about? There's no baby." She gently pushed me back down onto the bed, "You collapsed, Cass. Callum ran to get General Ren."

"Why- why would he get General Ren? I'm fine." I lied through gritted teeth. I wasn't fine, I realized. Something was wrong with me. I could feel it, just beneath my skin, something stirring in me. It made my skin feel too tight, like I might burst at any second.

Callum and General Ren rushed through the door, "Are you okay?" General Ren asked worriedly, pulling a chair up next to the bed.

"I don't know," I said, hating how pained my voice sounded, "It feels like I'm going to burst out of my skin."

"It's your magic." Callum said, grinning slightly.

I shook my head, wincing at the pain that rattled in response, "You said I didn't have any magic. You said you couldn't sense anything in me."

General Ren's brows furrowed, turning to Callum, "How is that possible?"

"I think…" He looked to me, "When you were holding the amulet, it was almost like…like a veil was being lifted, and your magic was stirring underneath."

"I.. I don't have magic." I said, my voice shaking, "I would know if I had magic all this time."

"Unless…" General Ren said quietly, "Unless someone sealed it away."

"Why would someone do that?" Adarra asked, holding my hand tightly.

General Ren's face darkened, "I'm going to write a letter to Grand Elder Ira. If he did this, he has some explaining to do." Before I could say a word, he stormed out of the room.

"Why is he so angry?" Adarra wondered out loud.

"I've never seen this before, but it seems like it could be dangerous." Callum said, "Based on what you said, Cass, it sounds like it's been building up for nearly 20 years. If it had been kept in much longer, it could have some serious consequences."

"How do I make this stop?" I choked out. The feeling wasn't painful, per se, but it was wildly uncomfortable.

He looked pensive for a moment, "I think that using the magic should alleviate it. This is all uncharted territory, so I could be wrong, but maybe think of your body as a sponge, and the magic is the water soaked into the sponge. Right now, you're drenched-hence the feeling like you're bursting out of your skin. Using the magic should act like wringing out the sponge and give you some relief." Adarra squeezed my hand gently in comfort.

I sat up, wincing, and nodded. "Okay…how do I do that?"

"You just…hm." He said, bringing a hand to his chin and thinking, "I've never had to explain this before."

I scoffed, "Glad to be your test subject."

"It's…" He tried again, "It's like this. Close your eyes, and *feel.*"

I did as he said. With my eyes closed, I focused on the overall feeling of discomfort. I zeroed in on it and realized that the feeling I had was not really all over, but there was a pocket, and from that pocket, it was projecting outwards. "Okay, I have it." I said quietly.

"Okay, now focus all your energy on that, and *pull.*" Callum said, not sounding all that confident.

But I did as he said, and unsure of how I would pull, I envisioned myself taking my hands and physically pulling from the pocket.

Adarra gasped. My eyes shot open, and I was almost immediately blinded. My hands were…glowing.

Callum was looking at me, awe in his eyes, "Cass…you have light magic."

I was feeling the relief almost immediately, the pressure on the inside of my skin lessening considerably. I turned my hands, looking at each side, "Well, that's a fun party trick, but what's the point?"

He shook his head, "This hasn't been seen in…in years. Light magic is part of the elemental magic family - it's different than healing magic or magic that requires incantations and spells.

There are legends of people who had this kind of magic. I only know because I used to read about them in my Grandfather's library. They were most often warriors - Elemental Warriors - they could take their element and shape it into whatever they wanted - a sword, a shield, a bow, and arrow…"

"Daggers?" I raised an eyebrow, and he chuckles,

"Yes, I imagine daggers would be possible too."

Now that the feeling of being about to burst open had subsided, I could think more clearly. Something dangerous stirred inside me. Hope.

"This could…" I shook my head again, letting out a disbelieving laugh, "This could give us a leg up on Aeron. This would be the last thing he's expecting." I stood, and grabbed Callum's hand, "Can you teach me?"

His brow crinkled in thought, "I *could*…your magic feels different than mine…but it should be the same basic principles."

Now that the pressure wasn't as intense, I noticed something…different about him. Surrounding his chest, there was a…presence. It was bright, but cool, and felt pure.

He cocked an eyebrow, "You're sensing my magic, aren't you?" I wasn't focusing on Callum exactly, but *around* him.

"It's so weird…" I said, my hand reaching out and hovering in the air next to him, "I can tell something is there, but I can't tell *what*." Adarra stifled a snicker, and I snatched my hand back, becoming aware of how ridiculous I must look. "Laugh all you want, Adarra, I can blind you now if I want." I raised an eyebrow.

"Yeah, I'll call you if I lose my coin purse in a dark room." She answered, picking at her nails in faux dismissal.

Rolling my eyes, I turned back to Callum, "What does mine look…or I guess feel like?"

"It's…pretty intense at first." He admitted, eyes hovering in the area around me, "But, now that you've released some of it, it's almost like a…like a radiant…mist." I frowned. Mist didn't sound very threatening. Callum put his hands up as if to say *hold on*, "Now that doesn't necessarily mean anything. Like I said, your magic is so much different than mine -this kind of magic could be deceptive on purpose, to not be perceived as a threat by others. Magic has a way of…protecting its' wielder."

CALLUM

I couldn't believe it. Cass had *magic*. I wanted to laugh, I was so giddy. I wasn't sure why I was that happy about it either – but somehow it made sense. The fact that she was the bearer of the Blade of Strattera, and therefore destined to defeat Aeron and his Shadow Guard, wasn't it poetic that Cass could wield *light* magic?

Perhaps that was why the sword chose her. It could sense the magic within her, even if she didn't know she had it yet. Though, I found it odd if that was the reason. Were all previous bearers of the sword also elemental warriors? No matter how much I tried I couldn't find any text that specified the requirements for a wielder of the Blade of Strattera.

I had a feeling that her hidden magic was the very reason the voice in Silverglade Castle did not deem her worthy. What were the words? *You cannot be worthy until you know what it is to be worthy?* Perhaps in her case, since she does have magic, it wanted her at her full power. This was all speculation of course. I shook my head. I would have to work as quickly as possible to find out all I could on elemental warriors and hope that their magic was at least similar to ours. I would need to coach her, to help her. This was my purpose in this war. I would be there for her until the end.

Chapter 22

The next day, I was sitting cross legged on my bed, flipping through one of the 5 history books Callum had brought me as the first step of his training. They were comically large, stacked one on top of the other on my floor, the fourth book reaching just about bed level. According to Callum, since he doesn't have any first-hand experience with Elemental Warriors, he figured that learning about them could give us some insight on how to proceed with training. I had never seen a history book - Aeron made sure to destroy any he could get his hands on, but General Ren told me that in the aftermath of the attack, he snuck back into the castle at regular intervals to salvage whatever books he could. The first 4 hours I skimmed through the first two books - nothing on Elemental Warriors.

My eyes were absentmindedly scanning the open book in front of me when something caught my eye. A paragraph titled

"*The Amulet of Vilin and the Establishment of the Kingdom*". The Amulet of Vilin…that was the amulet General Ren said gave Aeron all his power. Curious, I began to read.

"The 317th year since the establishment of the Silverglade Kingdom faced the worst mage rebellion the continent had ever seen. This rebellion was led by a man named Septimus Thanitem, who was discontent with the Shadowlands. For centuries the mages, though free to come to the 3 kingdoms, preferred to stay in the Shadowlands among their own people. It is also worth noting that the soil of the Shadowlands seems to allow for magic to achieve greater acts than in any of the three kingdoms.

According to castle records, Septimus had served as Grand Mage to King Edris Silverheart III but left the position within 2 months. Witnesses say he made a scene in the throne room, citing 'ridiculous restrictions' and returned home.

King Edris started to receive reports of unrest among the Shadowland dwellers; Septimus was going from settlement to settlement, convincing the mages that the land of Silverglade belonged to the mages.

The attacks on Silverglade started within the year, the mages making periodic attacks and claiming land, little by little. King Edris convened with King Dominicus of the Kingdom of Dragorah, and King Calvair of Eldoria. Knowing that if Silverglade fell, it was only a matter of time before Dragorah and

Eldoria followed, they sanctioned the creation of the weapon that we would come to know as the Amulet of Vilin.

The Grand Mage of Dragorah, Ferik Vilin, a talented elemental warrior, was chosen as the mage who would wield the Amulet against the whole of the Mage Rebellion, with all 3 kingdoms armies behind him. To balance the creation of such a weapon, there had to be a way to destroy the amulet - and thus the Blade of Strattera was forged. The Blade was made to be able to-"

I went to the next page- the words completely changed course, talking about the history of the Silverdrop Flower. I frowned, looking back and forth between the two pages. This couldn't be right, this- something caught my eye. Near the bottom where the two pages met at the spine…barely noticeable but looking close enough…yes. Someone had, albeit very carefully, ripped the next page out of this book. All I was left with was a barely-there remnant of a missing page.

I was studying the words that I *did* have when I heard a knock on the door - three short, hard raps. I was so distracted by the mystery of the missing page I failed to notice that it wasn't Adarra's regular 5 beat knock or Callum's slightly timid one - I called out, distractedly, "Come in!".

I didn't even realize who had come in until I heard Falcon's voice in front of me, "Due for a bit of light reading?" He asked, amusement in his voice. I looked up, he was leaning on the frame of my door, arms crossed, pointedly looking at the mountain of books stacked next to me. Man, I had forgotten how much I liked looking at his face. I hadn't spoken to him one-on-one since we got back from our mission; hadn't even seen him since I confronted General Ren in his office.

Falcon's gray and silver eyes were uncharacteristically playful, one brow raised, and a smirk slightly playing on his lips. He hadn't shaved in a couple of days - it looked good on him.

I placed an innocent look on my face, "What, you don't like my new bedside table?" I patted the stack of books next to me.

"So *that's* what we can use that library for." He said thoughtfully, "It's not like anyone's getting anywhere with the ward research."

"They aren't?" I asked, unable to keep the disappointment from my voice, "Maybe *all* the books are missing pages."

"Missing pages?" He repeated, pushing off the door frame and walking over to me, "What do you mean?"

I was all too conscious of how he leaned over me to look at the book in front of me. My breath caught in my throat as I tried to focus, "I finally found something good - about the Amulet of Vilin. Apparently, the original wearer was an Elemental Warrior, and just when it got to the Blade of

Strattera," I ran my finger down the ripped remnant of the page hiding in the crack of the spine, "it cuts off."

"Hmmm." His brow furrowed in concentration as he reached over to lift the book out of my hands, "May I?" He looked to me, so close our noses are almost touching. I swallowed, nodding. My goodness, what was wrong with me? He removed the book from my hands and to my utter and complete mortification, they were glowing.

His brows shot up, "That's new." He comments, and I hastily tucked my hands under my arms.

"I'm still learning to control it." I said offhandedly. Learning to control it - more like trying and failing to do anything other than make my hands glow.

"Yeah, General Ren filled me in." He commented, his eyes turning to the book, scanning the pages, "How…I mean, I know you'll do anything if it means you get your brothers back, but…how do you feel about it? Just because it's a means to an end doesn't mean you have to be happy about it."

I sighed, and to my relief, my hands had stopped glowing. "I'm not sure. I'm really blindsided by the whole thing." To put it mildly, "I don't even know who would have sealed away my magic or why. I just can't think about it, because if I do, I'll end up with more questions than answers and I don't have more room for questions."

He handed the book back to me, "I know. But just…don't forget to look after yourself too."

"I know." I said, a smile twinging on my lips, "I'll give you an updated answer once Aeron is 6 feet under."

"And there it is." He said, his eyes meeting mine, an easy grin spreading on his face.

I couldn't let him keep doing this to me. What about Liam? Liam. Whatever this was with Falcon, it had to be chemical. There was no other answer - we would only rip each other to pieces. Liam and I…Liam was comfortable, familiar. He was warm, and kind, and everything I had always thought I wanted.

As if he could sense the train of my thoughts, Falcon suddenly cleared his throat, "As to the reason for my visit, Foxglove." He said, breaking eye contact, "General Ren wants to see you."

Falcon brought me to General Ren's study, and rapped on the door sharply – 3 times, just as he did to my door. Without waiting for an answer, he pushed the door open, and peeked inside, "I have Cass here for you, Sir."

"Have you always called him 'Sir'?" I asked, raising an eyebrow, sidling under his arm through the open door.

He shook his head with a chuckle, "No, but he did always want me to call him 'Uncle Sir'."

I stopped dead in my tracks, trying to hold a laugh in, and noticing a little too late that it put me right under his arm, in between him and the door, "He...what?"

"I'm kidding." He said, and gently pushed me the rest of the way through the doorway, before following me in and closing the door behind him.

"Have a seat, Cass." General Ren said without looking up. There was a pair of half-moon shaped reading glasses sitting on the tip of his nose – I'd never seen those before. In fact, it was rather strange to see him like this at all – behind a desk, with mountains of paperwork.

I sat down in the seat on the other side of his desk, my heartrate increasing considerably. Did something happen?

"I wanted to let you know personally before I made some kind of announcement." He started, looking up from his paperwork and taking off his glasses, "Based on your performance on your latest mission with Commander Feldstrom, as well as the fact that you've been chosen by the Blade of Strattera, and in light of your new...powers - and obviously what I already know of your skill – you're being promoted."

A laugh escaped from me before I could stop it. I covered my mouth and looked back and forth between Falcon and General Ren, "Me?" I raised my eyebrows and gestured pointedly to myself. "Are you out of your mind?"

Yes, all of what he said was technically true...but there had to be someone else more qualified. Someone who had more experience than a 18-year-old girl. Sure, the Blade of Strattera had chosen me, but I was more of a weapon than I was the one who made decisions. Tell me who to stab and I'll do it.

Though, I supposed me having the power of an Elemental Warrior did somewhat tip the scale...not that I could do anything with it yet. The light in my palms flared as if to make a point.

General Ren's eyes fixated on my hands, a bemused expression crossing his face. "Once you get that sorted out, anyway." He shook his head and stood. With his hands behind his back, he started pacing, looking more like the General Ren I grew up with back in Everloom.

"You will be my left hand, and Falcon my right. He will be handling all matters of recruitment and building our army for our final assault on Aeron and the Shadow guard. You, Cass, once you get a hold of your newfound powers, will pick a specialized team who will be under your command. Whatever you need to get the first 2 gemstones to power the sword will be at your disposal. Once you two are ready, we will converge on Dragorah Castle, Falcon and his army will draw out Aeron and the Shadow guard, which will clear a way for you and your team to get in and get the last gemstone."

I swallowed. My own team? I had to admit I liked the sound of that. "So... after I get my magic under control I would be able to decide how I want to proceed? How I want to get the stones from each castle?"

Falcon pushed off from where he had been leaning on the door – did he always lean so much? "You won't have me to question your sword's feelings." Falcon said lightly, but I could sense the intention behind it. He was letting me know that he was wrong for how he acted back at the castle. Was he saying...he trusted me?

I took a deep breath. This was a lot to take in…was I ready for this? Probably not. But…It was what I needed. I nodded, "Okay. I'm in. I already know who I want on my team."

General Ren chuckled, "Why am I not surprised?"

I grinned, "Liam, Adarra, and Callum."

"You sure you want to put Liam and Callum on the same team?" Falcon questioned, "There seems to be no love lost between the two of them."

"I've got it handled." I said evenly, meeting his eyes.

Falcon rolled his eyes, "All of thirty seconds with a title and you've already got it down."

"What is my title anyway?" I asked, crossing my arms and turning back to General Ren.

"You'll be Commander, same as him." General Ren said, a twinkle in his eye, "While you will technically be the same rank as Falcon, I do encourage you to...defer to him if you are unsure on something." Code for: If he and I disagree on something big, it's probably going to be his call.

Despite not having any actual grievances with that decision, it took everything in me to bite back a retort. General Ren had that look on his face that I knew better than to argue with anyhow.

There was a quick knock on the door, and Falcon answered, stepping out. "There is one last thing I want to ask you about, General Ren." I've decided to bring up my dream – now is as good of a time as any.

"What is it?" He asked, sensing the seriousness in my tone.

"Two things." I started, "First, any word on who could have sealed my magic away?"

General Ren shook his head, "No. Grand Elder Ira said that since your parents settled into town with you as a baby, there wasn't a trace of magic in you."

Figures. Would be too much to ask for any sort of answer to why things are the way they are. "The second thing." I said, "I had another dream while we were gone." I started. His attention was fixed completely on me, "There was the same robed figure, and they told Aeron...I think it's Aeron...that the Mark is stirring and that it's almost time. Then Aeron said to begin the preparations."

General Ren's face had gone white. "I-" He started, but shook his head as if to clear the thoughts clouding it, "I've had my suspicions...but he truly can only be talking about -"

"The Mark of Alistair?" I asked, hoping to have my own suspicions confirmed.

He stopped and looked at me, "Yes. How do you know about the Mark of Alistair?"

Suddenly nervous, even though I had done nothing wrong, I wrung my hands in front of me, "Callum told me about it when I woke up from a nightmare. Apparently, I was talking about a 'mark' in my sleep." I said, looking down.

"So, it's true." General Ren said quietly, almost to himself, "I had my suspicions, but to have them confirmed..."

"You're telling me that Aeron thinks he has a royal child, and that's why he kidnapped all the kids?" I asked, prodding for more information.

He rubbed his temple and stared thoughtfully. He looked tired – more tired than I had seen him recently. "Yes."

"And you had suspicions all this time? Why didn't you say anything?" I tried hard to keep my voice level – as if I didn't feel some amount of betrayal at his lack of confidence in me.

"That's all they were –suspicions." He said, sitting down, "You've just confirmed it. I couldn't fathom why he would keep the children alive if he was looking for a royal child. But if he's waiting for the Mark to manifest itself..." He shook his head, "Aeron may have more nefarious goals than even I thought."

Goals *more* nefarious than kidnapping all the children in the kingdom? I wondered what he could be waiting for the mark for when General Ren spoke again, "Callum told you?" He was looking at me thoughtfully, "You two seem rather close despite having met each other not too long ago."

"So?" I asked, picking at my nails in faux indifference, "I'm a delight to be around. People love me."

He emitted a noise that I could only describe as a snort, "Sure. I just mean that even back in Everloom, you only let Liam get close to you, and you seemed even more...prickly before leaving with Falcon."

"And?" I questioned, not eager to answer the same question over and over again.

"And-" He said pointedly, "I'm just wondering how he got past all of your...defenses."

I sniffed. I supposed 'defenses' would be the correct word. "I don't know." I answered truthfully, "Almost immediately after meeting...something clicked. It's not romantic at all - but I know without a shadow of a doubt that I could put my life in his hands. Have you ever had that happen before?"

He shook his head, a small smile on his face, "No, I haven't been so fortunate. Perhaps it is magic related...perhaps it is simply fate. Time will tell."

Chapter 23

After I told Callum about my pending promotion, he moved our training schedule up. This kind of training was different than I was used to. Running laps, push-ups, sparring, I could handle that. But this magic...it was foreign to me. There was a lot of meditating involved which required me to be in my own head – something that I was not happy about.

This morning, when I showed up to practice, he told me to sit on the floor. Then he placed a glass ball on the floor in front of me and told me to illuminate it. I had scoffed, reaching to place my hand on it, when he stopped me, saying, "No hands."

"How am I supposed to light it up without using my hands?" I asked incredulously.

"Concentrate." He said simply. So there I was, in an empty room, staring at a glass ball. First he said to meditate. Envision the ball lighting up. That didn't work. Then, he said to try to collect the light from my hands and place it into the ball with my mind. When

I questioned how in the world I was supposed to do *that,* he sighed and asked me what sort of instincts I *did* have. To which I replied, "Obviously none, so let's approach this like I'm a child." To which he said, "Well, Cass, even children learning magic have some sort of instinct, so we are in uncharted territory here." I don't remember what else we said but included a lot of bickering. He left, saying that he would check on me in an hour.

I stared at the ball and willed it to glow. Nothing, Not even a flicker of light. My hands were having no problem producing their obnoxious white light, but the orb remained ominously dark.

What was I thinking? Of course, I couldn't do this. All I knew was how to destroy things – I was weapon to be deployed. Magic required creating, it required life. Anyone in the world would have been better at this than me. If my mama had been the one with magic, she would be unstoppable. Her very essence was light, and her soul was always full of joy. Bram, with his sweet disposition and love for others. Or even Kolby, with his humor and wit, and love for stories, could have channeled that into something productive.

A flicker of light caught my eye. The orb…it was starting to emanate a soft light. In my shock, the light vanished.

I concentrated on the orb again, and thought of my Ma, and my brothers. General Ren, my Pa, and Liam, and Adarra. Even

Falcon. The things that I loved about them, the things that would make them better Light Elemental Warriors than me and-

"Well, I'll be damned." Callum's voice came from the doorway, "You're doing it!"

I grinned from ear to ear as the orb pulsated with a light brighter than the lanterns in the room. "I know!"

Callum rubbed his hands together, "It's a start, but this is just the beginning."

"Again." Callum said, pacing in front of me, his hands behind his back. So far, I had been able to summon a ball of light in my hand, hold it for 30 seconds, and release it, dissipating into the air. It sounded simple, but it was taking so much out of me. Every time I used my magic, the sword on my back would sing in response.

I sighed, wiping sweat from my brow. "Control," Callum would say, "The first step is control." I focused back in on myself and imagined pulling a drop from the pocket of light. "Good." Callum said, "Now hold it."

I had to get this down. There was so much depending on me mastering this. Callum had even theorized that the voice back in Silverglade Castle could sense my magic within me but knew I couldn't access it – hence me "not knowing" what it is to be worthy. I could only hope he was right. That had to be it. If it wasn't - well, I could kiss any chance of ever seeing my brothers again goodbye.

General Ren said that only the bearer of the sword could retrieve the gems, so that was just one more way that I would doom us all if I failed to master this. I had to get this. I had to master this. I had to-

The light sputtered in my hands. "No." I said, opening and closing my hands as though that might summon the light back to me. "No, no, no. Come on!" The sword was utterly silent now. I shut my eyes tight and imagined pulling from the pocket of light again. I couldn't get enough air into my lungs. No matter how hard I tried, I couldn't summon the light again. The tightness in my chest grew stronger as I rubbed my hands together, "Come on, come on you useless thing-"

"Cass." A hand on my shoulder, "It's okay." Callum said quietly. "Breathe." Was I not breathing? I collapsed to my knees on the floor, my brain barely registering the sting of the hard floor as my knees made contact. I whipped the Blade of Strattera off my back like it was strangling me.

"Deep breaths." He said and started rubbing circles on my back.

"I can't...I - I-" I gasped in sobs, trying to get to my breathing under control.

"Focus on my hand," he said and continued to rub slow steady circles with an open palm.

I closed my eyes and trying to ignore the racing in my chest and the pounding in my ears, I focused solely on the sensation of his hand on my back. After a moment, my breathing started to regulate.

In, 2, 3, 4.

Out, 2, 3. 4.

In, 2, 3, 4.

Out, 2, 3. 4.

My heart rate slowed considerably. I blinked slowly and looked up at Callum, who was focused on my back.

"Are you using magic on me?" I asked, becoming more aware of the coolness that seemed to trail behind after his hand passes over my back.

"Just some light ice magic to help slow your heart." He said, still focusing on my back. Breathing continued to get easier the longer we sat there.

What had just happened to me? I sat wondering as our training session turned into a healing session. "Do you want to talk about it?" He asked me, voice steady.

"Talk about what?" I swallowed, willing him to forget the way he just witnessed me unravel in a way I had never unraveled before.

"What you were thinking about that made your magic retreat up inside itself." He said, removing his hands from my back and sitting down next to me.

I lost a breath. "I guess I was reminding myself that everything goes to hell if I can't master my magic – or at the very least get it under control. That I am the only one who can retrieve the stones to the sword that is the only weapon that can kill Aeron – which by the way, is also only able to be wielded by me. So, like, no pressure, right?"

"So, you psyched yourself out." He stated, matter-of-factly.

"Oh, is that the technical term for it?" I asked, his healing giving me some of my snark back.

He shook his head at me, but the small smile told me he was glad to see me back to normal.

Reaching back inside myself, I tried to pull from the pocket of light again. Callum let out a sigh of relief , "There she is." My hands were glowing as uselessly as ever, but at least I could access the power again.

Without any warning the door burst open. Liam came in, out of breath, leaning against the door frame, "Callum, Cass –

General Ren wants to see everyone. Something is wrong. Two of the spies guarding the outside exits never returned for shift change and..." He dissolved into a coughing, sputtering mess. I finally noticed the greenish brown smog that was pooling at his feet and spilling into the room.

"Liam!" I cried, rushing to his side, grabbing the Blade of Strattera with me as I went. Callum, close behind me, felt for a pulse.

"He's still alive." Callum confirmed, then looking around said, "This has to be some kind of gas to knock us out. It's definitely magical."

"We're under attack." I breathed, "How did they know where-" I started coughing as the smog swirled up around me.

"I don't know, but we have to get out of here." Callum said, pulling his shirt up over his mouth. I nodded, doing the same.

"You have to help me with him." I pleaded, pulling one of Liam's arms over my shoulder. Callum nodded grimly and did the same with Liam's other arm.

As we went down the hallway, the noises of panic and chaos grew louder. It was getting harder to breathe. We passed by people passed out on the floor, the brownish green smog caressing their bodies. My heart sank as I spotted Grigsby on the ground, passed out. I couldn't bring myself to search for Mullins or Selby. Callum faltered for a moment, "We have to keep going." I urged him, and promptly started coughing again. His face set in a hard line as he continued on.

We only made it a couple more feet before coughing overtook me. I dropped to my knees, bringing Callum and Liam down with me. Callum crawled to me, shouting something but I couldn't hear him anymore. My head was swimming, I couldn't separate the shouting in the background from the footsteps echoing in the halls around us or from Callum's voice.

Black boots came into my vision. I looked up. Captain Remus sneered down at me, with what had to be at least 50 or so Shadow Guard behind him. I tried to speak, but the words caught in my throat, choked down by the smog that was slithering into my lungs.

The last thing I saw before everything went black was Captain Remus snap his fingers and the Shadow Guard soldiers dispersed from behind him, carrying Liam and Callum away.

Chapter 24

My eyes opened slowly, the darkness around me disorienting my senses. I was laying on a cold, stone floor, my body ached in places I didn't even know I had. A small groan escaped me as I tried to sit up.

"Cass?" A female voice asked in the darkness.

"Adarra?" I questioned, my voice groggy.

"Oh, thank the gods, Cass. I didn't think you were going to wake up." She embraced me tightly.

The dimly lit torches on the walls came into focus. "Where...where are we?" I choked out. I couldn't believe this was happening. How did anyone know where our base was? Did someone sell us out?

"I don't know." Adarra said, "I think we're still in Stalton though."

"Have you seen anyone else? Or looked around?" I questioned.

"No. All I can tell is that we're in a cell of some sort. That window," she pointed to the barred window directly above us, "faces a forest. I think it's the forest on the outside of Stalton."

I reached for my power, my hands further illuminating the sparsely lit cell. At least we weren't chained to the floor – there were cuffs in the corner that indicated that could have been a possibility. Outside the barred door, there was a small table and a chair – presumably for a guard to sit in. For now, though, it was empty.

I could work on sawing the bars off that top window. I reached for one of my daggers – gone. Of course. Heart dropping further, I reached to my back. They had taken the sword as well. "No." I whispered in horror. The one thing we had to defeat Aeron – gone.

And then – my heart stopped. What had become of my Ma?

Enraged, I flew to the bars of the cell, gripping one in each hand. "REMUS!" I screamed with all my might. No. He would not take my brothers away from me again.

My voice echoed in the otherwise empty room. "Cass-" Adarra started, and I all but snarled at her, making her go quiet. After a moment, I screamed again, "REMUS!"

A second later, I heard footsteps approaching. Remus sauntered in, a trio of Shadow Guard behind him. "Oh look, the rat is awake."

"Rat?" I spat, "Who are you calling a rat, you filthy, low-life-"

Remus clicked his tongue at me, "Be careful what you say to the one who holds the key to your survival in his hands." He dangled the keys to the cell in front of me. "Besides, what else to call creatures crawling beneath a city, infesting it with traitorous ideals and royal assassination plots?"

"Ha." I barked, "He killed all the royals. Putting a crown on his head doesn't make him one."

"You do well to mind how you speak of our King." Captain Remus said slowly, arching a brow.

"Where's my sword?" I snarled through the bars, no doubt resembling a caged animal.

"*Your* sword?" Captain Remus laughed. "That sword belongs to the royal family – Master Aeron - and you stole it. I'm keeping it safe for him until we travel back to Dragorah."

My heart sank in my chest. Remus took a step toward me, "Sir, it's too dangerous-" one of the Shadow Guard said, but Remus held up his hand, effectively silencing him. He stepped until he was right in front of me.

"It didn't have to be like this, you know," Remus said, almost softly. "You could have been my prize. Such a shame to see a face like yours go to waste."

I spat at his feet "Go. To. Hell."

He shook his head, "Temper, temper. Lucky for you, that rebel leader of yours isn't as loose lipped as you are."

Was he talking about Falcon, or General Ren? Nobody was supposed to know that General Ren was the head of Luminous Storm.

"Falcon is twice the leader you'll ever be, *Captain*." I said the last word mockingly.

Something flashed in his eyes, "I see." He turned on his heel, his entourage following behind him. Looking over his shoulder, he said, "There will be a public execution in four days. Trilithia will know what happens when its leader is betrayed."

Adarra gasped behind me. I sank to my knees as the door to the room slammed shut behind him.

In the next 24 or so hours, based on the light changing outside, I gathered 4 things from the Shadow Guard assigned to our cell block.

1 – There were about 40 of us taken captive, the rest escaped or died.

2- All the mages were kept in a separate area with wards blocking them from using their magic.

3- They, for whatever reason, could not sense my magic.

4- In 72 hours, Falcon Feldstrom would be executed in front of the entirety of Stalton.

They were a surprisingly gossipy bunch if you flattered them enough. Between empty promises and eavesdropping, I was able to formulate a plan to stop the aforementioned execution from happening.

"Food." The Shadow Guard grunted, tossing two plates into our cell. Without another word he left, locking the door to our block behind him.

During meals was one of the few times Adarra and I could talk without being overheard. There was hardly anyone occupying the table and chair outside the cell, but someone was nearly always stationed outside our door – except for mealtimes. "I have a plan." I whispered. Adarra raised an eyebrow in response. I looked at the soggy bread in my hand and desperately wished for Cook's delicious food again. "We're supposed to witness the execution," I whispered, "They don't know about my magic. We wait until the perfect opportunity for me to use my magic and create a miraculous escape for Falcon and everyone else involved."

Adarra winced as a lump of gruel worked its way down her throat, "How are you going to do that? You can hardly even make your hands glow."

Before I could answer, there was a flash of black in the corner of my eye. My head shot to the barred window above us, and I nearly choked on the slop I was eating. "Ayla?" I managed to get out. Was she...bigger?

Lightweaver, I am relieved to find you. The voice echoed in my mind – the voice was female – light and airy.

Adarra looked at her, brows furrowed, "How did she find us-"

I shook my head, "I think I'm having an aneurysm. I just heard a voice in my head."

You are not damaged in your mind, Lightweaver. It is I, Ayla.

"I... you couldn't talk to me before." I stammered, suddenly questioning my reality. Adarra looked at me like I had indeed lost my mind.

I am your Elemental Guardian, Lightweaver. We guardians only access our full powers when we have a bonded warrior – and until a few days ago, your power was sealed away.

"But you...you left me." I said, with more sadness in my voice than I meant to show.

I was angry and frustrated that I could not do the one thing I was born to do – protect you. I foolishly left seeing as I could not communicate with you and couldn't use my power anyway. But now, though we are not soul bonded yet, being in your proximity gives me this small dose of power...

In a flash of light, she vanished from her spot behind the barred window, and reappeared right in front of me. I jumped back in surprise, and Adarra let out a little shriek, quickly covering her mouth. "I- she-" Adarra stammered, and finally got out, "a magic fox?"

"Apparently she's my 'Elemental Guardian'," I said with a grimace, "And she can use her magic better than I can."

Do not despair, Lightweaver, the voice echoed in my mind, Ayla's head tilting at me, *you could not reach your full potential easily without me there.*

"Where were you? Why didn't you come find me after my magic was released? Do you know what happened to my Ma?"

She looked sorrowful, *I could not come back as there were too many shadowed ones lurking about. I wished desperately to warn you, but they were searching for an entrance, and I did not want to reveal a way in to them.*

"I wonder how they found us..." I trailed off, shaking my head, "And what about my Ma?"

I watched from the shadows as they observed her. They left her where she was – a mage said he was the one who placed the curse on her and that she would not wake up.

My heart stopped. The mage who placed the curse on Mama was...here? I could get answers, I could-

"Elemental Guardian?" Adarra suddenly said thoughtfully, "Did you read anything about Elemental Guardians in your books?"

I shook my head, "No, but there wasn't that much on them to begin with."

Ayla placed a white paw on my leg, the symbol on her chest beginning to glow. *Only the exceptionally powerful need Elemental Guardians to help channel their magic. Otherwise, it is too much power for one body to handle.*

"Powerful?" I scoffed, "I can hardly make my hands glow, as my oh-so-helpful friend pointed out."

You did not have me before. Ayla said and settled onto my lap.

"Is this weird now that you can talk –" But suddenly all her white fur was glowing so bright I thought it might blind me, "What's happening, Ayla?"

Cassandra Brightwood, called Foxglove, Lightweaver, and Little Fox, will you bond your soul with me, allowing both of us to reach our full power and fulfill your role in defeating the Evil Tyrant who calls himself Aeron?

"I- what? What is soul bonding? Is it the only way I can beat Aeron?"

It is the only way that you will be able to use your power at its full potential without burning out – and that is what you need to defeat Aeron, she answered me.

Was it even a question? If this was the only way for me to defeat Aeron... "Yes." I answered, my voice serious. "I will soul bond with you, Ayla." At my words, a rush of power overtook me, room encasing in bright white. I swore Adarra's eyes grew two sizes.

I felt...more energized. Like I had eaten a feast and gotten days of good sleep. "What...what is this?" I asked Ayla as I feel around for my power. The light came easily to my hands now.

We are soul-bonded now. I have eaten and slept well these last few days – you have not. I transferred some of my life-energy to you so you can be at full strength before the serious one's execution.

I shook my head, "Ayla, won't that make you too weak? How will you protect yourself?"

Ayla blinked up at me, *If I was healing a serious injury, it might hinder me, but since it was mere exhaustion, I will be fine after I sleep.* She hopped off my lap, *I will come back at your next mealtime to practice your magic. It will be too obvious with a guard stationed outside your door.*

"Ayla. Do you know where the other members of Luminous Storm are being held?" I asked, an idea popping into my head.

Yes, I passed by their cells when I was coming to you. The serious one is in his own cell, and the kind one is grouped with the other mages. The scarred gray one is nowhere to be found.

My heart dropped – where was General Ren? And what about the one person she didn't mention?

"What about…what about Liam?" I asked, my voice shaking.

Ah, the jealous one? He is with the other non-mages.

"That's what you're calling him? The *jealous* one?" I asked incredulously. Adarra snickered. But a wave of relief hit me. Everyone was safe and accounted for. Except General Ren…

I merely call humans what they are. You can tell that to Soft Heart over there. Ayla quipped, tossing her head in Adarra's direction.

I covered my mouth to stifle a giggle, "She calls you 'Soft Heart'" I said to Adarra, whose mouth drops open, and a small sound of indignation escaped her.

I turned back to Ayla, "Ayla, can you bring me 3 scraps of paper and something to write with?"

You wish to send a message? Her head tilted at me.

"Yes, I need to send one to Falcon, Callum, and Liam – they need to know to be ready for whatever we're going to do."

She flashed out of our cell quickly and reappeared with a sheet of paper and a thin piece of charcoal in her mouth. I quickly ripped the paper into 3 pieces and scribbled a note on each of them.

"There." I said, admiring my cryptic message.

"Will they know what that means?" Adarra asked, peering over my shoulder.

"Falcon will." I smiled. He would know. "Callum, I'm sure will, and Liam…we'll just have to see."

I folded each piece in half and Ayla gingerly took them in her mouth, careful as to not pierce the pages with her teeth.

She rubbed her face against my arm and said, *Do not despair, Lightweaver, we will get your mother to safety, get your brothers back and clear the blight from this land.*

Her words filled me with hope, and I watched her in awe, "Wait, Ayla." I stopped her, something she said before, during the Soul Bond, stuck in my mind. "When has anyone ever called me 'Little Fox'?"

Is that not what your father would call you? Without another word, and with another flash of light, Ayla disappeared out of our cell.

FALCON

I stared at the stone wall in front of me. I couldn't believe we had gotten so complacent. How had this happened? I was sitting on a stone floor of the solitary confinement cell. I believed we were still in Stalton – I was chained to the floor though, so I couldn't look out the window to verify. I just hoped my uncle got out okay. And Cass. Gods, if that Captain Remus got his hands on her…my stomach turned.

A flash of light in the corner of my eye drew my attention. A flash of gold eyes and- "Ayla?" I asked incredulously. The fox was sitting on the ledge of the barred window of my cell, holding…a piece of paper? How on earth did she get in here?

The fox leaped nimbly from the ledge and landed on the floor, taking dainty steps to approach me. "What is it, girl?" I asked, hating that I'm talking to a fox.

The fox dropped the scrap of paper out of her mouth and

nudged it toward me with her nose. I scrambled to open it, and in a familiar script, read…

In these current conditions, foxglove is an extremely dangerous flower.

My face broke into an unrestrained grin. I didn't know how or what she had planned, but if anyone could pull it off, she could.

Chapter 25

Ayla stayed true to her word and was back the next morning at mealtime. She delivered each message, stating that Falcon (after the shock of seeing her teleport) immediately had a huge smile on his face and thanked her, Callum (who, at seeing the teleportation, looked at her like he found a missing piece of a puzzle) gave an exasperated sigh and said, "Well Ayla, if she dies, I guess I'll take custody of you."

Liam, it took him a second, she said, (*"an embarrassing amount of time passed"*) but he seemed to piece it together and seemed more worried than anything.

Now that we were training, she was sitting in front of me, her front paws together, tail swishing behind her. *It is not within you, Lightweaver, it IS you. You control it as you would any other limb you possess.* She said, her white-tipped ears perked high. I noticed that whenever I would use my magic, the symbol on her chest would glow.

It was the day of the execution – Ayla had come every mealtime to practice with me, to teach me how to use my magic. When I would question how she knew any of this, she would simply respond, *Instincts, Lightweaver.* I did not push the issue.

At least the magic was easier to summon now - now that I wasn't trying to pull it out of myself but instead use it within myself. Ayla described me trying to use my magic without her as a flood trying to escape through a pinhole. Her soul-bond allowed me to widen that exit in a way that I could use my magic efficiently.

The plan was to simply create a forcefield of light that would protect everyone while we made our getaway. I was finding that the more I practiced, the more creative I could be. I could change the density of the light, shape it into different forms like Callum had said, and project it onto other items without using my hands as a light source.

"Can you ask her why she's black if she's supposed to be a *light* elemental guardian?" Adarra asked, already on her 4th question of the day.

I swear the fox sighed. *What is darkness but the absence of light? In all things, we must be balanced.*

I relayed the message back to Adarra, who said, "Does that mean...you could remove the light from a space, creating darkness?"

I paused. That was actually a good idea. I raised an eyebrow at Ayla. *It is a rather advanced technique, Soft Heart, but it is possible.* Her tail swished, *I promise I will teach you if we make it past today alive.*

I shuddered, "She said if we survive today, she'll teach me how to do that."

Adarra grimaced, "That's a nice vote of confidence."

Sooner than expected, we heard footsteps echoing down the hallway that led to our cell block. I nodded to Ayla, who quickly blended into the shadows.

A Shadow Guard I didn't recognize came in and unlocked our cell, flanked by 3 other guards.

I raised an eyebrow at Adarra, "I think they're afraid of us."

One of the back guards wagged a finger at us, "No funny business, ladies. Captain Remus assured us that you're not a danger to us without a weapon... but no funny business."

MARK OF THE FALLEN

Adarra and I were being led down a long hallway in what I could only assume was the Stalton city jail cells. There were two guards in front of us and two behind us, monitoring our every move. The hallway was dark – lit only by the few torches lining each wall. Our steps echoed with growing anticipation. By now, Ayla should be back with Mama…hopefully our plan would work.

As we reached the end of the corridor, I held out a hand to Adarra and squeezed. She looked at me, tears in her eyes. Ayla was right – she was a Soft Heart. I winked at her, and quickly dropped her hand lest the guards catch on.

The guards in front of us opened the door at the end of the hallway – my eyes burned from not having seen direct sunlight in 4 days. As we exited, we were joined by 2 more Shadow Guard, one on each side of us so now we were completely surrounded. The one on the left pushed me when he didn't think I was moving fast enough. I tripped and landed on my knees, causing all of us to come to a sudden halt. I glared at the Shadow Guard who pushed me. I couldn't see his face since he had his helmet on, but he seemed like a jerk.

As we went further into the city, the crowd became denser, and eerily silent. Our guards pushed into the crowd without warning, which earned a defiant shout from some – until they saw who had pushed them. Then they went silent as they moved further out of the way for us. Anyone who dared to look up wouldn't meet our eyes. I wondered if any among them were the ones who betrayed us.

We made our way through the crowed, which was all gathered around a platform in the city square. Captain Remus stood front and center, his arms crossed and staring at the stage behind him with sick satisfaction. My heart lurched in my throat when I saw the Blade of Strattera strapped to his back – MY sword.

To the back left of the stage, the mages were gathered, clustered into a circle of wards to prevent them from using magic.

To the back right, the warriors and spies were gathered, with their hands tied in front of them.

Surrounding the back of the platform, making sure that nobody got out of line, were all the Shadow Guard that stormed our base with Captain Remus. My heart fell when I realized I didn't see any mages with the Shadow Guard – the mage who cursed Mama wasn't here after all.

I found Callum's eyes first, his gaze meeting mine with imperceptible nod. I scanned the other side for Liam. He met my eyes, another nod. My heart dropped when Captain Remus moved off to the side and revealed Falcon in the center of the stage, stripped of his armor and in just a linen shirt and trousers, hands tied behind him. His hair was free of its usual intentional messiness, and under his eyes were darker than I had seen them. Did they even feed him?

Falcon spotted me. His eyes stayed on me as we were roughly escorted through rest of the crowd. His eyebrows knitted together, as if trying to figure something out. I winked at him, and the darkness fled from his eyes, and he seemingly let out a sigh of relief. I had this. This plan *had* to work.

We were roughly pushed into the platform, and I oofed as my midsection made contact with the edge. "Thanks boys." I said roughly as I climbed onto the platform, helping Adarra up as well. We clung to each other as we were then roughly directed to stand off to the left of Falcon.

"Now that we're all here." Captain Remus started, giving me a pointed look, as if *I* had an effect on when we got here. He addressed the crowd around him, "You have all been requested to witness what happens when our King is betrayed. We were recently alerted to the presence of rats in your sewers." He looked around the crowd as if waiting for cheers or boos. When none came, he continued, "We are not one to proceed with an execution unfairly, so let us have the one who alerted us verify that we have the right people."

A murmur ran through the crowd. My heart raced. Who had betrayed us? Why had they betrayed us?

I almost threw up when a Shadow Guard soldier practically dragged Landry out next to the platform. With a sound of shock Adarra clung to me tighter…and I didn't think this was part of the act. "No." She whispered in disbelief. So *that* was how they got into the base - they used the entrance through La 'Bells.

"My good sir." Captain Remus said, walking over to him, "Is this man the leader of the rat rebellion?" He asked, a disgusted look on his face.

Falcon's face was set in a hard line, giving away nothing. Liam had a look of betrayal on his face that I was sure mirrored my own.

"No." Landry said loudly, "That's not the leader. I've never seen him before." What? Why was he trying to backtrack now?

There was a flash of rage across Captain Remus' face before he schooled his features again, "I would rethink your answer, sir."

Adarra and I gasped as another Shadow Guard dragged Belle out, knife to her throat. Belle, pregnant with their child, looked out at us with no fear in her eyes. "It's not his fault!" She shouted out at us, "They made-" Her words were cut off as she winced in pain, the knife at her throat pressing further against her, drawing a line of blood.

"Shut up, you stupid woman." Remus spat, and turned back to Landry, "Now – think very, *very*, hard. Is this the man the leader of the rebellion?"

Landry looked from his wife to the platform and his eyes landed on me. I understood. They would kill Belle just like they killed Liam's parents if he didn't confirm who Falcon was. So, I did what I would want anyone to do for me if I was in that position. I gave him a nod. *It's okay.*

His bottom lip quivered as he looked back up at Captain Remus. "It is." He said, his voice breaking.

The guard holding Belle let go and she rushed to him, hands on his face, "It's okay, Landry. It's okay." She looked to me, apology in her eyes. I motioned my head away from the platform, *get out of here*. Her eyes widened, but she nodded. Subtly pulling Landry back from the guard.

"There you have it," he declared, circling back to Falcon, "The rats." He motioned to everyone on the stage, "And, the King Rat." He pulled Falcon's head back by his hair, exposing his throat. Falcon's face was emotionless – he was not going to give Remus the satisfaction of seeing him squirm. But when Remus mimicked running his knife across Falcon's throat, I had to exercise restraint from throwing myself at him. Adarra gripped me tighter.

Remus carelessly let go of his hair, slightly pushing his head forward in the process, knocking him onto his face,

"Whoops," he said, laughter in his voice. Since Falcon's hands were tied behind his back, he wasn't able to catch himself and he was only able to turn his head to avoid smashing his nose into the floor. That earned a gasp from the crowd and a grunt from Falcon.

This wasn't an execution, this was a mockery, and Remus was having too much fun. I tried to restrain myself, but when he just *left* him there – I couldn't help it. I rushed forward, detangling myself from Adarra. I hurried to Falcon's side, gently pushing him back up onto his knees.

He looked at me, his silver eyes burning, "Foxglove, you have to know I-" Before he could finish his sentence, Remus pulled him back again.

"Your husband, was it?" Captain Remus sneered clearly referring back to when he saw us in Kleidis. A Shadow Guard pulled me back and practically threw me at Adarra where we clung to each other again.

"Do you want to know how we even discovered you hiding here in Stalton?" He asked, practically puffing up his chest.

"No." I said, knowing that he would tell me anyway.

"There was a triggered spell on Silverglade Castle." He paused, waiting for my reaction. At my confused look, he continued, "Aeron thought it would be prudent if a tracking spell was triggered on anyone who trespassed into the castle to…poke around."

My breath caught in my throat. A tracking spell? That meant…we did this…no, I did this. I insisted on going into the castle and gave them our location that led them straight to us. But… "How did you know it was us? It could have been anyone." I choked out, my cheeks burning.

"There is a mirror in the castle that has a twin. Its twin is…in our possession. We are able to see whatever happens in front of the other mirror." He said proudly, as if I'm going to congratulate him on his cleverness in catching us.

I swallowed. I couldn't believe we did this. That I did this. This was on me. Me. Me. Me. If I hadn't insisted we go into the castle, this never would have happened.

Remus clicked his tongue at me, "You used to be so much more fun."

A muscle in Falcon's jaw feathered at that comment. "Then go find someone *more fun* to capture." I sighed. I couldn't focus on why we were here. I must focus on our plan to get us out.

"This is boring me now." Remus said, a hand on his stupidly manicured beard. He held out a hand and one of the Shadow Guard placed a sword in it. "On with the execution." He said, pushing Falcon's head down. "This is what happens when our king is betrayed!" He proclaimed to the crowd, before raising the sword above his head, perpendicular to Falcon's neck. I peeked desperately at the rooves of the nearby buildings, and finally spotted Ayla atop one of them – the symbol on her chest beginning to glow. *Are you ready, Lightweaver?*

I swallowed, gathered up all the power that I could into the center of my chest. I poured my hurt, my fear, my regret into it. I also poured my love, my protectiveness, my devotion into it. For Bram. For Kolby. For Adarra, Liam, and Callum, and for General Ren, Mama. And for Falcon. And I held it there, waiting, trying not to let all overtake me. I waited. The sword started its downward arc – and I let the power explode out of me.

Chapter 26

An undead monster, making its way toward a crying baby. A hooded figure on the ground. I had seen this before. The woman under the hood closes her eyes for the last time as the monster reaches for the baby...

The moment the undead's decaying finger makes contact with the baby, there is an explosion of white light, burst forth from the amulet that is now out of the folds of the blanket. The light travels outward like a wave and disintegrates the undead where it stands. The woman lying on the floor could almost look like she is smiling. Her last-ditch effort to put the baby further out of danger had worked.

The amulet stopped glowing, evaporating into nothingness as if it had never existed at all. It had served its purpose. The blankets, having been rumpled, had fallen back around the baby's head, revealing a sparse crop of newborn hair – red. Upon the disintegration of the amulet around her, the hair framing the baby's face turned white.

I blinked, trying to push the vision I had just had from my mind and ignore the sudden burning on my arm. Could I have hurt myself during the blast? My burst of power left the area around me in shambles. The crowd had run away, Captain Remus was on his back, as well as the rest of the Shadow Guard, knocked back by the blast. There was a Shadow Guard, the same one who had bumped into me earlier, behind Falcon, pulling out his sword.

I couldn't help but grin as the Guard cut the ropes that were holding Falcon's hands behind his back. Just like I couldn't help but grin when I slid the daggers out of my boots that that same guard had slipped me when he pushed into me earlier, causing me to "trip" and giving me an opportunity to hide them.

Next to me, Adarra pulled out throwing knives. I raised an eyebrow – I'd have to ask her how she got those later.

Ayla dropped her shields surrounding my allies and we moved. Adarra released 3 knives into the three Shadow Guard who had managed to get up, each one hitting their throats, they all fell to the floor, choking on their own blood. I needed my sword. As Adarra ran to retrieve her knives, I ran for Captain Remus, who was just starting to come to. I was almost there when I heard – "Cass!"

Falcon cried out, and I only had a moment to brace myself before I was tackled by a Shadow Guard.

The Shadow Guard straddled me, trying with all his might to force his sword down on me – I only had my daggers to hold him off. His weight was crushing my lungs, forcing the air out of them. We were met in a stalemate, my daggers crossed in front of me, his sword coming down on them. I chanced a glance to the side, desperate to make sure the rest of our plan was being executed.

Ayla was lifting the wards surrounding the mages, the chalk markings on the platform glowing intensely. There was chaos around me as the Guard who freed Falcon started to cut the rope from the wrists of the other warriors. Anyone who was freed immediately turned on the surrounding Shadow Guard forces who were coming to their senses. Liam rubbed his wrists and grabbed a sword from a fallen Shadow Guard. His eyes met mine, widened, and he started towards me, but he too was apprehended by another guard.

Although I had only been down for a few moments, my arms were starting to strain as I pushed back with all my might against the Guard on top of me. His eyes were filled with hatred, his face close enough that I could smell his putrid breath. How was I going to get out of this?

A rush of air filled my lungs as the Shadow Guard straddling me was pulled off with no more consequence than if he was a ragdoll. My eyes darted to the one who saved me – Falcon. Worry etched in his brow, he grabbed my hand and pulled me up. "We need to-" I started to say, but without letting go of my hand, he pulled me to his chest, put his rough hand on my cheek, and kissed me.

And despite the turmoil around us, despite the desperation of our situation, there was hope in that kiss. There was promise of something greater, something more. My heart sped up more than it did when I was on the brink of death, and the butterflies in my stomach had nothing to do with the battle raging around us. I knew that this was a "if we die, this is how I feel" kiss. So, I kissed him back. And as quickly as it happened, we pulled away. He held my eyes for a moment; we would take about this later - if there *was* a later. There was a battle to be won.

I turned back toward Captain Remus, whose back was now to me. He was blade to blade with the Guard who had freed Falcon. "Traitor!" Remus screeched. The battle was growing more fervent – we had been slightly outnumbered in the beginning, but now the wards around the mages had been broken, allowing them to join the battle and turn it in our favor. Callum was quickly tending to any injured on our side.

Taking advantage of the distraction, I flew for Captain Remus, my dagger coming down behind him. Just before I made contact though, he whirled on me, knocking my dagger out of my hand with his sword. Shocked that he sensed me coming, I glanced at my dagger, then back at Remus. The smirk on his face prompted me to do what I'd been dreaming of doing since I first saw him. I reeled back and punched him in the face – which was clearly the last thing he was expecting since he didn't even think to put up his hands or try to block me.

The hit sent him stumbling back into the Guard he had been fighting, who promptly put him on the floor. He tried to get up, but the Guard put his sword to Remus' neck. "You dare defy your Captain? Your King?" Remus spat, inching backward to get away from the tip of the blade being held to him.

At that, the Guard removed his helmet, "You're not my captain." General Ren spat, "An Aeron sure as hell isn't my king."

"But! He – You-" Remus sputtered. At that, I removed the Blade of Strattera from his back, its blade singing to me as I touched it. It felt like a piece of myself had been returned. I weighed my other dagger in my hand as I considered how I would use both of them. Yes – this would definitely work. I moved to bring an end to Remus once and for all, but General Ren stopped me, "No – we need him alive."

"Well, this will keep him here." I deadpanned, grabbing my fallen dagger from the floor, and sticking it into his thigh.

He screamed in pain, "You can't do this to me! I'm Captain of the Shadow Guard! I am Beauford Remus the third! I…"

I turned away from him, "You'll heal." I threw over my shoulder and took in the battle surrounding me. There were ten or so guards left fighting. It looked like we only had one or two casualties.

Liam was engaged in combat with a soldier that stood at least 6 inches taller than him. Falcon cut down the one he was against, and eyes shooting to me, and then on the ground at Captain Remus next to me, he announced, "SHADOW GUARD!" the fighting ceased, "Your Captain has fallen! If you surrender now, we will only take you prisoner – not kill you."

Something in the air shifted as each of the Shadow Guard soldiers' eyes turned completely black, and they all spoke in unison, "We do not surrender to vermin, or to anyone." The wind started to blow, and pitch-black clouds rolled in to cover the sky. A chill ran down my spine as I watched each of them tear the black stone off the front of their armor with their left hand, "We give our lives to the service of Master Aeron so that his reign may not be threatened!"

Captain Remus looked just as confused as we did, and a gasp caught in my throat as each of the Shadow Guard ran their weapons across their own necks, their blood spilling out and as if guided by magic, flowed into the stones in their hands. The stones that stayed suspended in the air as the Shadow Guards bodies fell, one by one, felled by their own hand.

Ayla, what's going on? I called out inside my head.

Ayla flashed in front of me, earning a surprised shout from anyone who witnessed it, *It is Aeron. This is magic triggered by a certain number of conditions. I assume it is to ensure no survivors.*

I gulped. No survivors.

I felt Callum come up beside me. "I don't know what's going on Cass, but this is dark magic. It must be Aeron's doing." I nodded, my mouth set in a firm line. As the blood entered the stones, a black stream of what looked like smoke spilled out, growing and pooling together. Falcon came up on my other side, "What the hell is going on?" He muttered. Liam and Adarra made their way over to us as well, murmuring to themselves.

The smoke continued to pool on the ground, but I also noticed that it started to build up. It grew taller, and taller, until it was taller than most of the buildings surrounding us. General Ren ran up to us, "We need to evacuate the town."

Falcon whirled on Remus, "What is this?" He demanded, kneeling down, and grabbing him by his collar, ignoring the cry of pain from the dagger in his leg.

"I... I don't know!" Remus sputtered, "I've never seen this before!"

I sense the truth on him, Lightweaver. He does not have the same stone as his subordinates. Ayla looked at me, *This method must only be reserved for the lowest ranking soldiers.*

"Ayla said he's telling the truth." I said, and everyone except Adarra looked at me like I was crazy. "It's…I'll explain later. She can do more than just teleport."

The smoke was now shaping itself into some kind of…monster. From what I could tell, it stood on two legs and was building itself 4 arms. Selby, standing with Mullins and Grigsby, threw a rock into the smoke – it passed straight through. How were we going to fight this thing?

Falcon roughly released Remus and he fell backwards, crying out again as the fall jostled the dagger in his leg. He stood and faced all of us. What was left of Luminous Storm. We were running out of time before whatever that thing was made a move. "We created this rebellion to make a difference. To right the wrongs Aeron, and so many of his followers have committed. Today, the end has begun. Every move we make will have a direct impact on saving the children and bringing down Aeron. We start with protecting the people of Trilithia. I need ten people to go back down to base and pack as much as you can into a carriage. We'll take the Shadow Guards." His eyes shot to me, and he took a deep breath. "Cass has been promoted to Commander as well. She will lead the onslaught against this…whatever this is. I will lead the evacuation effort." I nodded. "Adarra, Liam, and Callum, stay with Cass. Everyone else, come with me. We need to make it to as many houses as we can. We meet by the south entrance of town. Let's go." He walked up to me as the rest of the rebellion made their way towards houses and grabbed my hand at my side. "Survive. Please." Was all he said to me, his silver eyes shining with desperation. I nodded, he dropped my hand, turned, and followed the soldiers to lead the evacuation. I turned to General Ren, "We need to get my Mama."

General Ren nodded. "I already moved her during the days you were imprisoned. She'll be with us when we travel." He hurried after Falcon.

I let out a breath, a weight lifted from my shoulders. My relief was short lived, however, as the beast being formed by the smoke let out a guttural groan. I quickly turned to my most trusted friends, "Callum, you stay in the back and heal from a distance when you can. If there is nobody to be healed, send whatever attacks you can from afar."

Callum nodded, "Got it."

"Adarra, take your throwing knives and my daggers and use them sparingly – I don't know if the creature will solidify once it's in its final form or they will just pass through."

"What will you fight with if you give me your dagger?" Adarra asked, worry etching her brow.

"I've got the Blade of Strattera." I said, the blade singing in response as I twirled it in my hand.

"Liam." I said, turning to him, "You fight with me - we hit it close, and we hit it hard. We might have to re-evaluate but for now…this is all we've got."

Ayla, stay close to me. I look to the fox, her white symbol on her chest glowing.

You couldn't stop me if you tried.

I turned to face the beast when someone else spoke, "Did you all forget about me?" Remus. We forgot about Remus.

"Adarra, you can take the remaining dagger from Remus' thigh." I said, moving to remove it myself.

"He could bleed out." Callum said, "You could have hit a major artery."

"So, heal him." I said coldly, "Just enough that he doesn't bleed but leave it enough that it still hurts." I looked back toward the smoky being who was growing larger by the minute. "If this thing starts attacking you leave him, I don't care if he bleeds out."

Callum nodded grimly, and kneeled down next to Remus, beginning to tend to the wound in his thigh.

I scanned the form of the shadow. It had to be almost complete. I observe the growing shape – it had no legs and its base was wide, like the bottom of a mountain. Its torso was formed with four arms – each as long as its body was tall. My gut tightened when 6 glowing red eyes opened on its face, and its jaw unhinged like a snake, and a deep voice echoed, "You have failed me, Remus. Let us hope you find mercy with your captors, for you will find none with me." The beasts body hardened into a black body with scales covering all its flesh. With that, the beast let out a guttural roar that shook the entire town.

Chapter 27

Two long arms swept across the platform we were on, Liam and I managed to roll out of the way, and it narrowly missed Adarra and Callum.

"Callum, leave him!" I shouted, landing on the stone floor of the town square. I rolled off my back and back onto my feet. I swiped at the tendril and narrowly missed.

"Almost there!" Callum shouted; his attention fixated on Remus' thigh. I seethed. Callum would risk this battle…for *Captain Remus?* There was probably some "healers' code" involved but did it really apply to the likes of *him*?

The arms swept again, on the opposite side, this time catching Adarra and knocking her backwards. She flew back and knocked into a wall, falling to the ground.

"Adarra!" I cried, narrowly missing another sweep of the limbs. This was not going well. Liam leapt forward and brought his sword down on one of them. Right before it made impact, though, there was a shift in the arms' visibility. It went straight through and clanged on the stone floor. So, it could become intangible at will. Great. How were we supposed to kill something we couldn't even hurt physically? Callum left Remus on the ground and rushed to Adarra's aid. Good.

Ayla, stay out of sight but do what you can from afar. I called out to her. This battle was getting messier than I thought it would.

"On your left!" Liam shouted, as the second set of tendrils swept at me again. This time, they caught me in my midsection and wrapped around me, knocking the wind out of me, and lifting me up off the floor. I gripped the arm, my heart racing.

I writhed in panic, kicking my legs as it lifted me to its face. I stared into six glowing red eyes. "Cass!" I heard them all cry below me.

Do not just sit there, Lightweaver. I heard Ayla's voice command me. Right. My light magic – and this beast was made of shadow. I willed my hands to glow – for my magic to listen to me – but nothing happened.

"This is the one who has caused so much trouble?" The voice chuckled darkly, "I must have very weak soldiers indeed."

I tried not to shrink back under the scrutiny of the monstrous face, "You know, a leader is only as good as it's army." I spat.

"You-" The voice stopped at a shout from below.

"Use that bloody sword!" Remus was shouting at me. I glanced down to my hand. Right. My blood pumping too loudly in my ears to question why he would help me, I raised my sword and brought it down on the tendril surrounding me. There was a slight hiss as the tendril around me turned back into a shadow, dropping me from a height that was surely too high to survive from.

So that was why Remus suggested I attack. So I would fall to my death. My stomach jumped into my throat as I started to fall back. I turned my head to the side and made eye contact with Liam, who had a look of pure horror on his face. I thought I might have heard Remus curse, but it was hard to tell with the wind rushing in my ears. I couldn't believe after making it this far, this was how I was going to die.

About 6 feet left to fall, and my speed suddenly slowed. I was now *floating* down from the beast, and my eyes searched for the source of this phenomenon. Callum, still up on the platform, was holding his hands out to me, chanting under his breath. I was slowly lowered down to the ground.

Have you forgotten our lessons, Lightweaver? The magic is not the weapon, YOU are the weapon. Ayla came next to me as my feet touched the ground. She pressed her nose into my leg, and I felt a renewed energy growing in my chest. I was the weapon. Right. My magic was no more a tool than my heart, or my soul. It was an extension of myself.

The beast recovered quickly from the blow and started swinging again. Liam was attempting to get close to the body but would get swept away just as soon as he took a step.

Callum's attention was on Liam, quickly sending streams of healing magic to Liam every time he was knocked back, "Maybe try something else?!" He shouted over the roaring of the beast.

Remus remained on the ground, hands grasping his leg, and looking up at the monster in either horror or disbelief – maybe both.

Adarra was trying and failing to throw knives into it – the section the knives were aimed at would turn intangible just before reaching the beast.

I put the Blade of Strattera on my back. Then I closed my eyes and focused all my energy. I imagined the light pouring out of my palms, becoming malleable enough that I could shape it into whatever I wanted. I opened my eyes, and I was holding two daggers made of pure light. I gripped them – they didn't feel like they weighed anything at all.

I ran towards one of the sweeping arms, managing to nick of them. It kept moving though, the blades having done no more damage than if it was a regular dagger.

I observed another arm sweeping towards Adarra as an idea hit me.

"Adarra!" I shouted, straining between focusing my energy to reshape my weapon and forming the words to Adarra.

"Kind of busy!" She said, jumping up far enough to avoid the sweep of the limb.

"Aim a dagger for the base of the arm! Don't throw until I say!" I shouted, my weapon almost complete. Her brows furrowed but she nodded and readied her knife.

"Callum! I'm going to need you catch me again!" I shouted, He wiped his brow and nodded as well.

I held the weapon in my hands – a giant war axe that I normally wouldn't be able to wield – but this one was made of light. I took off at another run, going towards the arm that was just about to start sweeping towards them again, "That one!" I shout, motioning my head up towards it.

I jumped just as another tentacle went past me and I landed on top of it – the beast was so focused on Liam that it didn't even sense me. I ran up it with all my might, towards the base of the arm.

"NOW, ADARRA!" I screamed, as I launched myself into the air, the axe over my head.

The base of the arm was coming closer, and Adarra's knife was headed right for it. The beast chuckled darkly, "Do you tire of failing?" It turned to shadow right as the knife was to make contact.

Just as I planned.

I arced toward the section of shadow and brought my axe down through it. The blade cleaved the shadow, the whisps left behind hardening into flesh.

There was a scream that shook the town as the arm fell from the body, its base sizzling. I continued to fall, and just as he was supposed to, Callum caught me again, and lowered me gently to the floor.

The screaming made way to a screech, "LIGHTWEAVER!" The voice rang out – an accusation. My feet touched the ground and rounded on it, readying my axe. "How is this possible?! I destroyed them all when I wiped out the royal family years ago!"

My rage flared – and I swear that I felt some of Ayla's emotions as well, "Well, I guess you missed one." I shot back, and took off at a run again, towards another arm.

It seemed to have learned from last time though, and refused to turn to shadow, not allowing me to cleave through it completely. I continued to hack away, but nothing would significantly slow it. Retreating, I observed our situation.

All three arms were now focused on Liam, as he deflected as best he could, with Adarra hurling her remaining knives at the ones that got too close to him. Callum was focusing on the two of them, sending stamina and healing to them.

This wasn't working. We weren't *getting* anywhere. Even if I could cut off the rest of the arms, that wouldn't kill it. The beasts jaw unhinged as it let out another roar. That was it.

I took a chance. I ran towards Liam and Adarra, narrowly avoiding the sweep of the arms. I grabbed them and threw a wall of light behind us that should act as a shield to keep the beast out – as long as I could hold it. We made it to Callum in one piece.

"What are you-" Callum started, but I cut him off. "We need to regroup." I said, out of breath, "This isn't working." I winced as the beast continued to beat on my wall of light. Adarra's hair was sticking to her face in places, a sheen of sweat across her brow. Liam had a bloody lip and a cut above his eyebrow.

"What do you propose?" Adarra asked, brow arched.

"Well, I figure anything will die if you cut off its' head." I said, and turned to Remus, "Right, Captain Asshole?"

He apparently knew better at this point than to correct me on his name, for he just nodded, and nervously said, "I don't know any information that would indicate that wouldn't work."

I nodded, satisfied with his answer. Speaking quickly, as my shield was weakening by the second, I turned to Callum, "We know you can catch me. What about launching?"

"Like…into the air?" He asked nervously, wiping the beads of sweat from his brow. This battle was taking a toll on him. He was used to the quiet life of healing the occasional sick person – besides the fight we had when Remus found us he probably had never seen a day of battle in his life. A week of training after getting here wasn't enough to prepare him for this.

Ayla, can you do anything for Callum? I called out in my mind. She appears next to me in her usual flash of light.

Tell him to hold out his hand. She commands, the symbol on her chest beginning to glow.

"Hold out your hand, Callum." I said, motioning toward Ayla, indicating that she had given the direction.

Callum looked quizzically at her but held his hand out all the same, and Ayla pushed her nose into his hand. There was the same white glowing as when she transferred some of her energy to me. Adarra and Liam looked on in awe. It only lasted a few moments, but when the glowing ceased, Callum rubbed his hands together, "Yeah, I could probably launch someone now."

"Good." I grinned, looking at all my team, "Here's the plan."

My shield finally gave out, everyone started attacking with renewed vigor. Adarra had pulled every available blade off the fallen shadow guard and was hurling them furiously at the beast. Callum was launching a series of attacks from afar.

"Where is the Lightweaver?" Its voice boomed.

"She went to go get help!" Adarra yelled between blades, "You're in big trouble now!"

Yes, she really was made for performing. The monster chuckled darkly again in Aeron's voice, "You fools. The Lightweaver was your only chance at beating me. You will all be dead before she returns."

I ran behind the buildings surrounding the square the battle was taking place in, pacing my breathing. They just needed to distract it long enough for me to reach its back. I caught glimpses of the battle as I passed behind the houses. Adarra's blades passed through shadow, doing no more damage than a gust of wind.

You are ready, Lightweaver. You will not fail. Ayla's voice echoed in my mind.

I would not fail. I would not fail. I *could* not fail.

I spied the rear of the monster through the next opening of buildings and tried the back door of the next building.

It was unlocked.

I ran into the house, looking for stairs. I ran up as fast as my feet could carry me. A window, a window, I needed a window. I searched the rooms until I found a window that faced the back of the building and opened it.

I poked my head out and looked up – part of the roof was hanging over.

Perfect.

I sat on the windowsill, my top half out of the building, and hoisted myself up on the roof. I peeked my head over the top, and spotted Liam crouching behind Callum. I shot a small ball of light up in the air – not enough to catch the beast's attention but enough to be visible – if you were looking for it.

Callum and Liam looked at each other at the appearance of my signal. They waited for an opening - Liam took off at a run and jumped with all his might. Propelled by Callum's magic, he flew straight towards the creature's head. The roof tiles creaked under my feet as I shifted forward, readying myself.

"You insolent creatures." The voice echoed, "You never learn from your mistakes, do you?"

Liam grinned as he swung his sword, and just as we counted on, the monster turned his head to shadow.

I launched myself forward, "Yes, we do." I breathed, midair, sweeping my axe made of light straight through its neck.

A guttural scream hardly made it out of its throat before the shadow was cleaved through, turning to flesh, and again sizzling as the head fell off its shoulders and onto the ground.

My fall was slowed by Callum's magic, but not nearly as slow as before – probably because he had to slow Liam's fall as well.

I was approaching the ground at an alarming rate, "Callum?!" I cried out, just as a body crashed into mine, pushing me off to the side with it, lessening the impact of my fall. I grunted as we landed on the ground, rolling from the combined force of my fall and the impact of catching me midair. I was flat on my back – a little dizzy. I turned to see who swiped me out of the sky, and was met with a dazzling pair of silver eyes – Falcon.

"I thought I told you to survive." He said softly.

"I did." I smiled, and sat up, staring at the corpse of the shadow beast. It was slowly disintegrating into shadow, floating upwards into the air, as if it had never existed, and the clouds were slowly clearing away.

Falcon got to his feet and held his hand out to me. His rough hand was warm in mine as I grasped it, pulling myself up.

"You came back." I shifted my stance, a hand on my hip, "You didn't trust me to handle it?"

He huffed a blunt laugh, "No. But is that hard to believe I would worry for you? My Uncle has a handle on everything else for now."

"How is-" The words caught in my throat as I was overtaken with blinding pain in my forearm. I gasped, grasping my arm and dropping to the floor. My head was buzzing I was in so much pain.

I heard voices crying out, "Cass! Cass!" But it sounded like their voices were under water. Everything was slowly fading away until I was falling…falling…falling… there was nothing left but the searing pain and darkness.

Chapter 28

I was standing in darkness. Well, not so much standing as I was…existing. Was I even existing anymore? My arm didn't hurt anymore. Did I die? Maybe this is what came after death… I could sense my body though, for my heart was pounding rapidly.

"Cassandra." A woman's voice spoke - soft, but emanating authority.

"Who's there?" I asked, blindly turning around.

"Do not be afraid, child." A soft caress on my cheek. I blinked – and there she was. In front of me, radiating a gold light was the most beautiful woman I'd ever seen. She couldn't have been much older than me. Her eyes, green like the forest, stared intimately at me. Her fair, freckled skin was complemented by the sage green of her gown, which was regal in appearance. A gold diadem shaped like the points of the rays of the sun sat atop her rich copper hair, that flowed in loose waves down to the middle of her back. The glow coming from her was odd…but it was comforting.

"Am I dead?" I blurted out, "Is this the afterlife?"

She chuckled and shook her head, "No, Cassandra, you are not dead. You are, in fact, very much alive."

"Who…who are you?" I asked, my voice barely a whisper.

"That will become clear in time." She said, her eyes crinkling slightly in a small smile. "You are quite the warrior."

"I try as hard as I can." I said, finding myself desperate to be sincere.

"That is all anyone can do." She nodded, still smiling that odd little smile. "Still, it takes someone with exceptional skill to create and wield weapons of light after only having access to their power for a couple of days."

"Yeah, Ayla says-" I stopped midsentence. Wait. What did this woman know about being a Lightweaver? "Are you an elemental warrior? A Lightweaver? Could you-?"

The woman shook her head, "No, I am not." My face fell, but she continued, "But someone very close to me was." There was a note of sadness in her voice. A note that I recognized all too well.

Before I could stop myself, the words found their way out of my mouth, "Did you love him?"

She seemed taken aback at first by my question, but then nodded, her eyes relaxed, "Yes, I did. More than I have ever loved anyone."

My heart dipped at that response. "Who…who are you? To me?"

"Call me a guardian if that is what sates your curiosity. Or a guide." She conceded.

"A guide…?" I mused. She seemed to know a great deal about me, "Do you know anything about the visions I've been having?"

"Who do you think sent them to you?" She asked, raising a brow. Ah.

"What was that vision I had when I unleashed my powers? Was that baby…was it-" I was quickly interrupted by a shuddering in the space around us.

"We are running out of time. For now, know this. You are awakening. You must trust your visions. And lastly…" She trailed off, as if unsure if she should speak the words. She continued quickly, "Lastly, your mother might not be held by a blood curse, but your blood IS the key to lifting what keeps her under."

I faltered, "How do you know any of that?"

She shook her head, "There is no time. I must complete the rite that was started by the gods generations ago."

MARK OF THE FALLEN

My brows furrowed, "Wha-" before I could get out my question, she grabbed my forearm, right where the burning pain had been that sent me into this…wherever I was. I reeled as the pain resumed in my arm and my vision started turning white. I thought I glimpsed something illuminating on her arm as she grabbed me.

"Long may…" her voice faded out as everything turned white.

My eyes blinked open rapidly. I was back in a dark space, but this was not the empty darkness of the void I was just in. There was a soft glow on the ceiling of the…tent? I sat up, holding a hand to my head to try to placate the dizziness. Where was I? How long was I out for? I could hear voices outside. The sound reminded me of overheard conversations in the mess hall back at base. I looked down at myself. I was not in the tattered clothes that I had fought the shadow beast in – fresh clean smelling white linen shirt, and brown pants. I looked at the tent I'm in – it is bare besides a brown leather armored corset thrown over a chair next to me, and a glass of water on the seat of the chair.

I stood, chugging the water and running some fingers through my hair – I'm sure I looked a mess. I started to lace the corset up and thought to call out, *Ayla? Where am I?*

You finally wake, Lightweaver. There is much to discuss. Her voice rang with relief inside my head. I smiled – the softy.

Okay, where are you? Where's Callum, General Ren, Adarra? I asked, fumbling with the laces of the corset more than I usually do.

It is best that you come outside the tent. Her voice is quieter than normal. But heeding her words, I took a step outside, blinking at the sun. There were people milling about, it seemed to be dinner time. The sun was setting over a set of mountains, which explained the glow in the tent. If Ayla was here and calm, I couldn't be in any danger – but I didn't see anyone I recognized. And there were a lot of people. More than we ever had at the base at Luminous Storm. Hundreds.

It seemed that I caught the attention of one person, who had been talking, for they just stopped and stared. This one person created a ripple effect and within a few moments the entire area was silent, turned towards me and staring.

Motion through the stillness caught my eye as Callum made his way through the crowd, "Cass!" He exclaimed, catching me in an embrace.

"What's going on?" I asked, too confused to appreciate the relief on his face.

He pulled back, shaking his head, "I can't really explain. General Ren can though."

"Well, where is he?" I questioned, feeling more than slightly perturbed at all the eyes that were still staring.

"Here." General Ren said, coming around a corner, followed by Falcon, Adarra, and Liam.

"Why are they all staring?" I asked, rubbing my arm.

"This is why," General Ren said, grabbing the arm that had been in pain and pushing back the sleeve of my shirt, revealing the same symbol that had been on General Ren's amulet, and the wall at Silverglade Castle. Marked in what could have been black ink - three circles all overlapping – 2 on the top, one on the bottom, with an intersection of all 3 in the middle. Before I can say a word, General Ren lifted my arm up, exposing the Mark for all to see. "All hail Queen Cassandra, the rightful heir to the Kingdom of Trilithia, and the bearer of the Mark of Alistair!"

My eyes widened and my heart pounded as I watched hundreds of men and women drop to their knees – a wave of submission – and declare in a singular voice, "Queen Cassandra, long may she reign!"

ACKNOWLEDGEMENTS

A great many people have encouraged and helped me on this journey of writing my book. My mom, my grandma, my friends - but none more so than my husband, Dominic. From high jacking car rides so I can read him the latest update to the book, to sitting and letting me talk through important parts, to giving me ideas of his own - this man has been my number one fan since the conception of the idea of this book. It has gone through numerous rewrites, character changes, and lore changes - but Dominic has been with me through them all. I love you, Dominic. I couldn't have done this without you.

You gave me the courage to pursue my story.

BOOK 2 OF THE FOXGLOVE CHRONICLES

IS COMING SOON